A New Kind of Zeal 3
The Crux of Salvation

Michelle Warren

Statement:

This novel is a work of fiction. Any resemblance of a character to a person living or dead is a coincidence, apart from those clear characters of inspiration from two thousand years ago. Likewise, the organisations, positions and places explored do not represent any current reality today, but rather represent a fictional future.

INTRODUCTION

This novel follows the events that took place in the novels 'A New Kind of Zeal' and 'A New Kind of Zeal 2 – The Price of Redemption':

Two and a half years have passed since Kensington confronted his son Alex in Saint Peter's Cathedral, Wellington. Alex has been studying at Victoria University, while the Prime Minister James Connor continues to lead the nation from the Beehive. Rachel Connor has been training to become a Physician, while her husband, John Robertson, remains attached to the Cathedral with Bishop Mark Blake.

Tristan Blake has been watching Alex. The young man, now twenty, is locking himself away in his room in Mark Blake's home, studying. Tristan sees the legacy of Alex's past: a past Alex seems to be trying to hide. What might become of him?

Rau Petera remains on the shores of Oriental Bay, offering good news: but Tristan is watching and waiting. The nation has suffered an upheaval, and has settled in a kind of peace – but Tristan is uneasy. Alex's strength is growing, even as he hides: his potential power over the nation is growing. Tristan sees in Alex his father Kensington: he sees the threat Alex has not yet overcome.

Trouble is brewing overseas; trouble is brewing within. Kensington is beginning to take a greater hold. Powers are rising: the world is at risk of war. What fate will beset the nation? What forces, in the midst of the growing darkness, will win?

CONTENTS

CHAPTER ONE: Graduation

Alex stood still.

Behind him stood the historic cream stone of the Law Faculty of Victoria University. Just across the road, a little in the distance, stood the Beehive. Alex lingered, passing his eyes over the ten stories of the grey hive: settling on the ninth story, near the top – the office of the Prime Minister.

In front of him was the graduation procession for 2032: hundreds of graduates from the University, wearing black academic gowns in the December heat, with different coloured hoods: light blue, yellow, orange...

He frowned, and glanced down to his own black gown – reached to finger the purple coloured hood sitting across his back. Then he moved forward, to join the throng.

They processed down Lambton Quay, through central Wellington. Family members were shouting and waving, from the path – holding up cameras and cell-phones to take photos. Alex avoided the shots. From time to time he glanced across the following crowd, as if he was expecting to see someone: a face, smiling at him – maybe...maybe...He swallowed, closed his eyes, and then made himself look and move forward.

They moved down Lambton Quay, through Willis Street, across Mercer Street and finally gathered on the brick pavement of Civic Square.

Alex looked up at Wellington Town Hall. The cream stone pillars had just been newly painted, after the entire building had been strengthened for earthquakes. His classmates were nearby, in their black gowns and purple hoods – he could hear their laughter. He wandered over to them: to their smiles. And then it was time.

They filed into the building.

Excitement filled the air: the excitement of victory – of achievement; of success. He looked around the students' eager faces: he sat down.

Soon it was time to rise: for the national anthem.

God defend New Zealand...

Alex's mind drifted...away from the resonant voices in the concert hall, to another chamber, to the robes of the Governor General, Anita Mayes, as she carried the golden mace...

"Welcome!" The Chancellor's voice rang out. Alex drew his attention back to him – to his colourful robes, and his strong voice as he led the gathering.

It was time for the Chancellor's speech. They sat, and Alex listened – acknowledgements, thanks; recognition of the students...He glanced up to the balcony above them: to the faces of the families. Only two seats per student...why hadn't he invited Mark and Tristan Blake? They would have come, he was certain: he'd been living with them for two years. And yet...and yet...

Family. Could he see? Eyes, watching? A familiar face? He thought he could see...no, no: it was just a dark shadow. It was nothing.

7

He settled back into his chair: but then they were being called to their feet. Now the Chancellor was directing them to be capped.

Alex reached down to the black cap tucked inside his left arm – he grasped it to his head. Graduated! He had made it! And now the Engineering Faculty was being called forward.

The Masters graduates stepped up onto the stage and received their degrees. Then his classmates were being called, in alphabetical order.

Nervously Alex watched them walk up to the Chancellor, shake his hand, take the scrolled degree, and move off the stage. And now his name was being called.

"Alex Kensington," the Chancellor said, "Bachelor of Engineering with First Class Honours, and the Anderson award for top of the final year."

Kensington. The name lingered in his mind. He thrust himself forward.

Eyes were upon him: too many eyes. He fixed his eyes on the stage – he concentrated on each step, rose to the top, and reached hesitantly out his hand to the Chancellor.

"Congratulations, Alex," his voice said.

"Thank you," he whispered, and reached out and took the scroll, and the medal, and walked across the stage toward the descending steps.

Something flashed before him. He gasped, and stiffened, and stumbled on the top step, but then a hand was on his arm.

"Easy," a voice whispered, and he looked up into Tristan's green eyes: into his grin. "Security," Tristan continued wryly. "Had to find some way in, being army and all."

"Worried about their safety?" Alex muttered back under his breath, tipping his head to the graduates as he walked smoothly down the steps past him.

"From you?" Tristan whispered. "Now you've aced IT?"

"My father would be proud," Alex choked – and now he turned, and returned to his seat.

The ceremony continued. Tristan's eyes were wandering across the room: Alex watched him. The soldier had found a way, shrewdly positioning himself to protect Alex, acting the older brother: but why? Why?

Maybe because…because…

A chill passed through Alex's body. He closed his eyes tightly. No: don't let Selena in – not yet! Not here.

He was twenty now…it had been two and a half years. Would the shock ease? Would it ever ease?

He drew his attention back to the ceremony. The next person was graduating, and then the next. It seemed endless. More speeches. And then, finally, finally, it was time to leave.

They rose to their feet – they followed the professors and teachers back out of the building.

Now they were back in Civic Square.

Alex looked around for Tristan: he was still there, he was sure, somewhere in the background, watching him and the crowd.

His class mates were grinning, talking quickly. They grasped their caps – they threw them, as one, into the air. Alex took his off and clutched it to his chest.

It was over. Finally over.

The graduates moved away with their families – Alex guessed they must be having lunch. He stood in the courtyard as the others disappeared. He looked back up at the Town Hall. And then he wandered away.

Where to go? To lunch? MacDonald's? He held on to his cap, and wandered through the streets, back down Lambton Quay toward the Law faculty...then eventually found himself standing in Molesworth street, between the Beehive and St Peter's Cathedral.

Home. This place felt like home.

He walked up the steps before the stone church: he moved through the glass doors.

The Cathedral was silent, and empty. The new stained glass windows shone many colours: red, blue, green – images of Christ; images of Peter, of John, of Paul...Reflections of reality: evocative light. Alex took in a deep breath. Water! Water for a thirsty soul. He drank in the air – he breathed in the Spirit of the sanctuary. And now he wandered down the central aisle.

Jesus was there, in the heart of the Cathedral, the innermost place: painted on tiles, stretched out on the cross, with the crown of thorns on his head. Alex looked at him, and then at the altar before him, covered in white linen: Christ's offering – the offering of his life.

Here...here his father had...had...

Suddenly deep breathing took him. He looked up again to the stained glass windows: the windows he had shot out – the windows now restored. Breathe! Breathe! His father was hitting him again! As he had already hit him so many times...

"Oh, God," he pleaded, but he forced himself closer to the altar: here he had chosen Christ! Here his father had pressed the gun to his head, pulling the trigger! Here his father's body had been violently seized from him just in time by Tristan's bullet.

Now agony took him. He reached out to grasp onto the altar: he sank to his knees, and pressed his head against it. Breathe! Breathe! He looked up at Christ, on the cross: suffering! His wrists, pinned! His feet, fixed! His side, pierced...

Alex's chest ached: his father's knife twisting in his side. The chalice! Where was Christ's chalice? Where was Christ's life? It was there, lying on the altar: silver, filled with wine.

This is my blood, given for you...

He reached for Christ's blood: he drank. He sank into the altar: he cried. Again! His father kept coming to him, again and again, even beyond the grave! So many times: why must it be so many times? A thousand deaths!

But now Joshua was before him, in his memory: standing before him – his brown eyes finding him, his gentle smile easing him.

"You are my brother," he said. *"Shine my Light! Carry the cost."*

A thousand deaths! A thousand resurrections. A reason! A reason for the pain! A greater purpose, and…and a calling.

Alex reached now beneath the black gown with his right hand to his trouser pocket. Here the five bullets were still with him, even now, even with his graduation after over two years: deformed – used. He had sent these into Joshua's chest, through Tristan: through the Prime Minister. And yet Joshua had known: and yet he had willingly taken Alex's bullets; and yet he had chosen for it to be so.

Alex could see him now, in his mind's eye: staggering, in the street between the Beehive and the Cathedral, his face bloody, clutching onto the ancient cursed crown Selena had thrust upon his head – carrying the crown of Alex's inheritance: embracing Alex's death into his own grave.

"You saved me," Alex whispered, grasping the bullets, and the pain seized his chest yet again, but he continued through the pain. "You took my curse onto yourself, and you overcame it."

Now he lifted himself away from the altar back to his knees, looking again to Jesus on the cross: clutching the bullets in his fist to his own heart. Joshua was only a representation! Only a translation of a much older reality – a reality he had touched in childhood.

"I will love you," he said, "now and always: I will follow you, whatever the cost! Whatever the cost."

And he rose to his feet.

The altar was before him: the silver chalice, sitting again on top. Alex tilted his head, looking at it: the necessary sacrifice – the whole offering. Why had he done it? To draw the inherited darkness of humanity onto himself: to overcome the corruption, passed on from generation to generation; to transcend the inevitable death of body and soul.

"Do it," he whispered, reaching out to touch the altar – to find the polished wood beneath the white linen. "Save us from ourselves, before it is too late."

He gazed at the altar – at his own fingers, touching the wood – and then, suddenly, he acted. His academic cap was still tucked, forgotten, in his left arm – his degree and medal clutched in his left hand. He reached now – he laid the black cap on top of the altar, and added his rolled up scroll and medal. He reached to draw his hood and gown over his head, and laid these also on the altar, over his qualification.

"Four years of work completed in two years," a voice said behind him, and he turned to look at Mark Blake. He was standing quietly, in his purple bishop's tunic: as if he had been there for a while, even waiting. "You are talented."

Alex shrugged his shoulders, and turned back to stare at the gown.

"Top of the class," Mark's voice said, moving behind him. "You would do well overseas."

"Meaningless," Alex muttered, staring at the hood: the purple. "It's all meaningless."

"How can it be meaningless?" Mark asked. "I watched you work hard for all you have achieved."

"I have achieved nothing," Alex said. "Nothing of importance."

"Not so," Mark said. "You have knowledge…"

"This kind of knowledge is meaningless," Alex said, staring at the degree, lifting it again in his left hand, "compared with what he did: compared with what he knows." And he pointed the scroll toward the cross, and now tossed it back on the altar.

Now Mark was alongside him at the altar: now Alex looked up at his face – his gentle sad smile, looking down at the academic gown.

"You could use your great talents," Mark said. "You could use them for good. All knowledge can be used for good."

"Do you think I won't use my knowledge for good?" Alex asked.

"You could help humanity."

Now Alex stiffened. "As if the only thing I have to offer humanity is my mind."

"I didn't mean…"

"Even priests treat Christ as if he's a piece of…"

"I certainly didn't mean…"

"He saved my life," Alex said curtly. "He overcame my father's evil in me. There is nothing more important than that, Mark: everything else is rubbish, compared with grasping him – compared with knowing him. I don't care about my degree anymore: you, of all people, should understand why."

Alex saw Mark grimace, but still the words poured out of his own mouth.

"I don't care if people treat me like a piece of shit," he said. "I don't care if people call me idiotic for leaving their values behind – I don't care if you think I'm useless without my degree…"

"Alex!" Now Mark's face had creased into a frown – now his voice was filling the Cathedral.

Alex caught his breath, staring at him – fear! Always the fear…He reached out to clutch at the altar.

Mark's face softened before him. "You're misunderstanding me," he said gently. "I am not your father."

Pain seized Alex's chest. He closed his eyes.

"I know you're not my father," he whispered. "That was never your responsibility."

11

"Again misunderstanding…"

Alex shook his head, and opened his eyes again. Mark…he had always offered himself! And Alex had always resisted. For two years they had danced the dance: Mark offering, Alex refusing…How could Alex accept anything from him? When…when he had used him to get to Joshua…when…when Selena…

He looked quickly away.

"It's time for me to move out," he said woodenly. "I've relied on your hospitality for too long."

"Son…"

Tears pricked at Alex's eyes – he quickly squeezed them away. Son? Son?

"Look at me," Mark said, and Alex struggled, and turned back to Mark's kind face.

"I have no claim over you," Mark said. "Your heart is your own."

"I…" Alex whispered. This man! This man had done so much for him! Could he not reciprocate? Could he not offer him love in return?

"But if I did have a claim," Mark continued, "I would be proud."

Alex felt his face contort as Mark continued.

"Not because of the hard work," he said, "though that is admirable. Not because of your grades, though they also are admirable. But because you survived hell, Alex: you survived hell, and escaped corruption."

Now Alex reached out a hand to his arm.

"I'm sorry," he whispered, and tears suddenly filled his eyes. "I'm sorry."

"I know," Mark whispered. "But it wasn't your fault."

Pain seized Alex's chest again. "I could never replace her," he whispered. "You do know that, don't you?"

Mark's blue eyes widened. "I never expected that. I never required that."

"I know, but…"

Now Mark interrupted him – now he was grasping Alex's hand in his own: now his eyes were finding him.

"You were a son to me," he said, "even if I could not be a father to you. I understand, Alex! I understand. You still love your true father."

Shocked, Alex stared at Mark's eyes: at the truth in them – Alex's truth, naked, laid bare.

"I have loved," he whispered, desperately, desperately holding down the tide – instinctively returning truth for truth. "I have loved you too, and I'll always appreciate…"

"I know," Mark interrupted. "I know."

"It's just, I can't keep going like this."

"I know."

"Pretending," Alex said. "Pretending."

"I know, Alex," Mark said.

Alex held his eyes. He trembled. Speak? Speak? "It's not okay," he said. "It's not okay, with my family, or with me, or even with anyone else. I see the reality in

12

here, and I see it out there. The World is in trouble, Mark: broken, half blind, struggling and straining to be delivered into something better, and he knows it." Now he gestured to the cross. "He knows it, and he's done something about it…"

"I know we have troubles," Mark said. "I know we're in trouble. I'm a priest: a fallible, corruptible, rescued priest."

Alex looked at him – at his exposed face, at his honesty. Why was it so difficult?

"I do love you," he whispered, and now he clenched his left hand into a fist. "I'll always love you, for taking me on, despite everything I've done."

Now Mark's face shifted into sadness. "And I will always love you," he said. "As I have always forgiven you."

Tears blurred Alex's eyes. "I have to move out," he said. "I need to move out, now."

"I know," Mark said. "It is the right time. But help me to understand, Alex." And now Mark grasped his shoulder, his face turning serious. "Why are you choosing this path?"

Alex frowned, and turned again to look at Jesus on the cross, releasing his left fist.

"It is the only way," he said. "The only way to overcome cursing and death."

"This is the hardest path," Mark said, "this 'Way'."

"I know," Alex whispered. "I know."

"It will strip you bare," Mark said. "It will chew you up."

"I know," Alex said, looking at Jesus's face: at the blood – at the crown of thorns.

"It will test you like nothing else," Mark said. "All of your weaknesses will emerge – all of your agony will emerge. You will be like a lamb led to the slaughter."

Alex's vision blurred – he took a deep breath, and turned back to find Mark's gaze intensified.

"You will be just like him," Mark said, gesturing to the cross, his own eyes still wet – and now the bishop stepped back, and released Alex from his grip.

Alex stared at him, and then shifted on his feet. "A broken lampshade," he whispered. "You do know that, don't you? I'm just a broken lampshade."

"So much the better," Mark murmured over him. "So it was with Paul."

"Paul?" Alex asked, looking back up to the stained glass windows: to Paul, the missionary, overwhelmed by the light of Christ, carrying it beyond the borders of Israel.

"The thorn in the flesh," Mark said. "God's strength in Paul's weaknesses. All the pieces are in place. We must look to Paul now."

Alex reached out to touch his face.

"A bearer of the light," Mark said. "The light for the Gentiles. Shine it well beyond the church, Alex: shine Christ's light to the very ends of the Earth."

And now Mark was praying over him.

Alex closed his eyes. Light! Light, in the darkness: light, in the growing darkness...

"Today is your graduation day, Alex," Mark said. "Today is your choice: which path will you take? May God bless you and keep you, in choosing the hardest way. May he make his face shine upon you, and give you peace."[1]

"Amen," Alex whispered – and he straightened his shoulders, grasped Mark's hand, and walked down the aisle, leaving his academic gown, degree and medal far behind.

---

[1] Numbers 6:24-26 Paraphrased.

CHAPTER TWO: A Vocation

Rachel stood in the medical ward.

It was early: the ward was still quiet, at the end of night shift. She wandered over to a window, in an empty room, and gazed outside toward the hills of the Hutt: to the bright pink sky of the rising sun.

"Congratulations, Dr Connor," a voice said from behind her. "Your first day as a fully qualified specialist."

Rachel turned to face him. Her father was standing leaning casually against a bed: the top of his shirt unbuttoned, his tie, for now, abandoned. He was smiling gently at her.

"Your mother would be proud," he said – and Rachel stiffened and turned back to the window.

"Don't," she said, drawing her white coat more tightly around her.

"You did it all yourself," her father said.

"Sure did."

"I couldn't be more proud."

Now tears pricked her eyes. She stared up at the hills: at the lightening sky. She quickly blinked the tears away.

"Finished a year early," James Connor said. "Trying to beat your brother?"

Rachel frowned, reaching to finger the stethoscope on her chest: cardiology grade! The stethoscope of James Lester...

Suddenly she was in St Peter's again, staring up at John, clutching the silver chalice of Christ's blood: suddenly she could feel James's gun to her temple.

"Who knows how much time any of us have?" she asked.

"I suppose as much time as we are given," Connor's voice replied.

The sun had risen. Confused, Rachel gazed at the light in the valley. The night time was over? It couldn't be. Not yet...The gun! The gun was still to her head...

"And what about you?" she asked, turning again to Connor, shaking the memory of the gun away. "You're actually acknowledging James as my brother now? After all these years?"

Connor shifted uneasily on his feet.

"I don't know..."

"You abandoned him."

Her father's eyes were set on her. "He went missing," he said. "I didn't know where he had gone."

"You didn't look for him," Rachel said, shaking her head.

"Of course we looked! Your mother..."

"Don't talk to me about her."

"She tried..."

"Bullshit. She was glad to see him go."

"Rachel!"

"She was glad to see him go!" Now rage filled her: now she jabbed her finger to the ground at his feet. "He was her child, Dad! He was my twin! But, no: focus on the good child – abandon the difficult child into some shitty life: let him rot in prison."

"He pulled a gun on you."

"I don't care." She shrugged his comment away.

"He was going to kill you!"

"Yeah, well who can blame him?" she roared, glaring at him. "Maybe he was just following his father's example!" And now Joshua Davidson's shooting was before her eyes: Tristan Blake, commanded by her father! Five bullets!

Now her father's face whitened: now his eyes widened.

"Rachel!" he cried. "I've already told you I'm sorry for that! I'm sorry for everything!"

Rachel felt her face contort: felt regret seize her chest.

"I know," she quickly whispered. "I'm sorry."

And now her father's eyes filled with tears. "This was supposed to be a good day, Rachel!" he said, jabbing his own finger toward the floor. "It was supposed to be a good day!"

"It's not a good day!" she said. "Not when there's nothing but dead bones inside!"

And now she pulled off her stethoscope – and now she dragged off her white coat.

"Don't," her father whispered.

"It's all a charade, Dad!" she cried. "All pretence!"

"No…"

"Why would I have anything to offer to anyone else?" she asked. "Why, when my own family…"

She shook her head, and tightly closed her eyes.

"I need time off," she whispered. "I need time."

"Then take time," her father's voice said, cracking.

"I need…" And she wandered back over to the window, now without her white coat, frowning: searching the hills and the sky. "I need…"

"Something stronger than humanity."

Surprised, Rachel looked back at him. Her words to Alex, after his decimation: after watching his father violently stripped from him.

"Come," her father suddenly said.

"Where?"

Connor smiled sadly. "To another kind of work."

"I'm needed here."

"Not yet," Connor said. "You've turned up ridiculously early for your first day, as I knew you would."

Rachel grinned at him – and then she reached out for her white coat, lifted it up and straightened it, placing it over the post of a bed, and grasped James's stethoscope into her pocket.

"All right," she said. "Let's do this your way."

And she followed her father down the corridor and out of the ward.

The Beehive was before her: ten stories of grey.

Rachel stepped out of her father's car and gazed up at the building, as he stepped out of the driver's seat.

"So, Prime Minister," Rachel said. "How's the state of the nation?"

Connor shrugged. "A whole lot better than it was straight after the disaster," he said.

"Which disaster?" Rachel muttered. "I'm starting to lose count…"

"It's all one to me," Connor said. "Temperature heating up, Davidson's movement, my…" he hesitated, and seemed to make himself continue, "my complete mess."

"You might as well say it clearly," Rachel said, as they wandered toward the entrance to Parliament.

"It makes me gag," Connor said, "but so be it. My arrangement of his assassination."

He seemed to shudder.

"And now, back again," he said. "It's been over two years, and I'm still feeling bewildered."

"It was Alex," Rachel said, remembering him now: the young blonde man, sagging on his knees, poisoned, in the Debating Chamber. "He exposed his father's plot to take over Parliament: he had you reinstated."

"I know," Connor said. "Kensington might have destroyed us all."

Kensington? Rachel suddenly remembered a worse image: Alex, forced back onto the altar of St Peter's – his father's gun to his head; his invasive kiss. *Shoot!* She had cried out to Tristan and James. *Save the boy!*

"His father?" she said. "Don't think about him: he was a malicious bastard! Like some kind of insidious force, setting us up, moving around and through us all, manipulating the pieces…"

"Like Satan?" Connor muttered. "As if there really was literally such a beast."

And now Rachel stopped. Who was that? Across the courtyard, sitting under a pohutukawa: a young man, staring at something in his hands.

"Dad," Rachel whispered, "I think it's him."

Connor stopped next to her, peering in the same direction. "Who?" he asked. "Kensington? Satan?"

And now his gaze seemed to settle in the same direction. "Oh," he said, "you had me worried for a moment: thought I'd be seeing some ghostly apparition, some red thing with horns…"

Rachel flicked her hand against his arm, and then suddenly seized him. Alex, here? Now? Why? Why now?

Connor shifted awkwardly against her, and looked between her and the young man.

"Listen, Rachel," he said quietly, "we all saw what happened to him. We all watched him traumatized."

"I was there," Rachel whispered, her gut twisting. The scream! His scream, after his father was torn away. "I was a part of it."

"We were all a part of it," Connor said. "And now he comes sitting outside of the Beehive, every morning: just spends hours staring into his hands."

Rachel frowned – and then suddenly looked at her father again.

"You brought me here for him?"

Connor smiled sadly at her. "Well, you are a fully qualified specialist now, aren't you?" he said.

"I..." Rachel stared at him, and then looked back to Alex, and frowned again. "I'm not a specialist in trauma."

"Are you not?"

Now she met the sorrow in her father's eyes.

"I'm sorry, Rachel," he whispered. "I don't know what else to do. But maybe you do. Maybe you know more than I do. Maybe you get it."

Rachel bowed her head and closed her eyes. "I don't know anything," she whispered. "Not really. I can't begin to save someone who has lost all of his family."

"If anyone knows what to do," Connor said, "it's you. You were there. You are a doctor. You've felt it too. You'll know what he needs. As for me, I'm just a politician who's feeling a bit nervous having the son of Kensington sitting repeatedly on my doorstep looking a little bit mentally unwell..."

Rachel grimaced. "Do it for national security?" she asked.

Connor held her eyes. "This is your chance, Rachel," he said. "This is your chance to try to stop the flame passing on before it is too late."

And now he was turning her: and now Alex's form, sitting under the tree, was in front of St Peter's Cathedral.

Rachel cast her eyes over the Cathedral: Alex had shot out the windows! But now they were replaced. She lowered her eyes to look at his forlorn figure, under the tree.

Her father's hand came to her shoulder. "You are a doctor," he said. "You will help him."

"All right, all right," she whispered. "I'm here. I'll try to help him."

And she left her father behind, and walked forward.

Alex was before her. He was little: she had forgotten how short he was, in contrast to the towering height of his father. He was sitting alone on the park bench, in jeans and an old T-shirt, staring down at his palms.

"Hey," Rachel said, and Alex lifted his head. His eyes widened, his face paled.

18

"Oh, shit!" he said – and he reached out to grasp the park bench with both hands. His body was stiffening: his breathing was quickening.

"Sorry," he gasped. "It's just, I haven't seen you since…since…"

Since the hospital ward, Rachel suddenly realized: after his near death, in exposing his father in Parliament – in bringing about the reinstatement of Connor.

A memory! She was reminding him.

"Sorry," she murmured – and now she sat down alongside him on the bench.

"Breathe," she murmured. "Breathe."

"Breathe?" he gasped. "That's what I already try to do…"

"Gently," she murmured. "Slowly."

And she laid a hand on his shoulder, and breathed deeply and slowly for him, and he followed her lead.

His tension was easing, under her hand. His breathing was settling. She released him.

Something had fallen, next to them: from his hands, in his shock, he had dropped something to the ground.

Rachel stooped down low to pick it up: it was sparkling, in the sun – a golden chain. She lifted it quickly, and there, hanging from it, was a golden crucifix.

She lifted it up in front of his face – he looked at it.

"Staring at this a lot?" she asked – and he took a deep breath, and took it back into his hand.

"This was my mother's," he said, and Rachel tilted her head.

"Your mother was Catholic?" she asked.

"Both my parents were Catholic," he said.

Rachel grimaced. His father! His father was also Catholic.

"We're Anglican," she said.

"I know," Alex said. "This is your Cathedral." And he gestured behind them, to St Peter's.

Rachel glanced up again at the church – and then looked back to Alex, grasping the crucifix in his hand.

"What was your mother like?" she asked, and he bowed his head closer to the crucifix, closing his eyes.

"I only have early memories," he said. "She died when I was seven."

"How did she die?"

"She was shot," he whispered, and Rachel stared at him. His mother shot, too?

"Unbelievable!" she cried – and he opened his eyes, wrapping his arms around himself.

"It's as if my whole family was cursed, from that moment on," he muttered. "My father found her! He found her. That's…that's when everything changed…"

He was starting to shake. Rachel watched him, frowning. His eyes were starting to drift…

"Alex," she said, and he shook his head.

"What?" he whispered.

19

"Look at me."

He seemed to drag his eyes to her: and now fear was filling his gaze – and now the breathing was quickening again.

"Breathe," she murmured, "remember? Breathe."

He reached to grasp her hand to his shoulder, and followed her deep breathing. She held his strained gaze, and soon he was still.

"You haven't dealt with this," Rachel said gently. "You haven't dealt with any of it."

"How do you deal with it?" Alex asked, grimacing, looking away. "The one who murdered my mother killed my entire family."

"Did they ever find the one?"

"I don't know," Alex muttered. "I think they shot him. But that doesn't fix anything…"

Now his face contorted. "Nothing was enough for my father," he whispered. "It didn't bring her back. Nothing could bring her back. God…" And now his body tensed again, as if in anticipation. "God himself must pay…"

"God?" Rachel asked.

"He hated him," Alex said.

Rachel grimaced again. Enough of his father: time for his mother! There must be more about his mother. "What was she like, Alex?" she asked. "Your mother?"

His eyes found her again: widening, his brow breaking into a crevice.

"I remember," he whispered. "Blue eyes, looking down at me…strong arms, holding me… warm, and gentle, with the crucifix! The crucifix always lying on her chest…"

Rachel reached out a hand to lay her fingers over his face.

"You will see your mother again," she said. "Joshua was alive, after death. We both believe in a resurrection."

"And what about my father?" Alex asked, rising to his feet, stepping back away from her touch. "Will I see him again?"

Rachel swallowed. In that moment she remembered again: Alex stretched out on the altar, Kensington with the gun to his temple.

"Why would you want to?" she breathed, and Alex frowned.

"You think he was a psychopath," he said, and Rachel shifted uncomfortably before him.

"Was he not?" she asked. Kensington, a psychopath? Of course! Or…or something worse…

"I knew him!" Alex said, and his young face was contorting. "I knew him, before he changed! A psychopath doesn't change!"

Rachel frowned, and lifted herself to her feet before him. "Alex," she started carefully, "he had a gun to your head."

"So did James Lester," Alex said. "He had a gun to your head."

Rachel stared at him, and swallowed hard. "It's not the same!" she cried. "James changed!"

20

"Only after shooting my father!" Alex said.

"He was going to kill you!" Rachel cried – and now Alex was shaking his head.

"And what's your great solution now, doctor?" he cried back. "If you're going to stop my escape, what next?"

"What?" Rachel breathed.

"Don't you get it?" Alex cried. "You, a doctor? Don't you get what it's like? Every living moment I feel him! Every night I see him being shot! Even studying at twice the pace didn't take it away!"

Rachel stared at him – watching him start to pace, agitated, before her.

"You still love him," she breathed. "You actually still love him."

Now Alex stared back at her.

"What is it with you people?" he cried. "Why must you keep twisting the knife deeper? So what's next, doctor? Alcohol? Drugs? Maybe go to prison for distribution?"

Rachel gazed at him – and then reached out to his hand, and opened his instinctively clenched palm: the crucifix.

He looked down at it. He sank heavily back down on the bench.

"I don't understand," he whispered. "Why did he have to make life so difficult, Rachel? A battle! It's such a battle…"

"It's like a race," Rachel said, sitting next to him on the bench. "We've got to get to the finish line…"

"Why such pain?" Alex asked. "How could he allow such pain?"

Rachel hesitated – and then reached out to take his hand in her own, with the crucifix sitting between.

Alex looked down at their hands together.

"You're crossing all professional boundaries now, doctor," he muttered wryly.

"You're not my patient," Rachel said.

"Then what am I?" Alex asked. "If not a patient you are counselling?"

Rachel frowned, tightening her grip on his hand. Pain! Her own pain! His pain. To say it would inevitably bring more pain, yet she must. She must.

"Brother," she said. "You are my brother."

"Oh, God," he whispered – and his body stiffened, and he seized his hand away from hers. "Selena!" he cried. "She's dead! Protecting me! Saving me! Making herself my sister!"

And Rachel again saw Selena's body, lying stabbed on the black altar of Kensington.

She quickly reached for James's stethoscope, and tossed it from hand to hand. Work? Relief in work? Distraction? Withdraw the offer?

"I should go," she said. "I have a job to do."

Silently Alex sat next to her, grasping hard the crucifix in his own hand, closing his eyes tightly. "Then go, doctor," he whispered. "Go and save everyone else."

Rachel frowned at him. "You'll be okay now," she said. "Surely you'll be okay."

And she lifted herself again to her feet.

21

He was still there, on the park bench, now drawing his knees to his chest: now hiding his face in his knees, and wrapping his arms around his legs. Just a boy! In that moment she could suddenly see him so clearly – just a boy, sitting quietly, clutching at the crucifix…

A broken, beaten, traumatized boy grasping for relief…

Gripped, Rachel gazed at him.

The stethoscope, counselling, medication…surely all could help. But he was truly a boy, sitting right there: lost, homeless, broken…And he had the power to change their nation, for good or for bad.

This was her brother.

Perplexed, she gazed at him: and then his eyes found hers. He was changed, now: suddenly changed. He was lit up, inspired beyond himself – suddenly knowing more than he should know. And then, equally suddenly, something seized her: love, all consuming – all committed. A brother! This was the brother she could help!

"Well?" he asked. "Still believe in redemption?"

"Yes," Rachel whispered. "Yes, I do!"

His smile widened: but then came another change – sudden exposure, so striking, so young, so vulnerable, that she held her breath. Surely he had not risked uncovering himself so profoundly as this to anyone, not since…since his mother had died…

"Then help me, Rachel," he whispered, his face naked before her. "You couldn't help Joshua in his death, you couldn't help your brother, but you can still help me. I trust in God, but I know…I know I need your humanity too, if I'm ever to succeed…"

And instinct drove her to his side.

She reached for his hand, with the crucifix: she folded their clenched palms over his chest.

"I will help you," she murmured, and his eyes swiftly filled with tears. "I will stand in the place where your mother could not."

He trembled, in her hands. "Mother of God," he whispered.

"Human," Rachel murmured carefully to him. "I am only human."

"Humanity was torn from me," he whispered. "Oh that I might have it back again."

"I will stay with you," Rachel said. "I will protect you."

"Forgive me," Alex whispered. "Forgive me."

He was a man now: a young man. He turned, and gazed at the Cathedral. He turned, and gazed at the Beehive.

"I think we should go," he said. "It begins with your father."

"My father?" Rachel murmured.

"He holds the keys to the nation," Alex said. "And the connections to the World."

"And the keys to his car," she muttered wryly. "I'll need to get back to the hospital, to prepare."

"Then prepare," Alex said. "Do what you must, and let's see together what God will do."

And he grasped her arm, and moved them both forward toward Parliament.

James Connor sat in his office.

On his desk was the photo of Pam and Rachel – Pam's floral summer dress; Rachel's floral shirt, and jeans. Smiles...

James frowned, and reached to finger the frame – to touch each face. Two years ago...two years ago he had sat here, in this spot, sweating with the broken air-con and the global warming, before everything had hit the fan with his handling of Joshua Davidson. The air con was working now: his room was pleasantly cool. He glanced out of his window to the trees outside: the sun was shining, Christmas was coming.

And yet...and yet...

There was a movement. Connor jerked: fear! Why fear? He looked quickly to the door, but it was Patrick Clarkson. Connor breathed a sigh of relief.

"Clarks," he muttered, gesturing to a chair. "How's that rearrangement of the Socialist Party coming along?"

"I could tell you, but I'd have to kill you," Clarkson muttered, sitting opposite him, and Connor shot him a wry glance.

"A little too close to the bone, Pat," he said.

"Yeah," Clarkson muttered. "Sorry."

"That bastard Kensington had my daughter at gun-point," Connor said. "How the hell did you let him infiltrate your party?"

Clarkson's wrinkles seemed to deepen. Connor was sure he had lost even more hair.

"He checked out," Clarkson said. "His record was flawless, and superlative."

"'He comes as an angel of light,'" Connor muttered – and he rose to his feet, and wandered across to the window.

"Satan?" Clarkson said, behind his back. "Don't get all superstitious on me, Jim. Hold it together: you're still our Prime Minister."

Connor leaned heavily against the frame, looking to the street outside: to people walking freely past Parliament, and to the Law School beyond. In that moment he saw Rachel, on her knees, at the altar of St Peter's – with James' gun to her head.

"He manipulated my family for his own purposes," Connor said. "Whether literal or metaphorical, Patrick, he was as Satan to me."

"He's dead now," Clarkson said. "The threat is over. I've weeded out the corruption from my party, Connor. It's a new day. We must put this chapter behind us."

Connor frowned, staring out at the University.

"His son is still alive."

"Jim," Clarkson said. "Don't crucify the son for the crimes of the father."

"No," Connor muttered. "I have something else in mind for him."

And he turned back to Clarkson, and walked back to sit at his desk.

Now Clarkson tossed a folder in his direction.

"Here," he said, and Connor frowned, reaching for it.

"What's this?" he asked, reaching to open the brown cover.

"More intel from the Communications Security Bureau," Clarkson said.

"How do you get this stuff before me, Clarks?" Connor complained. "You make a mockery of our systems: the Leader of the Opposition informs the Government?"

"That's democracy for you," Clarkson said. "But some things are more pressing than our systems, Jim."

Connor looked up to the warning in his eyes, grimaced, and looked down to the papers.

"So inform me," he said, as he began to flick through the folder.

"Unease."

"Yes," Connor said. "No surprises there."

"Networking."

"Yes."

"And this." Now Clarkson reached out and halted the pages – pointing to one paragraph, underlined.

Connor stared at it, and then looked up into Clarkson's eyes.

"Oh, shit," he whispered.

Clarkson's face was controlled: professionalism? He was choosing professionalism, at a time like this?

"It's a potential scenario we have known for decades, though in a different context," Clarkson said. "It is everything we once feared."

"These bastards are playing with fire!" Connor said. "Why do they do this? Why do they hold the fate of the rest of us under siege?"

"They don't see the rest of us," Clarkson said. "Only their own security. Only their own interests."

"Do they know?" Connor asked. "Do they know that we know?"

"Not that we know," Clarkson said wryly, "but, Jim, if they do this, if they go ahead with this move: it won't matter anymore which party is informing who – nothing will matter anymore."

Connor stared at him: at his grim severity. He rose to his feet.

"What are you suggesting...?"

"You know what I am suggesting."

"I can't."

"You must."

"I can't!" He walked again over to the window: to the sun, and the people walking freely outside. "If I get this wrong, Clarks, I'll precipitate World War Three!"

"We're already at war, Jim," Clarkson said quietly. "The War is already here, on all continents: in all nations. The war is already taking place within our boundaries."

"No," Connor whispered. "No." And he closed his eyes, and leaned his head against the glass.

25

"A different society," Clarkson said. "Different ideologies. Different worldviews. How to hold them all together? How to co-exist? Some don't want to coexist, Connor: many don't want to coexist."

"Extremism," Connor whispered – and he opened his eyes again, looking across to the School of Law. "I made a mistake once. I mustn't make it again."

"Inform the other side of the threat," Clarkson said. "Inform the other side."

"Political suicide," Connor said. "They are not our allies. We will be cut off from both sides."

"There can be no survivors from a nuclear holocaust, Jim," Clarkson said. "We will be collateral damage in some else's quest for self-defence. You fear terror? It doesn't get more terrifying than that."

"Yes it does," Connor whispered, and now he saw James's gun again to Rachel's head: and now he saw Kensington's gun to Alex's head. "There is a greater terror than annihilation, Clarks."

"Assimilation."

It was another voice: familiar. Connor looked quickly to his door, to see Alex standing there, frowning, with Rachel behind.

"This is a matter of national security, young man," Clarkson said. "You should not be here."

"The door was unlocked," Rachel said, her eyes finding Connor. "Sorry, Dad, but I need your car."

Connor almost laughed – the relief! Relief: a moment of sanity. His daughter!

"She has free access," he muttered to Clarkson, as he reached into his pocket for his keys. "Knocking is always wise, but perhaps we should not have been discussing matters of national security so casually…"

"Assimilation," Alex repeated. "The greater threat than annihilation is assimilation."

Connor was drawn by his blue eyes: an intensity so similar to that of Kensington, yet without the control.

"What do you mean?" Connor asked, leaning over Clarkson, passing his keys to Rachel.

"You know what I mean," Alex said, holding his eyes. "We are still at threat from within."

Chills went up Connor's spine. Kensington! Alex was talking about Kensington.

"Superstition," Clarkson muttered. "I was blind, Alex, before: I'm sorry you had to expose yourself to danger in the Debating Chamber to make me see it – to uncover your father. You did us an important service: but you are not a part of the Debating Chamber anymore."

"Is he not?" Connor asked – and Clarkson frowned at him.

"Systems, Connor," he said. "Let's not go throwing the baby out with the bathwater."

"He is Kensington's son."

"Yes."

"He knows how he thinks."

Clarkson shifted on his chair. "I'm not sure that's an asset, Connor," he said.

Connor glanced back at Rachel – at her frown – and then looked at Alex.

"I am the Prime Minister," he said. "The Prime Minister you reinstated."

Now Alex shifted uncomfortably on his feet. "I only undid the damage I had caused," he said. "You are the Prime Minister the people chose."

"Then, here," Connor said – and now he reached for the folder on his desk and thrust it into Alex's arms.

"Connor!" Clarkson cried. "What the hell are you doing?"

"Protecting national security," Connor said, holding Alex's bewilderment. "You aced four years of IT in two years, and came top in your class."

"You've been watching me," Alex said, and Connor nodded.

"Wouldn't you, in my position?" he asked, and Alex nodded.

"Yes," he said. "I would."

"Read this document," Connor said. "Tell me if it's real."

Alex frowned at him, and then looked down at the papers in his hands.

"I'm not as qualified as the Communications Security Bureau," he said, while he began to read.

"That doesn't matter," Connor said. "I know what you can do. I know what you were doing, before you went to University."

Alex's gaze returned to him, troubled, before the eyes dropped again to the document. He was skimming! Skimming very quickly, page after page – and then he finished, and his eyes were looking around, his hands reaching instinctively.

"Here," Connor said – and he turned the monitor on his desk toward Alex, and handed him his keyboard.

"Jim!" Clarkson said. "This is about national security!"

"Did you not see what he did?" Connor replied, gesturing Alex to his own seat. "He put himself in harm's way to secure our freedom, Clarks. We were going down."

"I know that, Jim, but this?"

Now Alex's eyes were on him. The window: the login.

Connor held his eyes. "Do you know how to hack into this?" he asked.

"Yes," Alex said plainly. "But it is illegal."

Connor studied his eyes. "You are capable of overriding the law, but choose not to?"

"Yes," Alex said.

"Why?" Connor asked.

"Because it is a law others have chosen."

"Boundaries," Rachel's voice said behind him. "He is respecting the boundaries, irrespective of threat of punishment."

"Fine," Connor said. "Be my guest." And he typed in his own name and password.

Now Alex had legal access.

27

Connor watched as his fingers sped across the keyboard – as his eyes quickly moved across the screen: as rapidly changing windows appeared.

The National Communications Bureau – the intelligence...

Alex frowned – and then he rose to his feet, gathered up the papers, and passed the folder back to Connor.

"It's fake," he said. "The intelligence the bureau received is fake."

Connor stared at him, and then glanced across to Clarkson's wide eyes.

"What do you mean it's fake?" Clarkson asked. "We have internationally acclaimed specialists in the field..."

"It's manipulation," Alex said, his face stern. "Someone is trying to make you afraid."

And his gaze was fixed on Connor.

"To what end?" Connor asked, and Alex smiled sadly.

"You know to what end," he said.

Connor stared at him, but now Clarkson was logging out of the computer and turning the screen away from Alex.

"That's enough," he said. "He's a cocky youth too secure in his own opinion to be ready to advise."

Connor frowned, studying Alex's blue eyes. Cocky? Sure, capable of this, but right now? Right here?

"Rachel?" Connor asked – and now Rachel was alongside him.

"Yes?" she asked.

"Interpret him."

"What?" she said, her face flushing.

"For the sake of national security, Rachel: interpret him."

Alex's eyes widened – was that tears? And now he looked away.

"I'll be going now," he said.

"No," Connor said. "Look at me."

Alex swallowed, and looked up, and held his eyes, but something was happening: something else.

"He's lying," Clarkson said, and Rachel shook her head.

"No," she said. "It's not that."

His breathing was quickening: fear? Fear of being found out?

"Stop this," Rachel said. "You're interrogating him: he is not the enemy."

"I have to know the truth," Connor said. "For national security."

Now Alex was wrapping his arms around himself.

"Something to hide!" Clarkson said. "Come on, we can't trust this youth."

"That's enough," Rachel said.

"Interpret him for me," Connor said.

"That's enough!" Rachel said. "He's not a lab rat!"

"Neither one of you are leaving this room," Connor said, feeling anger suddenly rise up, "until you interpret him for me!"

"Who the hell do you think you are?" Rachel suddenly cried out. "Hitler?"

28

Now Connor stared at her. Hitler? He fell back a step.

"How dare you?" Rachel cried, jabbing her finger at him. "How dare you use him? How dare you manipulate me?"

Use? Use? Connor shook his head, trying to clear it – but now Alex's eyes were before him: his blue gaze intensified further through the tears.

"It's him," he said.

"What?" Connor asked.

"Kensington," Alex said. "It's him: his methods. I recognise him."

Connor swallowed as he held his eyes. "You mean me?" he asked. "I look like Kensington?"

And now Alex reached out to grasp his arm. "Assimilation," he said. "Assimilation is the greater threat than annihilation."

"To become like Kensington," Connor said, looking at him – grasping the hand on his arm. "To become like Hitler. I see it now: you're right. I'm sorry."

And Alex nodded, and withdrew his hand.

Clarkson was still sitting in front of them: Connor watched his eyes move from Alex to himself, while Rachel still stood rigidly at his left side.

"I've always thought you might become a Hitler, Jim," Clarkson said wryly, "so that part isn't exactly news, but what's all this about Kensington?"

"He's set up systems," Alex said. "Corrupted programmes I couldn't find when I did a sweep after he died."

"You're saying this intel is one of his corrupted programmes?" Clarkson said.

"Yes," Alex replied. "I recognise his signature."

"But…how can we know we can trust you?" Clarkson asked – and now Connor looked again at Rachel.

She was fuming. "You have got to be joking," she said. "You brought me here for this?"

"No," Connor said, taking her arm – moving her away from Clarkson and Alex. "I'm neither that conceited nor that clever."

"You came to the hospital just to…"

"No," he said. "Rachel – I'm not Kensington."

Her eyes: he had her attention now, even as his own eyes blurred.

"I will read you before I read him," she said. "Tell me the truth."

Connor took a deep breath and then held her eyes.

"The intel," he said. "It suggests a nuclear missile will be launched in eight days, toward a target…"

"Where, Dad?" Rachel asked – and he leaned over and whispered the answer in her ear, and withdrew to look at her widened eyes.

"Oh, dear God," she whispered. "That would be cataclysmic."

"I could tell them," Connor said. "Should I tell them?"

Rachel frowned. "But they will give a pre-emptive strike."

"Maybe," Connor said. "Or maybe they will just show themselves ready, and the attack will be diverted…"

29

"Equal defence, equal knowledge…"

"But Alex says it is fake, Rachel: that the intel is false. If so, I might precipitate disaster if I act: false news of an imminent attack, fear precipitating a pre-emptive strike, igniting an escalating nuclear exchange, sucking in all the allies in its wake. But if the intel is true, and I don't act, Rachel, I might be sitting back watching World War Three unfolding before our eyes, when I could have prevented it: when I could have balanced the stakes."

Rachel grimaced, but now Alex's voice sounded. "You're missing the point," he said. "You're focusing on the wrong enemy. It's not either side of a tit for tat nuclear exchange that we should fight: the real enemy targets deeper and harder."

Connor looked back to his serious young face – and now Alex stretched out his arms, before them.

"He's telling the truth, Dad," Rachel's voice said.

"How do you know?" Connor asked, holding Alex's intense gaze: his open gesture.

"You know politics, he knows computers," Rachel said, "but I know him, Dad."

And now Connor glanced back to his daughter: to her insight. "I know you know him, Rachel," he murmured. "That's why I knew you could help him."

"You were genuine?" Rachel asked. "About helping him?"

"Of course," Connor said. "I'm not Kensington, Rachel: I'm seriously not that much of a bastard, at least not yet."

And Rachel grinned, and Connor grinned back – and then he turned back to Clarkson.

"Here," he said, handing the folder back, and Clarkson rose to his feet. "We've got work to do."

"Should we use him?" Clarkson asked, and he gestured to Alex. "He can recognise his father's signature. He says his father is the real enemy."

Rachel was moving toward Alex, and Connor frowned. Use him? Use Kensington's son? But now Rachel was turning.

"It's his choice," she said. "It always must be his choice."

And now Alex walked over to the window and looked outside.

Connor watched his back. How would it be for this young man? Almost killed by his father, now constantly seeking out his signature to save the nation again and again from his corruption?

"It's like a life sentence," Connor muttered under his breath. "But surely there is an end to it: surely there must be an end."

Alex was silent, and then he turned: and then he grimaced.

"I'll help you," he said. "I'll help you for a time, but only for a time. And when the right time comes, I will move on."

"Very well," Connor said. "Do what you can."

"Then do it with me," Clarkson said. "Your father's hand was most clearly outworked through my party. You will be able to most effectively clean up through our routes."

Alex took a deep breath and released it. "All right," he said. "I'll do it with you."
And he followed Clarkson out of the door.

Rachel was lingering. Connor stood silently, and then she met his eyes.

"I'm sorry," she said, "about the Hitler thing. I just couldn't stand…"

"You were right," he said.

"What?" she asked.

"You were right," he said. "I needed you to tell me."

Rachel swallowed. And then she moved toward the door.

"You know, Dad," she said. "This thing with Alex: it will take its toll. It's not just a normal job for him: it will never be just a normal job."

"I know," Connor said.

"He…he needs…" She was hesitating, and he smiled sadly.

"He needs you," he said gently. "Already you defend him as family."

"Adopted, I guess," she said. "Adopted."

"So be it," Connor said. "Watch out for him."

"I'll return your car and catch the train."

"Okay."

"I'm resigning for now."

"I know."

"I…" And now she hesitated again, and the continued. "I love you, Dad."

He smiled sadly at her, and nodded.

"And I love you, Rachel," he said. "Everything I have is yours."

She gazed at him, smiled again, and then was gone.

He was alone, in his office.

Troubled, he moved back to the window and looked outside. Again, people moving, freely, down the sunny street. Blissfully ignorant that he might have just ended their lives, were it not for Alex's intervention.

"Who knows how much time we have?" he muttered to himself, and then he turned away from the window and back to his computer.

CHAPTER FOUR: A Response

John Robertson stood in St Peter's Cathedral.

The church was quiet. John stood in the central aisle, and looked up to the red, green and blue of the stained glass windows above. Christ was feeding the masses. Peter and the others were in the boat with Christ, surrounded by the storm. Paul was being blinded by the light...

John gazed up at the windows, and then lowered his eyes to look at Jesus on the cross, with the crown of thorns on his head. He remembered Joshua, kneeling in the street between the Cathedral and Parliament, wearing the ancient metal crown on his head: drawing all darkness to himself – drawing it, carrying it, into the grave, that others might be relieved of it.

The pain! The pain of the offering! The pain of Tristan's bullets, throwing his body back to the ground! Choking! Choking! And yet, the peace! The peace of the realization of that offering. "It's finished," he had said to Rachel, with a smile. "It's sorted!"

The death...and then his return.

John still remembered that morning: he had been there, lying against the white stone wall next to the church, dozing at Joshua's grave – he had awoken. Joshua! His smile! Surely a dream! Surely his deepest desire! And yet, Joshua had drawn his hands to the bullet holes in his own chest – and yet Rau had appeared, and had seen him too.

John wandered now forward to the altar – he reached out his fingers to touch the white linen, and the silver chalice of wine and plate with wafers on top.

The body and blood of Christ...the offering, to carry the sin of the World into the grave and to overcome it, that all might be given the chance to truly live.

He fleetingly closed his eyes. "Have your way," he prayed. "You are the Master of everything good: have your way."

And he went down to his knees, pressing his head to the wood of the altar: offering himself in return.

Peace filled him: peace, and love. He smiled into the altar. And then he lifted himself to his feet, and turned.

Mark Blake was standing behind him. John cast his eyes over his purple bishop's tunic and then lifted his gaze to Mark's blue eyes.

"Greetings, Mark," he said.

"Greetings," Mark replied, the corner of his mouth lifting. "Good to see you, John."

"Good to see you too," John said. "Office work getting a bit tedious?"

"Great to have an excuse to get out of the box," Mark said.

"Hope you don't mind..."

"Of course not," Mark said. "Hope I'm not interrupting..."

"I always love..."

"Of course you do," Mark said.

"This is his house," John said, gesturing around the church. "His home. His family."

"Where else would you be?" Mark asked.

John smiled at him – and then heard another voice, from the back of the church.

"That's right," she said. "Where else would you be? Not in a 'real' job, that's for sure."

Mark's eyebrows lifted, his smile widening, and then he bowed his head to John.

"That's my cue," he said. "Make way for the wife." And he backed away to the side aisle, and disappeared down the corridor behind the choir stalls.

John turned – and now Rachel was striding down the aisle. Her long brown hair was a bit messy around her shoulders: he liked it that way.

She arrived: her white cheeks a bit flushed, the stethoscope just visible in her trouser pocket.

"Ah, John…" she began, reaching for his arm. "There's something I have to tell you."

"What's that?" he asked, and her blue eyes set on him.

"I've resigned," she said.

"What?" he asked. "But you've only just started as a consultant…"

"I've resigned," she repeated, and John searched her certain face. Was she still in pain? Still carrying the trauma of everything that had happened? She held it to herself: always so very close to her own chest.

"Is it about Joshua?" he asked. "Or James? I thought you were feeling better…"

"So many issues," Rachel said, smirking. "Hard to keep track! No, it's not about Joshua or James – I'm feeling much better about them. It's about Alex."

"Alex?"

And now Rachel was gesturing down the centre aisle.

John followed her gesture: and saw the young man sitting in the very back row, on the aisle, his arms crossed over his chest – his face looking ashen.

John swallowed. Alex was in his mind, lying over the altar, his father's gun to his temple…

He was there again, now: sitting, quiet, almost deathly still.

"He looks terrible," John muttered to Rachel.

"He is terrible," Rachel said, "some of the time. Much of the time."

John gazed at the compassion in her face. She was giving up her job for him?

"The money…" Rachel began.

"We'll cope," John said. "We can still use the money I got from selling my business."

"I don't know how long…"

"I know," he said. "Do what you have to do."

"Us…He…"

John smiled sadly at her. "Think I'll get jealous?"

33

"No," she said. "Of course not. But…it'll take a lot, John…"

John frowned, and then reached out to take her hand and walked with her down the aisle.

Alex was before him: seated, looking a little stiff. He was staring forward toward Jesus on the cross and the altar – the place where his father had been snatched away.

John remembered – he was reaching out to him, while Kensington was about to pull the trigger: reaching out, and then there was a shot – and then Kensington's body was taken. And then…then Alex screamed…

John reached out to him again now – to touch his shoulder…

Alex stiffened, and shook John's fingers off. Now Rachel was reaching – now she was laying a hand on his shoulder, and his posture seemed to ease a little.

How old was he now: twenty? And Rachel was fifteen years older. Almost…almost old enough to be his mother…

Alex trusted her.

Fascinated, John looked between them – and then sat himself quietly next to Alex, looking forward, shoulder to shoulder.

Alex's gaze was still intense: still fixed on the altar.

"What do you see?" John murmured, and Alex shrugged slightly.

"The altar," he said. "The chalice. The cross."

"No," John said. "What do you really see?"

Alex swallowed, and closed his eyes tightly. "More than I want to see," he whispered.

"Share it," John said quietly. "Share it, so you needn't carry it alone."

"There is no one to share it with," Alex whispered. "No one strong enough: no one wise enough."

John suddenly wanted to grasp his hand: he resisted – knew Alex would shake him off. He glanced up at Rachel's hand on his shoulder: a doctor. Was she strong enough? Was she wise enough?

"Support," John said. "We will give you support."

Alex shrugged, and opened his eyes again – looking back at the cross.

"For a time," he said, "and then no more."

John looked up to Rachel's eyes: to her determination. She was drawn! Wholly drawn to his side: to help him. Why? It was as if she was bound to him, bound to his fate: she had been there – she had risked her life to cry out for his salvation.

And now…now she was putting her career on hold for him.

Why?

Was he to her a son? No, surely she was too young. Was he…oh, yes, of course: a brother! He was a brother to her…

"She won't leave you," John said. "Once she makes a decision, once she bonds, there's no going back…" And he grinned at her, and she smirked back at him.

Alex's expression softened for a moment. He glanced up at Rachel's face.

"Thank you," he whispered. And then his face changed again: and then he was looking again at the cross.

John noticed him gripping something in his right hand. A golden chain…and, yes: a crucifix. He nodded at it.

"Catholic," he murmured.

"My mother's," Alex said back.

"The Protestant cross is usually empty," John said – and now he reached toward Rachel, to the plain golden cross lying hidden on her chest. He held her eyes, her knowing consent, unhooked it, and pulled it down on his hand, hanging it before Alex's eyes. "Why is the Protestant cross empty, Alex?" he asked.

Alex tore his eyes away from Jesus on the cross to the empty cross hanging before his eyes: John watched his confusion.

"I don't understand," he whispered, and John nodded.

"You will," he said quietly. "One day you will." And he passed the empty cross back to Rachel.

The young man…he was caught somehow, in that place: John could see – caught in the crucifixion.

"Stay here," John murmured. "Stay as long as you like."

"I'd better be going," Alex said – and he rose to his feet, and turned away toward the glass doors.

John glanced at Rachel, who was following after Alex.

"Are you going back in there?" she asked, and Alex shrugged.

"It's what I have to do," he said. "It's what is needed."

"Then I'll go in there with you," Rachel said.

Alex glanced back at her now, smiling sadly. "You should stay here," he said. "My father's thoughts are not for the faint-hearted."

"Am I faint-hearted?" Rachel asked, smiling wryly, and John watched Alex's face stiffen, as if with some cursed memory.

"That's not what I meant," he said. "Selena…" And Rachel shook her head.

"I'm not Selena," she said. "I am an adult."

"That doesn't matter," Alex said. "He is powerful: more powerful than you are."

"You speak as if he is still alive," John said, and Alex glanced to him.

"Is he not still alive?" Alex asked. "In my heart and mind?"

"He needn't be," Rachel said. "He shouldn't be."

"Shouldn't be?" Alex asked. "He's my father."

"Alex…" Rachel began.

"He is my father!" Alex cried out – and his voice filled the entire cathedral. John watched Rachel's eyes widen – then he stepped forward.

"Keep us around you," he said, and Alex shook his head, as if to clear it.

"What?" he asked.

"Keep us around you," John said. "Both of us."

Alex frowned at him. "You don't understand me," he said. "Even you."

"Then help me to," John said.

"I wouldn't wish it on anyone…"

35

"Help me to!" John said – and now he reached instinctively to grasp Alex's hand.

A shudder passed through Alex's body – he quickly, immediately, threw off John's hand.

"Don't touch me!" he said, and John swallowed as Rachel again reached to lay a hand on Alex's shoulder: as she calmed him.

"I'm sorry," John said.

"You don't understand me," Alex said. "You have no idea what you're dealing with."

"What am I dealing with?" John asked.

"Me," Alex said simply. And then, suddenly, he laughed.

John gazed at his sudden lit face. Where did that come from? Humour? Humour, in the midst of intensity?

"You're not so scary," John said, and now Alex's face intensified again.

"You have no idea," he said. "No idea."

"You are not the same as your father, Alex Kensington," John said.

Now Alex was staring at him – now he swallowed.

"I hope and pray that that is true," he whispered – and he looked up to the cross, turned, and thrust open the glass doors before him.

John looked again toward Rachel. She looked perplexed.

"Well?" John asked. "How's his mental health?"

"His mental health?" Rachel asked. "I was hoping you'd tell me how his spiritual health is."

John frowned, looking after him. "His spiritual health," he murmured. "He is in pain: sometimes spirit-breaking pain."

"Yes," Rachel said.

"And yet," John said, "there is more."

"What more?" Rachel asked.

"There's something about him," John said. "Something…"

"…powerful," Rachel finished.

"For good or for bad," John said. "Something powerful."

Rachel was holding his eyes, and smiled sadly.

"And you?" John asked. "What do you see in him?"

"A broken boy," Rachel said, shrugging slightly. "A broken boy who needs care."

John nodded. "And so you have responded," he said. "As inevitably you would."

"Inevitably?" Rachel asked.

"Well," John said, "you're a sucker for hard core cases."

And now he broke into a grin, and now Rachel hit him on the chest.

Suddenly, instinctively, he drew her to himself. Alone! In that moment, in the church, they were alone! He felt her breath quickening on his face – he lowered his lips toward her…but then the church doors were opening again.

"Well?" Alex's voice said. "Coming with me into the pit of hell?"

John drew back, released Rachel, and watched her turning toward Alex.

"Okay," she said. "I'm coming."

"I'll be here," John said to them both. "Right here."

"Okay," Rachel said. "I'll see you soon."

And she followed Alex out of the church and away, toward Parliament.

CHAPTER FIVE: Love, Light and Fear

Tristan Blake stood on the sand of Oriental Bay.

In front of him, Rau Petera was still standing on that same rock: lifting his voice to the crowd. Tristan cast his eyes over the many faces: Maori, Pakeha, Pacific, Indian, Chinese, Filipino, Korean....thousands! Many thousands were cramming themselves within the tsunami retaining wall of the beach, spilling over into the calm sea behind Rau, forming silhouettes for the light reflecting off the water...

"Good news!" Rau cried at the top of his lungs, his voice lifted in the gentle sea breeze. "Joshua Davidson is alive! We killed him, in our fear, but he was stronger than our fear. We killed him with our darkness, but he was stronger than our darkness."

Tristan reached into his own jacket pocket: his rifle, the weapon he had used to execute Joshua, was gone. What was in its place? Empty space? His fingers groped about, searching for the familiar trigger, seeming lost without it...and yet...and yet...

He looked again at Rau's brown face, radiant in the sun – he felt his own face responding: his own smile dawning. It didn't matter! It didn't matter that his defence was gone! He had thrown it away, into the Hutt River – he had chosen trust instead. Trust in what? In life after death? In a kind of life stronger than death?

He remembered Joshua's face, as he had knelt before Tristan: as he had worn the cursed ancient crown Selena had thrust upon his head – as he had sweated blood.

"Father, don't hold it against them!" he had cried, lifting his face to God. "They really have no idea what they are doing!"

No idea...Tristan had sent the bullets into his chest. Joshua had received them! Had taken them into the grave. And then...and then he had overcome them...

"We saw him!" Rau cried out – a thousand times, with no less passion as he reached more and more with the news. "John and I saw him! We touched the bullet holes in his chest! He was alive! He is alive! And now..." He paused, and his warm brown eyes found Tristan, and Tristan saw the familiar tears form, and felt his own tears respond. "...and now we can live too."

Joy. Tristan could feel it: like a river bursting forth in his depths – life! Life, strong enough, true enough, to even transcend death! Eternal life! Everlasting life...

Rau's eyes were holding him fast. "Come!" he cried out to the crowd. "Accept this gift which God has offered: a new chance! A new way! Say goodbye to the old ways: the ways of death, of destruction – hand those ways over, let Joshua take them into the grave. Rise again with him into a new way: into a new kind of life."

A new life...

Now Rau was gesturing behind him to the water: now he was smiling at Tristan, and Tristan grinned at him.

Don't you dare, old man, he said to him through his gaze, and now Rau was off the rock and striding toward him, reaching out his hand.

38

"No gun in your pocket holding you back this time," Rau's muttered, and Tristan stared at the hand.

"Yeah, I know," he said, "but, come on: grown men holding hands?"

"Enough!" Rau cried. "You've procrastinated too long, boy!"

And he grasped his sleeve, and Tristan let him drag him into the sea, playfully flicking at the affectionate strong Maori grip on his arm.

"Wash away the darkness of the past!" Rau cried out to the crowd watching on the sand. "Wash away the guilt. God is offering a new start! God is offering a new life."

Now Tristan let Rau lower him under the water.

A wave covered his face. He stared up through the murky salt water to the sunlight beyond: and now Rau was pulling him up out of the watery grave with both fists on his jacket.

Tristan gasped, and stood, dripping, standing in the sea. A crowd was watching him – he didn't care. He lifted his face toward the warm summer sun: he closed his eyes, and took in a deep breath.

"Christ is coming," Rau's voice sounded alongside him. "Christmas is coming. He came once: he will come again. We look to his coming: we look ahead to the time when the true King will make all things right again."

Christmas…a mass of people gathered to receive Christ…

"Next time when he comes, he will not be as a baby," Rau said. "Next time, he will come as Lord."

As Lord…Tristan opened his eyes: he looked at Rau.

"But what does that even mean?" he said. "A Prime Minister? A human dictator?"

"An altruistic monarch," Rau murmured to him. "But with one key difference: this monarch carries within him the authority of God."

"God," Tristan murmured. "All powerful, all knowing, all scary…"

"Joshua, on his knees," Rau murmured back, "carrying your bullets that you might live."

Tristan quickly reached out a hand to his shoulder. "It's a frightening thing, Rau," he said, "the thought of Christ taking over…"

"There will come a time," Rau said, grasping Tristan's hand on his own shoulder, "when we will long for it to be so."

Rau was leading him out of the water.

"The vulnerable human being," Tristan said, "shot, killed, crucified, that we might live."

"He keeps his vulnerable humanity," Rau said, drawing him back onto the sand. "He keeps his divinity."

"How can a person be both human and God?" Tristan asked, and now Rau was turning to him: and now the brown eyes were sparkling.

"To not reduce Christ to mere humanity," he said, "and to not elevate humanity to the position of God: that is the task before you, Tristan. Because humanity is by no means God: and yet Jesus is beyond mere humanity."

Rau was grasping his hand. Tristan stared at their hands together, and grasped Rau in turn. The Maori priest grinned. "May God bless you, Tristan," he said – and then he turned away, to the others.

Tristan watched him for a while: his warmth, as he stretched out his hand to many – as he grasped many. Tristan was dripping, in the sand, but still warm. Christ: divine and yet human. How? How could this possibly be understood? And yet Joshua, on his knees, receiving Tristan's bullets – and yet Joshua, alive again, before Rau and John...

This could be understood.

He turned, and looked across the water: the sparkling of the sun, the lifting of his heart...

"Love," a voice said alongside him, and Tristan looked up to see John. "There is light, and there is love."

Rachel was next to him, pretty face; messy hair. She was grinning at him. Did she have light? Did she have love?

Tristan searched her. Rachel had almost died – Tristan had stood ready to protect her: ready to shoot his own comrade, James Lester, pointing the gun to her head. But something had happened in that moment – something profound. She had believed – she had trusted in Joshua's new life beyond her own imminent death.

Now her arm was around another's shoulders...

Tristan almost started. Alex! He hadn't expected to see him, here, on a Sunday morning. Last time Tristan had seen him appear in this spot, it had been with Kensington's gun...

Alex's forehead was forming a crevice: his eyes were moving quickly across the sand. Tristan had seen the signs so many times, since he had lived in their house: the fast breathing, the tension in his body, the...the harrowing look in his eyes...

"Hey," Tristan said, touching him on the shoulder. Distraction! Bring him back. "You must think I'm a dweeb, fully grown man walking into the ocean with all my clothes on."

Alex's eyes settled on him: his face broke into a quiet wry smile.

"I think I prefer the clothes on," he said.

"You should try it some time," Tristan said. "It's really quite refreshing!"

"I'll bet," Alex said – and now his eyes were following after Rau: and now he was wandering toward the priest.

Tristan returned to John.

"Love," he said. "I get Joshua's love: who wouldn't? A man dies to save you."

"That's the point," John said, the same light in his green eyes. "The love is there, as well as the light. The light can be frightening, if we are still in darkness, but the love gives us confidence."

"Yes," Tristan murmured – and now Rachel was wandering after Alex, and now Tristan wandered after Rachel.

She stopped, behind the young man: she reached out a hand to his shoulder. What was going on there? Tristan wondered, and he glanced back to John: but, no – the green eyes, perceptive, were wholly at peace. It was something else…something else, in the beautiful lady: in the doctor. Curious, he circled around the group waiting for Rau: he stood now facing Rachel and Alex.

She spotted him staring at her: he questioned her with his gaze, and a grin. She shrugged her shoulders, whilst keeping her hand on Alex – but now Alex grabbed his attention.

He had reached Rau, and his face, his young face, suddenly contorted.

Rau reached for him, grasping his arms as Rachel fell back a step. Alex's voice was rising! Rising, higher and higher, toward a scream.

John thrust himself forward – but Rau was drawing Alex toward the ocean.

"No!" Rachel called out. "The water! He's having a flashback: he might drown!"

"Leave the past behind," Rau said. "Be washed clean of it, Alex! Start again: a new birth – a new life."

"He's coming!" Alex cried. "You're not safe! None of you are safe!"

"Rau," Tristan said, stepping forward: reaching a hand to the priest, to restrain him. "I know what you're trying to do, but…"

"Joshua is stronger," Rau said – and now Alex was on his knees on the sand before him: and now Rau was grasping him to his own chest.

"I know Joshua is stronger," Alex whispered against him. "I know!"

He was crying, and Rau was holding him.

In wonder, Tristan watched them. This young man had been sent by his father to kill Rau: and yet he had resisted – and yet he had submitted to Rau's message instead.

And now Rau was comforting him.

Joshua had indeed been stronger. And yet…and yet Alex was not yet at peace…

He was leaning against Rau – and then he rose to his feet, and turned his contorted face to the beach.

"Please," he whispered to Rau, "you're meeting out in the open, getting stronger and stronger, and…and I don't want to see you die."

Tristan stared at him. Kensington was dead: he had shot him himself, with James Lester! Both had shot: two bullets, to heart and brain, saving Alex's life. No possible survival.

And yet, Alex was clearly serious. Surely delusional! Surely it was the potency of the flashbacks: they were real! Tristan knew the power of trauma. Each one was almost as strong as the original: fear, anguish, and the fear of it all repeating all over again…

Yet Rau was taking him seriously.

41

"Even if he should come," Rau said to him. "Even if he should rise from the dead, Joshua is stronger."

"You don't understand," Alex whispered to him. "None of you understand."

"Even if everything you fear comes to pass," Rau said, "God will overcome in the end."

"I know," Alex pleaded, "I know. But I can't bear to watch you die."

Now Rau was grasping Alex's forehead to his own – now his eyes were holding Alex's terror.

"Then look away," he said. "When the moment comes, look away."

Tristan stared at him as Alex gasped. "You know?" Alex cried. "You know already?"

"I know," Rau said. "Joshua told me."

And he pressed his nose into Alex's nose with a hongi. "Carry the light," he said. "When my time is over, Alex, carry the light for me: carry it for Joshua – carry it for God."

Alex was weeping, and Rau held him close to himself, face to face – and he breathed over him, and prayed, and Alex's tears settled.

Rachel gathered Alex into her own arms. John's face looked white, staring at Rau: Rau grasped his shoulder, and then turned away, and now he was facing Tristan.

Tristan stared at him – tears filled his eyes. He tried to blink them away.

"The boy is wounded," he said. "Always feeling his father's fists: always remembering his father's gun."

"He is," Rau said, holding his eyes. "But he is also gifted."

"So where does the trauma end?" Tristan asked. "And the gifting begin?"

"They are one," Rau replied. "He was broken open to testify to the light."

Grief seized Tristan – he hurriedly pushed it away.

"He's just feeling the pain!" he whispered, his throat constricting. "Just feeling the same pain…"

And now Rau's hands came to Tristan's arms.

"You need to be ready," Rau said. "When the time comes, you will need to be ready."

"I have no gun," Tristan whispered. "I have no defence."

"That is because physical defence will not be your role," Rau said.

"Then what?" Tristan pleaded. "What can an ex-army officer do but defend, or attack?"

Rau smiled sadly at him, and then reached to grasp his shoulders.

"You are an excellent man, Tristan Blake," he said. "You will know what to do, when the time comes."

And now he grasped his hand, bowed his head, and turned away.

Tristan stood alone on the sand. Thousands were gathered around Rau. Alex was backing away from the crowd, turning toward the street, now running. Rachel was

42

rushing after him, glancing back at Tristan with a troubled frown. John seemed to have gone: almost anticipating Alex, almost one step ahead.

Rau…Tristan quenched the sob in his throat. Brown face, warm smile, light in his eyes…It had begun with him! All of it…this crazy trip through life, and death…

Now another hand was on his shoulder.

He turned to find his father standing behind him, without the purple bishop robes – wearing a T-shirt and shorts, and a simple golden cross.

"Shouldn't you be in church?" Tristan muttered, and Mark smiled gently.

"I am in church," he said, and Tristan reached out to grasp the hand on his shoulder.

"Rau," he said, and felt himself trembling, and Mark's grip tightened on him.

"He's ready," he murmured, "as am I. There's a time to live and a time to die."

"I'm not ready to die," Tristan whispered. "And Alex looks like he's already dead."

"Alex will find his life," Mark said. "Keep watching out for him. Keep protecting him."

"I'm scared of him, Dad," Tristan said. "He goes through hell, again and again: I see what it could do to him – I see what it could make him into."

"His father's son," Mark said, and Tristan stiffened, looking at Rau.

"That bastard Kensington," Tristan said. "How could he do that, in front of all of us? How could he munt his own son? How could he…"

And now, suddenly, Tristan's vision blurred – he swayed.

"I'd want to kill him all over again," he whispered. "If I ever saw that bastard in the flesh…"

His father was supporting him. "Selena is alive," Mark's voice said over him: penetrating his giddy haze. "Protect your heart. Protect your mind."

Tristan took a deep breath, and his vision cleared. His sister! Dead, on Kensington's black altar! And yet…and yet…

"The light," Mark murmured over him. "Selena: the light, in the darkness."

"The light," Tristan whispered. "Her name…"

"It costs, to dare to shine light in darkness, Tristan: she knew that – she accepted it."

"We saved his body," Tristan said. "She saved his soul."

"No," Mark said. "She simply ushered him toward the only one who was truly capable of saving his soul: the one who had already saved her soul."

"It's all beyond me," Tristan said. "How can Alex survive it? How can he persevere, and not hate, and not fight, and not want to kill…?"

"He is like a child," Mark interrupted. "He still has some innocence, in the midst of overwhelming evil, but that kind of vulnerability needs protection."

"I will protect him," Tristan said, staring at Rau: finding Rau's eyes returning to him. "Even if it kills me, I will protect him."

"Without a gun?" Mark murmured from behind him, and Tristan turned to him.

43

His father. He looked sad, in that moment: smiling gently, and yet with sadness. Tristan searched his eyes.

"How do I fight this kind of battle, Dad?" he asked. "A battle of intangible forces: of evil and good within the same person – of darkness and light; of sin and sacrifice?"

"You fight it with humility," Mark said, "and with a willingness always to submit to the one who is greater: the one who is capable of overcoming all of our darkness with his light."

Tristan reached out to touch the golden cross sitting on Mark's chest, and then reached out to touch his father's face.

"May God bless you, Dad," he said. "May he make his light shine upon you, and give you peace."

And tears filled Mark's blue eyes.

"Likewise," he whispered – and his arms came around Tristan, and Tristan closed his eyes.

Peace: a peace without tangible weapons. He drew away from his father: he resisted the urge to search for his rifle in his empty jacket pocket. He turned, and glanced back to Rau, who was smiling – and then he turned away from the beach and toward the street.

CHAPTER SIX: A Revelation

John stood in St Peter's Cathedral.

The church was dark – the lights were out. John frowned. He looked around himself, at the wooden chairs, at the prayer books, at the red carpet. Quiet solitude…and yet…and yet something was wrong.

Frowning, he looked back toward the glass doors. It was out there. Swallowing, he glanced back to Jesus on the cross. Strength! Comfort. Courage: courage to face the truth. He closed his eyes, breathed in deeply, and then turned and thrust himself down the aisle and through the glass doors.

The street was empty. John lifted his eyes to the Beehive, and started. Flames! Flames, engulfing the building – flames spreading to Parliament House. Stunned, he stared. Real? Surely not real…there was a quality to the flames, as they began to engulf stone: a surreal, true quality…

Screams were rising in the air from the flames. John shuddered. Act? Move? He was fixed to the steps, outside the Cathedral – but there was something more: something worse.

A chill rose up his spine. He turned, on the steps: he looked. His vision was taken, through buildings, through hills, across a vast expanse of water, to another land: to a vast city, a ruling city – and an explosion.

A blinding flash of light. A vast invisible moving wave. Buildings collapsing, heat pulverising: millions standing, afraid, and then suddenly gone.

Then the dust…the vast dust of destroyed stone, of decimated people, thrown forcefully into the atmosphere: blood red, forming the shape of a mushroom…

"Oh my God," John breathed. "The beginning of the end…"

And he fell down to his knees, and slid down a few of the steps.

"John?" It was Rachel's voice. John shook his head. Normality? He turned, sitting on the step. The Beehive, the ten stories of grey: it was normal! The cream stone of Parliament House alongside, free from flames: free from consumption…

A hallucination? A vision?

"Democracy," John whispered "Freedom will soon be taken…"

"John," Rachel's voice said – and now she was shaking his arms. John stared up into her pretty face – normality! He could feel it returning. He took a deep breath, closed his eyes, and opened them again. Blessed freedom…

"John," Rachel said, her tone urgent. "We need your help."

And she was dragging him to his feet.

Alex was there. John stared at him: felt the same chill up his back. His eyes: death! Destruction.

"We have to get him out," Rachel said. "It's too much, John! The burden is too great – the cost is too high."

And now she was dragging Alex up the steps and through the glass doors.

John followed them into the Cathedral.

45

Alex was sagging, even as Rachel dragged him – even as she drew him all the way up the aisle, and released him next to the altar.

"No!" Alex cried – and his body stiffened, sinking to the ground, and now he was jerking: now his voice was lifting into a shriek.

Suddenly John remembered Selena, at the altar: body collapsing in his arms, voice lifting into a wail.

"It's not medical, John!" Rachel cried, distraught. "It's not a physical seizure, it's not the trauma: there's something else! Something spiritual."

John frowned, and moved himself forward.

Alex was writhing on the ground at his feet. John swallowed, crouched down next to him, and reached out fingers to touch his head.

Darkness suddenly filled his vision: there was no light.

Gasping, John pulled his fingers away – he could see again! – and now Alex's face was lifted to him: and now he was sneering.

"Do you think you are stronger than me, John Robertson?" he asked. "I have the power to destroy the world!"

John stared at the hard crevices in the young face. He looked up at Jesus on the cross, and back down to Alex.

"I don't think I am stronger than you," he said.

"Then I will kill you," Alex said. "And after you I will kill all."

"I'm not afraid of death," John said – and now he reached quickly for the silver chalice: and now he drank from it.

"Don't touch me," Alex said. "Don't touch me with him."

And now John thrust both of his hands on Alex's head: and now he lifted his voice to fill the entire cathedral.

"Get out!" he cried. "He doesn't belong to you anymore!"

And Alex screamed. "I hate you!" he cried. "I hate you, I hate you, I hate you!"

And he clutched at the hands on his head, and his body jerked, and John maintained his grip, and searched his eyes – and somehow the Alex he had known was struggling to emerge.

"Choose," John said, reaching again with one hand again for the chalice, still grasping Alex's head. "You must choose."

Alex's face contorted: a true contortion – his own feeling.

"Again and again," he whispered, "I will choose him."

And he reached for the chalice, and drank, and screamed, and beat his own chest with his fists, and sank down to the ground, wholly spent.

John placed the chalice back on the white linen, and sank down next to Alex on the floor, leaning against the wooden frame of the altar. Rachel was there – John looked at her face, with some relief: beauty! Beauty, in the midst of such darkness. He fleetingly closed his eyes, and then drew himself back to Alex.

The young man was lying still, on the ground, clutching the crucifix around his neck. John instinctively reached out to him – he touched his hair gently.

46

"It's unfair," he murmured over him. "Unfair that you should have to carry this much burden."

"It's just the way that it is," Alex whispered, and now his body was curling into a ball.

"I won't leave you to carry it alone," Rachel's voice said – and now John watched her as she leaned into the child on the floor: as she drew him into her own arms.

Alex's body started to shake – weeping took him like another seizure. Rachel held him: she began to rock him in her own body: she began to nurture him, almost as a baby to her own breast. John was captivated by her: light! Light, penetrating into Alex's darkness: clothing him.

"You will heal," John said. "With a new family, you will heal."

"I can't," Alex whispered, his eyes closed, his face buried, innocent and young, in Rachel's chest. "Any new family will never replace the old. I still love them! Mother, father, sister – I love Selena!" And now weeping took him again. "I love my Dad."

John gazed at him, speechless – and now Mark Blake was standing over them.

Mark eyes passed over Alex and Rachel. He went to his knees before Rachel – he reached out his fingers to Alex's face, in Rachel's embrace, and now Alex's eyes opened.

Mark's blue gaze met Alex's blue.

"Let me take you," Mark murmured. "Let me hold you."

Alex's face contorted, yet he nodded.

Mark, tall, reached out to take the small form of Alex into his arms. John was reminded again: that day! That terrible day, when Kensington had been taken from Alex – tragedy! The abuser was still loved! The abuser was still needed.

And yet, here was another: here was another father – the father John had seen, for Alex; the father John had lain Alex upon, in the midst of his trauma.

The bond had never set…and yet…and yet was this another chance?

Mark was offering, again: drawing Alex to his own chest – embracing him into his own arms, rocking him with his own body.

And Alex…Alex was weeping.

"You need humanity," Mark murmured over him. "You need humanity as well as Christ."

"Humanity terrifies me," Alex whispered. "Rape, torture, death…"

Mark's face was close over Alex's face. "Love," he murmured gently to him, and Alex contorted, but he still remained – gripping onto Mark's purple tunic, then, finally, releasing himself into sleep in Mark's arms.

Mark held him. John gazed at the image before him: the father embracing the broken son. He looked at Rachel, who was crying. And then he rose to his feet and looked around himself.

47

The church lights were back on. Frowning, John lifted his face to the stained glass windows. There were others…others he hadn't dwelt upon: Christ's second coming – light, in the midst of great darkness; in the midst of the end of the world.

"Mark," John whispered. "Do you think we will lose ourselves in the darkness? Do you think humanity is capable of destroying itself?"

"There has always been a battle," Mark's voice said, "since near the beginning: always a battle for the souls of humanity, between darkness and light."

"I saw a vision, Mark," John said. "A vision of the beginning of the end."

Now he looked back to the bishop's face: now he saw sorrow.

"There is a time for everything," he murmured. "A time for life, and a time for death."

"A time for the death of all?" John breathed, and Mark tightened his embrace around Alex.

"Sometimes death is needed," he said, "for a new kind of life. A better kind of life."

"A rebooting," John murmured. "A rebirth." And he looked back up to the stained glass windows. Images of people suffering, in darkness – but then, light: then Christ, on the clouds…

"'The lion will lie down with the lamb," Mark said, "'and a child shall lead them.'"[2]

And he embraced Alex more closely in his own arms.

John gazed at him: at the wisdom in his older face – at the strength in his repose.

"Accept death?" John murmured. "I can accept my own death: but accept death of the entire world?"

"Let your faith be stronger than death, John," Mark murmured gently. "Even if it should be the death of the entire world."

John took a deep painful breath, and turned back to Jesus on the cross. The burden of the world: an offer! An offer to carry the crimes of the world…And now John turned to look back down the aisle and out, through the glass doors, to the world.

"Choose the light," John whispered. "When the darkness hits, when our backs are against the wall, be ready and choose the light."

And he turned, went down to his knees, and pressed his head into the altar.

Alex stirred in Mark's arms.

Alive? Alex thought. He was still alive? Not yet dead?

He reached up to the older face above him – he touched Mark's sad smile. Mark rocked him gently again.

"Peace, Alex," Mark murmured over him. "Peace."

"Peace," Alex whispered back.

---

[2] Isaiah 11:6 Paraphrased

"I've adopted you," Mark said, his blue eyes gentle for him. "I've joined with you, to give you strength, Alex – so that you can do what you must do; what you long to do."

"What must I do, Dad?" Alex whispered, reaching his fingers up to the lines in Mark's forehead. "What do I long to do?"

"Find your first Dad, Alex," Mark murmured over him. "Find your true father."

Tears filled Alex's eyes: he trembled in Mark's arms.

"I lost him," Alex whispered. "He was lost."

"You can find him," Mark whispered back. "You have a gift. You must find him, Alex: you must reach him."

And now tears filled Mark's eyes.

"The lion will lie down with the lamb," he whispered. "A child will lead them. Your father is a lion. Your sister is a lamb." Mark glanced toward Rachel, and then his gaze returned to Alex. "And you are a child, Alex."

Alex gazed up at him. And now Mark was setting him separate from himself: and now he was reaching around his neck.

A cross: a golden cross. Mark unfastened it, and held it up in front of Alex's eyes.

"The Protestant cross is empty, Alex," he murmured. "Do you understand why?"

Alex tilted his head, looking at it. Empty! Relief from death…

"Christ is no longer on the cross, Alex," Mark said. "He doesn't need to suffer anymore. He has already carried the evil, for those who choose to give it. This is the resurrection, Alex. The resurrection! The hope, beyond death, to which we are all called."

Tears filled Alex's eyes. The resurrection! He could feel it! He could actually begin to grasp it…

"Here," Mark said, leaning closer to him with the cross. "Wear this next to your mother's crucifix."

And he was fastening it around Alex's neck, and Alex reached out to finger the flat cross on his chest.

"Give yourself fully into the light, Alex," Mark said, "and the darkness will never defeat you. Satan will never have his way through you. Overcome your father's evil with Christ's goodness."

And now Mark reached out a hand, and lifted Alex to his feet.

"You are a defender, Alex," Mark said to him. "A defender of humanity, not an abuser. A defender, even of your father's own humanity. But it will be at high cost, Alex. Be ready for the cost."

"The cost," Alex whispered. "Always a cost…"

"Leave Parliament now," Mark said. "Leave them, leave the focus of your father's attempts at control, and go out into the wider world: a world that will need your insight when the greater darkness comes."

And Mark leaned forward over him, and kissed his head – then he turned him, and launched him down the aisle toward the doors.

CHAPTER SEVEN: The Realization

James Connor sat in his office, on the ninth floor of the Beehive.

All was quiet. It was late. He glanced at Pam, in her floral dress – he looked back to his lap-top.

Kensington. Alex had worked diligently, though at high cost to himself: he had uncovered many false leakages – many pointers toward an impending Holocaust. His father had laid down many tracks toward destruction: Alex had curtailed them all. He had done it willingly: he had done it with pain. The eyes – the intensity of Kensington, but with pain. He was choosing pain, instead of…of assimilation…

Connor shut down his computer. He shoved his chair back away from the desk, rose to his feet and wandered over to his window. The light was fading, outside – only a few dark figures were wandering the streets: night time was falling.

He reached into his trouser pocket for his car keys – he stretched out his arms to yawn. Home time! It was almost Christmas! Christmas Eve! What might Pam have cooked tonight? Ham? Turkey? Fleetingly he wished for cranberry sauce, as he left his office behind.

The other offices were deserted: no one working late this evening. He reached the lift, and jabbed the button: nothing. That was odd. He tried it again, no light – frustrated, he turned and thrust himself into the stairwell.

The stairs were dark.

"What?" Connor muttered to himself. "Another fuse blown? Where's maintenance?"

He reached out with his hands – he felt his way along the wall of the stairwell, felt his way with his feet down the steps, and then, suddenly, his legs collided with someone.

Connor gasped, reaching out with his hands: a person, but not moving? He blinked his eyes, to try to adjust to the dark – he shoved the person aside, and tried to rush down the stairs. Nine flights! Get to the bottom! He must get to the bottom. Get into the light!

Panting, he clutched at the wall, his legs trembling, his feet moving – and finally he thrust the door open at the bottom of the stairwell, into the round hall, surrounded by windows looking out to the fading light.

Bodies. Bodies were scattered, all around.

"Oh my God," Connor breathed. He stared out of the windows to the street beyond – to the Law School beyond. Had no one seen? Just a few dark figures, still walking, oblivious! Oblivious to the crime! He reached out with his hands, turning over the body closest to him: the tea lady! A bullet wound, to her chest! Blood! Blood…

Shocked, he laid her back, and reached for another, and another…the cleaners, and his…his PA…

Connor stared at her young face. Sandra? Sandra had stayed late?

Dismayed, he laid her back down. A random crime? How long had they been lying there? Why…why had he not heard? A silencer? Why had he not been killed? And then, suddenly, a chill rose up his spine.

"No," he whispered. "Oh, please God, no…"

He rose to his feet – he turned. Dread seized him, as he looked toward Parliament.

"Please," he whispered. "No."

And he ran forward.

Security! Where was security? He ran down the wide curved staircase to the bottom, past the security entrance: dead! Bodies, lying at their station: the guards had been shot dead! He reached for the emergency button at the security desk: the silent alarm. Would it work? He could hear no response. The Army! Why was the Army not there? Why not there, now? Now, of all times? Now, at the point of crisis? But the courtyard outside was empty. There was no defence.

"No," Connor pleaded – and he turned: and now he ran.

The Debating Chamber! The Chamber of Parliament! Democracy! Freedom! He ran toward everything he believed in: he ran toward the heart of their nation. He thrust the doors open.

Bodies lay strewn over the seats. There had been no session planned! No debate he would not have attended: no session scheduled that day he would not have joined! And yet: and yet there they were, as if killed and then delivered into their different positions – as if gathered by an unholy shepherd, like sheep after the slaughter, ready for consumption.

Rigidly Connor approached the seats of his own party. He reached out to touch their unmoving bodies: surreal! Surely a nightmare! Surely not real. He shook his head. It couldn't be real. He turned, and walked across to the Opposition. Clarkson! Clarkson was there, his face grey, his eyes open and fixed, his chest…his shirt wet with blood.

"It can't be," Connor pleaded, reaching out with his fingers – shuddering with the touch of his blood. "Can't be!"

And now fear seized him. Look at the Throne? The position of the Speaker of the House? The position previously taken up by the Governor General, Anita Mayes? The position of authority for their constitutional monarchy, their order, for all the land?

"You have been flushed out," a low voice said, from the direction of the Throne, "like a rat, fleeing, trapped: but your ship is sinking fast, James Connor."

Terror seized Connor's heart. Clarkson was dead, and all the rest! All who had co-operated! All who had sought to bring Kensington down.

The voice! Was it Alex? Alex, turned mad? Consumed, at the last hour, by his father's malice? The son, entrusted with full access to Parliament, now powerful enough to take down their land?

"Look at me," the voice said. "Look at your conqueror."

51

Connor shook, staring at Clarkson. Pam! Had he killed Pam too? Rachel! Rachel...

"Look at your Nemesis," the voice said.

Courage! Connor thought. Have courage, to at least look at the murderer! Look at the destroyer! And yet, what courage? Based in what? Everything he had believed in was evaporating, before his eyes.

"Look!" the voice commanded, and Connor looked, and saw the bodies of the Speaker and the Governor General at his feet, and, sitting on the Throne, was Kensington.

He sat, tall, robed in black – his blue eyes intense, penetrating. He had the golden mace in his right hand.

"Impossible," Connor whispered, staring at him: at his iron face. "I saw you shot: I saw you killed."

Kensington smiled – and now he rose to his feet, over him. He grasped the golden mace between his hands and snapped it in two, throwing the pieces to the ground.

"You don't define my possibilities," he said. "I do."

"You were dead," Connor whispered. "You're only human!"

"Am I?" Kensington asked. "Only human?"

And Connor stared at his dark eyes, and felt the hairs stand up on the back of his neck.

"Oh, shit!" he cried – and now instinct seized him: terror thrust him away. Kensington was reaching! Reaching under the black robe.

He turned, and staggered out of the Debating Chamber.

"That's right!" Kensington's voice called out from behind him. "Run! Run, like a doomed rat: I know where you are going!"

And Connor threw himself through the corridors of Parliament, past more bodies, and out of the doors, onto the courtyard beyond.

Just a nightmare! He insisted to himself. It's all a nightmare! It had to be! He turned, to look back at Parliament: and now, before his eyes, the stone building exploded – throwing him off his feet, onto the street beyond.

"No!" he cried, and sobbing seized him: uncontrollable sobbing. He staggered back away from the carnage – he thrust himself up the steps of the Cathedral. The glass doors: they were shattered, with the blast! Connor threw himself over the shattered fragments.

"A sanctuary!" he cried. "Oh, please God, a sanctuary!"

And now he rushed down the aisle: and now he lifted his voice.

"Mark!" he shrieked. "Mark – I've seen the face of Hell! He's back! Kensington's back!"

Mark was there, on the other side of the altar! Purple robe, contorting face.

"Blakey!" Connor pleaded to him, falling to his knees at the altar. "He's taken Parliament! I'm not ready to die! I'm not ready for democracy to die!"

And now Mark was moving around the altar – and now the bishop was gathering him into his arms.

Connor clung to his tunic: clung to his blue eyes.

"Run," he whispered to him. "Run, Mark: he'll kill you straight after me."

"I'm not running," Mark said, his face steadfast. "I'm going to help you. I'm going to stay with you."

"Blakey," Connor whispered, shaking his head – remembering suddenly debates of High School: democracy. For the rich? For the poor? All of it was meaningless now! All meaningless.

"I was a bad leader," Connor whispered – and now he wept, and now Mark was rocking him on his knees.

"No," Mark said. "You were human."

"Tell Rachel," Connor whispered, clinging to him. "Tell Rachel I'm only human…"

"She knows," Mark said. "She knows."

"Thank God," Connor whispered, "she knows…"

And then, suddenly, he heard a shot, then felt searing pain to his chest: and then came darkness.

Mark held James in his arms.

His body was limp: his eyes lifeless. Mark swallowed, and reached to touch the bullet wound to his chest. He closed his eyes in prayer, laid James gently on the floor before the altar, and then rose to his feet to face the assailant.

Kensington was standing before him.

Mark met his dark eyes over the rifle. No silencer. No need anymore. Kensington was tall – Mark stood as tall. Black robes, and purple tunic.

"You stole my son," Kensington said through gritted teeth. "You corrupted him."

Kensington was back from the grave? Yes, of course…

"Your son is still your son," Mark said. "I was never a substitute."

"Damned right," Kensington said, "and I will have him back."

Mark swallowed, stretching out his arms. "He is an adult," he said. "Older than when you left."

"I will have him," Kensington said, "or he will have no one."

And now Kensington fired, and Mark stiffened: but the searing pain was to his wrist! He was thrown back against the altar: he gasped, and reached with his right hand to nurse the left, pressing it into his tunic – trying to stop the bleeding.

"You'd be proud of him," Mark whispered, fighting the pain. "He topped his class in Engineering."

"Proud?" Kensington said. "Do you think I care about his feeble achievements? I care about what he can do for me!"

And now he kicked Mark off balance – Mark grabbed the altar with his right hand, and now the rifle was firing again: searing pain, this time to his right wrist!

53

Agony! Mark clutched both wrists to his opposite arms pits, and rocked against the altar with the pain. What was Kensington doing? Through a red haze, Mark stared up at the stained glass windows to Christ, on the cross. Nails! Nails, to wrists and feet! Crucifixion.

"God help me," Mark whispered – and he dragged his gaze back to Kensington. The eyes were hardening further. Mark felt a chill.

"Don't," he whispered. "Don't touch him. Alex doesn't belong to you."

"All belong to me." The voice had changed – deep, guttural. Kensington moved his hand – and suddenly Mark felt himself lifted off his feet, and thrust back on the altar.

"No," Mark whispered. "Robert..." Was that his name? How did he know? Yes, Robert Kensington: Alex's father! His father, before...before he had lost his humanity...

And now the rifle fired again: a shot to his ankle.

Mark cried out. Red pain! His head lolled back on the altar. He stared up at Christ. Not much longer! Not much longer! But the man! The man, before him, supernaturally saved: resurrected by evil.

"Robert!" he cried out desperately. "Robert, where are you? Your son needs you! You don't belong to the enemy: not yet! Not Hell, yet! You've been given another chance!"

Another shot – this time to the other ankle! Agony!

Death! Death was nearing!

Kensington's face was over him now: the knowing smile, the domination.

"Your time is over," he whispered over him. "Peter is dead."

Mark stared up at Christ, now, behind the altar, behind him: at the crown of thorns on his head.

"Peter may be dead," he whispered, "but now we have Paul."

A flash of confusion passed through the eyes: humanity! For a moment, his humanity, restored. But then, suddenly, the humanity was gone again.

A shot fired: searing pain came to Mark's chest. And then came darkness.

CHAPTER EIGHT: Crisis

Tristan stood at Oriental Bay.

Tens of thousands had flooded the sand, pouring into the water, filling the streets beyond. It was Saturday morning! Early Saturday morning. Panic had struck the city: Rau Petera had rushed to the beach, word of mouth had spread, and now many thousands had followed.

Tristan frowned. Where was Rau? Tristan could see him, somehow, further forward, being pressed in from all sides. Tristan tried to jostle his way toward him, but was elbowed out of the way.

Mayhem! The Beehive! Parliament! The buildings were gone, in three simultaneous explosions! Where was the Army? Tristan glanced down toward the retaining wall, but there were no officers: no response. How? How could that be? Nothing!

And now, a massive crowd was pressing into Rau.

"Don't be afraid!" Rau's voice lifted urgently above the crowd. "We know tough times are ahead, but the light is brighter than the darkness! The light will overcome! Hold onto the light! Hold onto hope, trust in God: hold to the one who is greater than any calamity in this life."

Urgently Tristan looked around. Where were the others? Alex, Rachel, John...Connor! Surely Connor was dead, in the blast! Surely Rachel had lost contact. Reporters were still confused: still struggling to find the truth – to find something comprehensible to report upon.

"Joshua said a tsunami was coming!" Rau's voice called out. "But after the mayhem comes the rebuilding! After death comes life! A new day! A glorious sunrise! Hold on, though the floods come: dig your foundations deep, deep into the rock – don't be afraid! Your house will stand! Your house will stand, through hell and high waters..."

Tristan followed his voice: there! He spotted his brown face. Protect him! The crowds! The surging crowds, as on the day...on the day when Tristan had shot Joshua...

"You're not safe, old man," Tristan whispered.

"Death is only a doorway into new life!" Rau called out. "God is the Master of death and life! Don't fear the ones who only have temporary power over you: a greater One is coming! A Light that will consume all darkness! Be ready! Don't fear the Darkness: be ready for the Light!"

John was there, next to Rau: Tristan could see him, his face white; his hand reaching out to the Maori priest. What had he seen? He had seen something...

Where was Rachel? Tristan turned. There she was, in the crowd, her face contorted and wet, and yet turned away from Rau and John – turned toward another...

Alex. Tristan stared at the young ashen face. Had it been him? Alex's plan to blow up Parliament, on the eve of Christmas: to precipitate a massive crowd into church the next morning, Christmas day, to find…to find…

Alex's blue eyes found him: was it him? Harrowing pain.

"Please," Alex whispered. "They are coming."

"Did you set this up?" Tristan asked him. "Tell me the truth."

"I didn't," Alex choked, his face contorting. "I'm telling you the truth."

Tristan reached out to grasp his shirt in his fist.

"Did you use us, all of this time?" he asked. "To set yourself up in a position of influence: to gain access to Parliament, to set down the bombs, to plant the assassins."

"No," Alex pleaded, and now his body was tensing – and now he was beginning to shake. "I know who did this."

Tristan looked to Rachel: to the tears in her eyes – to her agony.

"What is it?" he whispered – and her hand came to his arm.

"St Peter's," she whispered back. "They're dead."

Tears filled his eyes: he urgently blinked them away.

"Who?" he asked. "Who is dead?"

"Dad!" Rachel cried. "My Dad, and…and your Dad…"

Tristan stared at her, through his tears. "How?" he asked – and now Rachel's eyes, wet, softened from the hard edge of grief into compassion: into sympathy for him.

"Shot," she whispered. "They were both shot. They were together."

Tristan stared at her. Shot? His father was dead? Dead, in St Peter's? Was his body still there? He should go! Go to him! Now!

He turned away from them: he set his eyes on the street. But now Alex's voice was sounding.

"Don't go to him," he said. "Don't go to St Peter's. Don't look."

"Why?" Tristan asked, staring down the street in the direction of the Cathedral.

"Because he was tortured," Alex whispered. "He was tortured first, and I know who did it."

Now fury seized Tristan. He turned back – he grasped Alex's shirt with both hands: he dragged him along the sand and pushed him up against the tsunami retaining wall.

"Who did it, Alex?" he asked. "You tell me to my face, who you expect me to believe did it."

"Tristan!" Rachel's voice cried out, alongside him – her hands reaching out to his fists. Tristan flicked her off – he stared into Alex's eyes. Terror! The boy was feeling terror.

"Stop it," Rachel said. "It wasn't him!"

"How can you know that?" Tristan asked. "He has all the ability to do it, Rachel! You can't see it, because you love him! You love the bastard son of Kensington: the one capable of transcending even his father's malice."

56

"Just because he has the ability, doesn't mean he did it!" Rachel cried. "You know that, Tristan!"

"He lost it," Tristan whispered, and now his entire body began to shake. "He lost it, and now everyone will suffer!"

Alex's eyes were widening. "Are you going to kill me?" he whispered. "Are you going to make me the scape goat?"

"This isn't his fault," Rachel said.

"He's coming," Alex pleaded. "You have to be ready: he's coming!"

"Bullshit!" Tristan cried. "It's all in your head! All in your beaten, bruised, tortured mind!"

"The Army," Alex pleaded. "He'll call in the Army, Tristan: you know it! Today! Today! A military state! A coup, disguised as real authority! On Christmas day!"

"No," Tristan whispered, shaking his head: squeezing tears from his eyes. "No, he's dead! You're mad! A dead man can't come back to life."

And now Tristan looked up – and now he could see the Army, in the distance, marching! They were marching toward the bay.

"He owns the Army, Tristan," Alex pleaded. "You know that! You know it."

"Oh my God," Tristan whispered.

"Fear is his weapon," Alex said. "Assimilation is his goal. Assimilation or annihilation."

"You know him so well," Tristan whispered, staring at the approaching officers. "How is it you know him so well?"

He glanced back to the young face, contorting.

"He is a part of you," Tristan said. "He can take you down."

"Do you want to watch him take me down?" Alex whispered. "Do you want to see it, before your eyes?"

"Black outs," Tristan said, frowning. "Times when you lose it, and make all of this happen." And he gestured up the street.

"Don't be ridiculous," Rachel said. "Are you trained in psych?"

"I have all my memory," Alex said. "I can account for all of my time: all of my thoughts."

"You killed them." And now agony seized Tristan. His brother! His younger brother. "You killed them all."

"No," Alex pleaded. "It was my father! He's back, Tristan! He's back!"

"He's back in you!" Tristan cried. "You sick bastard, he's taken over you!"

"No!" Alex cried. "No! Don't you see? You're all going to die! You're all going to die if I don't make you see! I'm not your enemy: the enemy is coming! He's coming, and you're all sitting ducks, if you don't listen to me! If you don't fight him!"

"Fight him?" Tristan said. "I have no weapon, and if I did, should I be shooting you?"

"No!" Rachel cried. "That's enough, Tristan! That's enough!"

57

Tristan turned to her: to her pretty, distraught face.

"You believe him?" he asked. "This traumatized, crazy, genius boy who scares the shit out of me? You believe him? He just shot our fathers!"

And now dismay seized him. His father! He was dead! No more family! All gone!

He swayed on his feet – and now Rachel's face, gentle, was before him.

"Hear me, Tristan," her voice said firmly. "Alex didn't shoot our fathers: he was with me! He's been with me for the last couple of weeks."

Tristan stared at her, trying to understand. He was with her? Still he shook his head.

"Doesn't matter," he whispered.

"I watched everything he did," Rachel said.

"He was stirring up trouble," Tristan said. "Pretending to undo his father's tactics, on his computer: conjuring up the final plan. Organising the assassins."

"Tristan, hear me," Rachel said – and he held her eyes as her voice continued. "It's not Alex who is delusional right now: it is you."

Tristan stared at her. He stepped back, and shook his head. Then he looked at Alex.

The young man had fallen to his knees in the sand. Now he was bowing forward, his head on his arms, at Tristan's feet.

"I've failed," he pleaded, and now the arms were moving over his head: now his body was rocking. "I haven't prevented the calamity: I haven't been able to stop him."

"It isn't your fault," Tristan instinctively replied: reaching out to the wounded brother – laying a hand on his back, suddenly clearly seeing the truth. "None of this is your fault. I am so sorry, Alex: I was a bastard. I'm so sorry…"

And he reached to draw Alex back up to his feet.

Rau's eyes were on him as he stood with an arm around Alex's shoulders, steadying him. The brown eyes: knowledge! Foreknowledge. His words to Alex:

When my time comes, don't look…

And now John's green eyes were before him: tense, anticipating.

"Death," he said. "We're all going to die."

"Move," Tristan said – and he tightened his grip around Alex's shoulders. "Move, now."

"What?" Rachel said, looking bewildered – and Tristan grasped her shoulder with his left hand, and ushered her toward the street: away from the coast! Away, but toward the carnage: they won't expect that! Move into the eye of the storm.

But Rau…

Tristan glanced back to his friend. The warm brown face was smiling at him: smiling, in the face of his own certain death.

"Ka kite," Rau called out to him. "Arohanui! See you on the other side!"

Tristan stared at him, tears welling up.

"Ka kite, old man!" he choked. "Arohanui!" And now he turned himself away from the priest, and thrust Alex, Rachel and John ahead of himself.

The streets of central Wellington were deserted.

"Hurry," Tristan whispered. "Hurry."

"Where are you taking us?" Rachel gasped.

"Into ground zero," Alex muttered.

Shots were sounding behind them! A barrage of shooting!

"Oh my God!" Rachel pleaded, instinctively turning, but Tristan tightened his grip on her shoulder.

"Keep going," he murmured to her. "You can't help them, Rachel, but you can help Alex."

She reached out for Alex's shoulder, and Tristan could hear John groaning. He reached out his other hand to him. It was as if John could see the deaths! In his mind, see them, in his heart feel them, though they were not present...

"Peace," Tristan murmured to him. "We will find our peace, somehow, some way."

And now they were near the end of Lambton Quay.

Parliament. Tristan stared. He had seen the footage on the internet, but to see it directly: rubble! Rubble in the place of their Constitution! In the place of their leadership, and order!

The Beehive had collapsed: Parliament House also. Chills went up his spine. The Army were stationed, around the rubble, and the Cathedral...the glass doors were shattered, and police were moving in and out...

"Move," John's voice now warned. "I saw the bodies, Tristan: I saw them with my own eyes. Don't go in there."

"Did you touch them?" Tristan asked.

"What?"

"Did you touch them?" His teeth were grinding.

"No," John said, looking confused – but now Tristan looked to Alex: to his widening eyes.

"You killed my father," Alex whispered. "It was you, and James Lester."

Tristan frowned, staring at the police.

"You would say this is his justice," he muttered. "His retribution. But a man can't come back from death, Alex. Kensington was dead. He still is dead. Some other terrorist group has done this: they will reveal themselves in time."

"Still you do not understand," Alex said. "Still you will not understand."

And Tristan frowned.

"Forces?" he said. "Other forces?"

"The real enemy has always been within our boundaries," Alex said.

And now a man emerged from the Cathedral: tall, wearing a black robe. He stood on the steps – and now he was looking directly at Tristan, smiling.

"Holy shit," Tristan whispered. "It's him."

59

"It can't be," Rachel's voice sounded. "It can't be!"

And now Rachel was rushing down the street, into the space between the decimated Parliament and the broken Cathedral.

"Rachel!" Alex's voice cried, and his body jerked toward her, but Tristan instinctively reached out and grasped him back.

"No!" he said. "No!"

And he held Alex bodily, struggling, against his own chest, and Alex sank against him.

"Explain this to me," Tristan whispered to him. "Explain this to me, Alex, because I can't understand this at all: how can your father be back? I killed him! I killed him!"

"Forces!" Alex gasped. "Forces you can't understand!"

And now Alex's body was starting to jerk in his arms: and now his face was contorting in agony.

"Oh, dear God," Tristan whispered to him, "you are innocent of all of this! You are innocent, and now the tormenter has returned, in full force: in supernatural force…"

"Save me," Alex pleaded, his face lifted to the sky. "I'm dying! I'm dying."

And now he sank down to the ground, curled up, and was still.

Tristan stared down at him – reached down a hand to his shoulder, as he looked up at Rachel approaching the tormentor. John was rushing forward: calling out! Calling out, and yet holding back. Rachel! This was Rachel's choice! This was Rachel's act.

She came to stand before the Cathedral. She looked up the steps to the man, towering above, in the black robes.

"You killed my father!" she cried out. "You bastard, you are hell-bent on destroying our nation!"

"Give me back my son," Kensington said to her, "or I will kill everyone before your eyes."

Where were the police? Inside! Inside the Cathedral.

Rachel shifted on her feet before him. "Your crimes are not my own!" she said. "I will not hand over an innocent boy into your destruction."

"He's not innocent, pretty girl," Kensington said, laughing. "Are you really so blind?"

"His crimes are dealt with!" Rachel called out. "He is redeemed!"

"There is no redemption," Kensington said. "There is only power: only survival of the fittest. And I am the fittest."

"You are not fit!" Rachel cried. "You are not fit to rule!"

"I will rule!" Kensington roared. "And you will be my bride!"

Rachel was staring at him now: Tristan was struck by her face – horror? Horror, at the suggestion? At the violation?

Now John stepped between them – and now Tristan left Alex, just for a moment! He rushed forward, grasped Rachel's shoulder, and drew her back.

60

"Leave!" he insisted. "You, and Alex: leave, now!"

Rachel looked dazed. She shook her head, staring at him.

"What?" she whispered.

"Take Alex and run!" Tristan said.

"Where?" Rachel breathed – and Tristan reached to grasp Alex to his feet, and moved them both forward.

John….What was he doing? Standing at the base of the steps of the Cathedral, looking up to Kensington.

"Salvation!" John's voice cried, carried on the breeze. "There is still salvation!"

"You are a fool," Kensington said. "I will take your wife for my own: I will strip you both bare, until you finally understand that there is only one God, and he is me."

"No man can be his own God," John said. "Humanity cannot save itself: it cannot transcend itself. And the Darkness will not endure forever."

"Actualized humanity is my greatest weapon," Kensington said. "My greatest tool."

"The Light will come," John said. "The Light is our only weapon: submission to the Light is our only surgical tool."

Now fury seized Kensington's face, as a contortion: striking a sudden intense fear into the heart of Tristan as he watched, powerless.

Kensington thrust out his hand – and, with an invisible force, threw John backwards, into the middle of the street.

Alex and Rachel: where were they? Running! Still running, through the streets. A horn sounded: a horn, in the distance…

Tristan suddenly realized he and John were one: defending! They were both defending the ones they loved, standing in their place.

"John!" Tristan cried out – and now the eyes of Kensington were on him.

Darkness. Tristan shuddered, and then he moved forward, past John: past his scrambling back to his feet.

"Go," Tristan whispered to him. "To the ferry. Quickly. Join the others there."

"Tristan," John said, reaching out a hand to him. "Don't go into the Cathedral. Don't look. He will have you. He will imprison you."

"I must go," Tristan whispered, staring at Kensington. "And so must you. Protect your wife, John – protect Alex. We need him: he's the strongest one of us, even while he is the weakest."

"I know," John whispered. "He is the key."

"Go," Tristan said. "Go."

And John fled, and Tristan walked up to the base of the staircase.

Kensington looked down at him: black robes, intense blue gaze. It was him: he was alive.

"Behold the army officer," Kensington said, "who killed his own father."

And he gestured toward the cathedral.

61

Tristan swallowed – go in there? Face the lies? Face the truth? He thrust himself up the steps, walking past the chill of Kensington, and entered the church.

Connor was lying dead at the altar. And...and his father was there, alongside him.

Tristan walked up the aisle, as if in a daze: he came to stop next to their bodies. His father! Blood, from both wrists and feet: blood, having soaked through the purple tunic, now old...dead for several hours. Sick! He felt sick.

Two police officers stood on either side of the bodies. They were wearing gloves: one was carrying a weapon.

Tristan stared at it. His rifle! This was the rifle he had thrown into the Hutt River...

"Here he is," Kensington's voice sounded behind him. "The murderer, returning to the scene of the crime."

"We are placing you under arrest," the other officer said, stepping forward, carrying handcuffs. "You have the right to remain silent: anything you say might be used against you in a court of law."

"The court of law?" Tristan cried, shaking, staring back at Kensington. "Haven't you people noticed? Parliament has been shattered: there is no law!"

"An anarchist as well," Kensington said, smirking. "A true enemy of the state."

And Tristan glanced down at his father. Dead! He was dead, and...from Tristan's own gun...

"Peace," Tristan whispered to him. "Rest in peace, Dad: please! Rest in peace."

And he was turned, by the officer, handcuffed, and ushered out of the church.

CHAPTER NINE: The Race

Rachel rushed toward the Wellington ferry, grasping onto Alex's shoulders: pushing him in front of her.

The horn was blowing! The ferry was preparing to leave.

"Hurry!" she cried. "Hurry!"

She grasped Alex's hand, and ran with him – along the coast, through the streets, into the ferry terminal, and across: over the barrier, past the protesting staff, into the retractable ramp and up. The ferry was ready to pull away: the ramp was starting to retract.

"Wait!" she cried, and she shoved Alex across the small gap through the closing door of the ship. He clutched at the doorway: he shoved the door back open, and turned to face her.

"Rachel!" he cried, stretching out his hand. She swallowed, looking down at the wharf many metres below, and then looked back to Alex's distraught face. Let him go? Stay behind, and face Kensington alone?

"Jump!" Alex cried. "Before it's too late!"

She stared at the growing gap: at the fall to the wharf below.

"I'm not an athlete," she whispered – and now she felt strong hands on her arms: and now she was being half lifted, half thrown across.

Alex had her: grasping her under the armpits, pulling her through the door. Rachel stumbled against him – she fell to the deck and then jerked up to her feet, turning around.

John! John was standing in the retracting ramp. He stared at her. The ferry was moving now! Pulling away from the wharf. He hesitated, backed away, and then took a fast running leap.

Rachel leaned through the door, over the metres of the ship below: where was he? Further back? She slammed the door shut, rushed past Alex down the corridor, found some stairs, ran down to a deck below, rushed outside, and found him hanging off the rail. Quickly she clutched at his arms, helping him to clamber up and fall onto the deck, while others stared.

Now the ferry had separated from the wharf.

Rachel grasped at John's shirt, as he staggered to his feet – she reached for the railing, and stared at the disappearing ramp. Then she turned, and rushed down the deck toward the bow of the ship, as the ferry pulled into the centre of Wellington Harbour.

Alex was already there, collapsed on the deck: pressing himself into the railing, his eyes closed, his breathing heavy. Beyond him were the waters, and a course…a course beyond Wellington, across the Cook Strait, to the South Island! Away! Away…

She was following him: following him on his course, but to where? To what? They had only what was on them: they had left everything else behind.

He was clutching at the crucifix on his chest now – his lips were moving. Prayer? He was praying? Rachel reached out fingers to touch his blonde curls. She loved him. In that moment, she knew – in that moment, again, she chose. She had risked herself for him: and John – John had followed her into that risk.

Alex was shuddering, in his prayer. Rachel knelt down before him: she reached out to his hand, clutching the crucifix – she laid her fingers over his. She closed her own eyes to pray with him.

She felt his forehead come to lean on her hand: she remembered, and reached to his chest to the empty golden cross – to Mark's cross. She gently opened his clenched fingers: she laid the empty cross alongside the crucifix, and closed his fingers over both.

"Hope," she whispered into his ear. "Hope for the resurrection, beyond this life: beyond this death."

"If there is no resurrection," he whispered back to her, "I am most to be pitied."[3]

"There is a resurrection," Rachel said. "You will find your life: you will find your peace."

And she drew him into her arms, on her knees, and he rocked against her, and his voice lifted into a wail.

"He's back!" he cried. "He's back, from the dead!"

She pressed her forehead to his. "He's alive," she whispered, "so that you can reach him: so that you can know him."

Agony was consuming him: his face was contorting, his body stiffening...

Rachel closed her eyes, reaching again for his hand: grasping his fist, with crucifix and empty cross, to her own chest.

She prayed. What words? No words. Groans – groans, with his pain: grunts, with his anguish. With tears, unspoken, she prayed to God – and now Alex was sagging against her shoulder.

She sat quietly with him – she held him, there, on the deck, hidden under the rail.

Now John was sitting next to her.

Rachel swallowed, looking at him. His face was white.

"I'm sorry," she said to him. "I never intended to put you at risk."

He frowned and lifted himself to his knees, looking over the railing across the water.

"It's not your fault," he said.

"If I'd just kept going," she said. "If I'd just pretended, just kept doing medicine..."

"Kept hiding?" he asked, staring at the expanse hidden to her. "It wasn't the truth."

"I couldn't leave him," Rachel said. "I couldn't ignore him."

"I know," he said.

---

[3] See 1Corinthians15:12-20.

"I…" Now she hesitated, and pressed herself on. "I'm scared, John…"

Now his gaze came to her: now he moved himself down to sit next to her – his shoulder against hers.

She leaned her head on his shoulder. She closed her eyes. The tears! The tears, welling up, silent, hidden…her father! Her father was dead! Shot! His power, his influence, his leadership, gone.

Pain took her – but John's arm was moving around her shoulders.

"Peace," he murmured over her. "Be at peace, Rachel."

Peace…her chest! Pain!

"It's a mess!" she said. "We're all in trouble!"

"There is another day," John murmured. "One day at a time."

"He's there, in the Cathedral," Rachel whispered. Kensington! Black robes, sinister smile. "He…he…" And now she shuddered, and closed her eyes.

John's breath was on her cheek. Instinctively she moved into it: lips! His lips. Gentle, love! Love…

Make love…

"Don't be afraid," he whispered into her lips. "Don't let him shake you."

"He said…"

"I know what he said," John replied. "You don't belong to him."

And now he entered her mouth.

Rachel gasped. Pleasure! Love. She received him. She breathed. There was nothing more: nothing more they could do. And yet this…this was enough.

He withdrew, and she leaned against him. Relief! Relief.

He leaned back against the bulkhead: he closed his eyes, frowning – Rachel knew he was praying. She reached to gently touch his face – she lifted herself away from him, to give him space.

Alex was stirring, in her arms.

Rachel looked down at his face. A child – for a moment, he was child, looking up at her, blue eyes wide. Then the moment passed: then the haunted youth resettled in him.

"Is it real?" he whispered. "Not just a nightmare?"

She felt her own face contort – she reached down to lay her fingers over his eyes.

"Oh that I could protect you from it," she whispered. "Oh that I could change it. But, no: it's real."

"I knew," Alex whispered, drawing her fingers away from his eyes. "I did everything I could to stop him."

"I know," Rachel quickly said. "I watched you."

"What more can I do, Rachel?" he asked. "I don't know what more to do."

She stroked his forehead: she massaged the crevices of his frown.

"Reach him," she said. "Reach his sanity. Reach his humanity."

"I can't," Alex said. "If I do, if I actually reach his humanity, he will kill me."

"He won't," she said. "If he sees you, if he truly sees you, he must respond."

65

"The rest are sitters," Alex said. "They have no idea: no idea how he operates – no idea how evil operates…"

"Show them," Rachel said. "Show him. Shine light in his darkness."

"He will kill me, if I shine light," Alex said. "He will kill me, if I expose the truth. He will subjugate all if I don't submit to him."

"You will save him," Rachel said. "You will penetrate his darkness."

"Hand me over," Alex whispered, reaching up to touch her face. "Hand me over to him."

Rachel felt her face contorting, shaking her head.

"No," she whispered. "Not if all the forces of hell are set against me: I will not hand you over."

Alex looked at her – and then he lifted himself away from her, and rose to his feet.

Rachel watched him as he stood against the railing – as he looked out across the water. They were passing the neck of the harbour: they were heading toward Cook Strait.

"New waters," he murmured to himself: and he closed his eyes, and took a deep breath.

"You will find yourself there," Rachel said to him. "You will overcome him there."

Alex's eyes opened, and he gazed into the distance.

"Mountains," he murmured. "I can see mountains…"

And he broke into a radiant smile. Rachel watched him, captivated by him, and he turned to her and took her hand.

"Faith!" he said. "Faith feels like a shield! Protecting us from evil."

"If there is such a shield," Rachel said playfully, "then there must also be a sword."

"A sword," Alex said, still holding her hand, looking out across the waters. Rachel followed his gaze: the South Island! She could just make out the coast of the South Island…

"Joshua's thoughts!" Alex said. "His ways. They are the weapon to refute evil: they are the sword."

"His thoughts, over evil thought," Rachel said.

"And a belt," Alex said, reaching to his own belt, in his jean shorts. "The truth…"

"The truth will set you free," Rachel said.

"Even if it kills you first," Alex said wryly back, but his eyes were still forward.

"A shield," he said, "a sword, a belt…"

Rachel reached a fist over her heart, and Alex glanced at her – at her fist.

"A breastplate," he said. "Purity, to protect the heart."

Tears pricked at Rachel's eyes – Alex smiled sadly at her, and looked again forward.

"Protection for the mind," he said.

"Some kind of cap?" Rachel suggested with a smile. "A sunhat?"

"A helmet," Alex replied.

"And readiness," Rachel said.

"Readiness?" Alex asked.

"To share," Rachel said. "To help."

Alex glanced down at his feet. "Shoes," he muttered. "I get the feeling we're going to be doing a lot of walking…"

Rachel looked down at her own leather black shoes, and at Alex's sneakers.

"I guess you're more ready than I am," she muttered, and he actually grinned.

"Maybe," he said.

She glanced over her own light denim shorts, and grimaced.

"No belt."

"Then use mine," Alex said – and he straightened, unbuckled and pulled out his belt, and gave it to her. "Truth."[4]

He stood, denim shorts now loose, his black leather belt curled up in his hand, extended out to her.

Rachel gazed at it – and reached out to take it. She reached for her own denim shorts – she inserted his belt. He was small – the tightest hole fitted her.

She felt secure. She looked back to him: to his young face, looking across the water. Her leader! This young man was her leader.

"You are finding yourself," she said. "You are emerging from the darkness."

Alex stretched out his arms. The wind, from the water, lifted his blonde curls – he closed his eyes again: breathed deeply again.

"Faith," he said. "Faith is the sailing: faith is the swimming. Faith, hope and love.[5] There is so much, Rachel: so much to reveal."

"Then reveal it," Rachel said. "Reveal it, and I will help you."

"I will reveal it," Alex said. "I will make it known, whatever the cost."

"Whatever the cost," Rachel repeated, "so be it. Make it known: make it known, to the ends of the Earth."

And her eyes followed his across the water: and now she too could see mountains.

---

[4] Ephesians 6:10-18 Paraphrased.
[5] 1Corinthians 13:13 Paraphrased.

CHAPTER TEN: Imprisonment

Tristan stood still.

He was dressed in grey prison clothes, his hands cuffed behind his back. A prison guard stood in front of him, a police officer, carrying his rifle, behind.

"What are you doing?" Tristan asked the guard. "I thought the pyjamas only came after conviction."

"You have been convicted," the guard said, grimacing, and Tristan glanced back to the officer behind him.

"I haven't had a trial," he said. "I demand a trial."

"The evidence is clear," the officer said, lifting his rifle. "The bullet in your father's chest, and in the Prime Minister's chest, matches your weapon."

Tristan shifted slightly on his feet. "The police are not the jury or judge," he said. "I demand a trial. I demand a lawyer."

The officer smiled, and Tristan stared at his dark eyes. There was something about them: something insidious – something familiar...

"Kensington owns you too," he muttered – and now he was being prodded forward, toward a cell.

The prison guard pulled out keys from his pocket: he turned a lock, threw open bars, released the cuffs, and prodded Tristan in.

He spun on his heel, as the bars shut hard in front of him. He gritted his teeth. The police officer and prison guard were watching him.

"Kensington has bewitched you," Tristan said. "He's a cunning bastard that way."

The officer smiled knowingly. "Whatever you say," he said. But the prison guard's eyes seemed different: resigned, but troubled.

"Everything is uncertain now," he said. "The future is uncertain. Justice is uncertain. The truth is unclear."

"The truth?" Tristan said to him. "Whose truth?"

The guard smiled sadly. "Whose indeed," he muttered, and now he turned away, his head bowed low.

Tristan watched him disappear down the corridor, followed by the officer, glancing back, still smiling. Kensington! Bastard! How far had his influence extended? Far enough to even rise from the dead? What the hell was that about?

Tristan frowned. He was cunning? That meant being more cunning again. Control! Take control. Think! Don't react.

He reached out to finger the bars – to grasp them, in front of him, in his fists: to feel their solidarity. Then he turned.

James Lester was standing in front of him: a wry smirk on his face.

"Oh, no way!" Tristan said, staring at his face. "You have got to be joking!"

"Well, well," James said. "Got up to some trouble while I've been away?"

"You?" Tristan spluttered. "I get to buddy up with you?"

"I'm a changed man," James said, spreading his hands out before him, grinning.

"You're almost as much of a bastard as Kensington!" Tristan protested. "I'd only be a bit surprised if you'd planted half the bombs yourself that took Parliament out, even from prison!"

"Don't be ridiculous," James said, his grin starting to fade. "You're delusional."

"Yeah, right," Tristan said. "This from the man who held my gun to Rachel's head!"

"I've moved on from that," James muttered.

"How's that?" Tristan said, now starting to pace backwards and forwards before him. "How do you move on from imminent first degree murder?"

"You tell me," James said. "You murdered Joshua Davidson."

"Oh, shut up!" Tristan cried – and he strode up to the bars and shook them. "Let me out!" he cried. "This is torture! One day with this prick is worse than any life sentence!"

And he banged his head against the bars – then made himself stand up straight. Hold it together! He turned, faced James, and slid down against the bars to the floor.

"Fine!" he said. "I'm stuck with you. Then let's get to the nitty gritty, right here: right now."

"Fire away," James said, smiling.

"Shut up!" Tristan said. "Listen! Kensington's back! We both shot him, and now he's back."

James frowned, and was silent. Tristan stared at his face – then James turned away, and reached for a stethoscope sitting on the ground. He sat himself down against a wall and stared down at it, in his hands.

"Kensington can't be back," he muttered. "That's impossible."

"I know it's impossible!" Tristan said. "We've both killed a lot of people, James: we're army. The dead don't come back. But this one has."

James's face darkened, staring at the stethoscope: silent.

"What, now you don't speak?" Tristan said. "Where's the torrent? I'm delusional, right? Off my face? On drugs?"

"Where's Rachel?" James asked, and Tristan grimaced.

"I sent her and Alex on," he said. "With John. I copped it myself, so they could get away."

Now James's eyes lifted to him: now he gave a quiet smile.

"Where?" he asked.

Tristan frowned, looking at him. "Why do you want to know?"

James shifted, and then pushed himself to his feet and wandered over to the bars, staring out.

"It's dangerous now," he said. "Something big is going on."

"Bigger than us?" Tristan asked.

"The foundations," James said. "All around us, the foundations…"

"Exploded," Tristan said. "We have no constitution anymore."

James frowned, staring out of the bars: holding the stethoscope in his right hand.

"Why are you here?" he asked. "Why have you come?"

69

"I was falsely accused," Tristan said – and now, suddenly, pain took him. He looked quickly away from James – he drew his knees up to his chest, and wrapped his arms around his legs, hiding his face away. Privacy! Some privacy...

"Falsely accused of what?" James's voice asked.

"My father," Tristan said into his knees. "Kensington shot my father, and set me up: sent me to prison, to carry his crime. My father's dead..." And now Tristan gasped. His father! Lying, shot! Dear God, shot, wrists and feet, and chest...

"Dad," he whispered – and he felt James's eyes upon him.

"You're father's dead?" he asked. "Like mine?"

"Like yours," Tristan said into his knees.

"Kensington's not my father," James said.

"No," Tristan muttered. "He's Alex's father: and Alex is out there, and so is Kensington, and the man's a...a..."

"Psychopath," James said – and Tristan lifted his head to look at him fingering the stethoscope.

"A psychopath can't come back from the grave, James," he said – and James frowned.

"Delusional," he said, and Tristan shrugged.

"Yeah, yeah," he said. "You didn't see him: you didn't get manipulated into jail by him."

"Did I not?" James asked – and Tristan frowned at him as he moved away from the bars and sat down again against the wall.

Tristan studied him. Where was he at? He had held a gun to Rachel's head: had been on the verge of killing her! But then...then Kensington had rushed in: had thrust Alex over the altar, had almost killed him. James had shifted, in that moment! Had killed Kensington instead! Had seen himself: had seen the threat he had posed to Rachel. Had handed himself in.

But now? Now he expected to know where Rachel was again?

"Why, James?" Tristan asked. "Why did you almost kill Rachel? What were you thinking?"

James shifted in discomfort, staring down into his hands: at the stethoscope.

"I don't know what to say to you," he said. "No answer will explain it adequately."

"Not good enough," Tristan said. "We're both in the same boat now. Tell me what happened."

"You like her?" James said, smirking, looking down, and Tristan grimaced.

"Don't change the subject," he said. "She's my friend."

"You seem to care for her."

"Don't manipulate me," Tristan said. "We are equals: we are comrades. Tell me what happened."

James's face contorted – and then he looked quickly away, through the bars.

"I lost it," he whispered. "She...she has that effect on me."

"What do you mean?" Tristan asked.

70

"I…" Now James gritted his teeth. "I love her."

Tristan stared at her. Love? Love with a gun?

"Bullshit!" he said.

"You're not a priest," James said. "I don't owe you any explanation."

"Like hell," Tristan said. "You were using my gun, James! You do owe me an explanation, right here: right now! Tell me the truth, soldier!"

James sucked in a deep breath – and then he turned to face Tristan.

"I was afraid," he said. "I was afraid, and I attacked a civilian instead of the enemy."

"And who is the enemy, James?" Tristan asked gently, watching him. Confession? He was confessing to him?

"I am," James whispered. "An autonomous agent, fighting only for himself. A cancer."

And he closed his eyes, and sat against the wall.

Tristan watched him. "In the army," he began, "you would have been court martialled."

"I court martialled myself," he said. "I am here."

"And now?" Tristan asked.

"Now?" James repeated, opening his eyes. "Now I would wish to fight for someone else."

Tristan gazed at him. Yes: yes, he was speaking the truth.

"As we once did," Tristan murmured. "When we were in the army."

"I would wish to return," James said. "But now I will never return."

"And neither, it seems," Tristan muttered, "will I."

James's eyes held his. "Would you wish to?" he asked. "If you had the choice?"

Tristan smiled sadly at him. "Never again," he said. "Never again."

"Why not?" James asked.

"Because I don't like killing people, James!" Tristan said, exasperated. "Even if they are our enemies!"

"What about Kensington?" James asked. "Would you kill him all over again, if you had the chance?"

Tristan watched him, frowned, and then rose to his feet, wandering himself back to the bars. Would he kill him all over again?

"It won't work," he muttered. "Death won't overcome him."

"He's more than human?" James asked, and Tristan shrugged his shoulders.

"I don't know anything about this," he said. "It's beyond me."

He glanced back to James: his face was set.

"What about you?" Tristan asked. "Do you know anything about this?"

James swallowed. "Some enemies can't be overcome by physical force," he said.

"Then what hope do we have?" Tristan asked. "What weapons? What strategies?"

71

James frowned, and glanced through the bars. "No hope, here," he muttered. "No weapons: no strategies…"

And he fingered the stethoscope.

"Rachel's left her job," Tristan said instinctively. Was that her stethoscope? He seemed to remember, she had given it to him.

James stiffened. "What?" he asked.

"Why do you love her?" Tristan asked. "In what way?"

"Why do you?" James asked. "In what way?"

Tristan blushed. "Fine, he said, "I'll go first. In a different time, in a different place…"

"…on a different planet," James interjected, smirking, and Tristan grimaced at him.

"She's married," Tristan said. "That's it for me. But I love her, and I'll keep loving her – friendship will have to do. You?"

James looked away, suddenly seeming troubled.

"Why did she leave her job?" he asked.

"She's with Alex," Tristan said. "She seems to be looking after him."

James looked quickly back at him. "Seriously?" he asked. "She gave up her job for him?"

"I think so," Tristan said. "Now, fess up: I've spilt my guts. What about yours?"

James's gaze intensified: Tristan thought he could actually see tears.

"It's difficult," James whispered, and Tristan nodded.

"So I see," he said. "Courage."

"I…" He started to writhe slightly. "It's like being stripped bare."

"We're both blokes here," Tristan muttered. "Even if I did see something surprising, who am I going to tell?"

"She's my sister," James whispered – and now he turned away, and covered his face with his hands.

"What?" Tristan cried out, staring at him. Sister? How could that be possible? "You held up your own sister at gunpoint?"

"Shut up!" James cried. "Shut up!"

And, suddenly, he was flying toward him – and suddenly he was punching him across the face.

"Whoa!" Tristan cried, reaching easily to restrain the fists. James was unfit! Imprisoned. "Take it easy, mate!" Tristan said. "You're one messed up bastard…"

And he suddenly, instinctively, embraced him.

James sank down to his knees, against him: Tristan followed him. What was going on with him? Something deep: something intense. Rachel's brother?

"I've got to get out of here," James whispered against him. "I have to get out."

And now he backed away from Tristan, and reached for the stethoscope.

The drum…Tristan watched as his fingers moved over it: as he began to dismantle it.

"James…" Tristan warned, wary – and now James was withdrawing a part.

72

It looked like a hairclip. Tristan stared at it.

"That doesn't look like it belongs," he muttered.

"That Rachel," James said, with his same old wry smile back again. "She'll hold onto things until they have totally fallen apart."

And now he reached for the lock of the cell.

"James!" Tristan whispered. "What are you doing?"

"What do you think I'm doing?" James asked.

"It's illegal!" Tristan said. "You'll be thrown back, for twice as long."

"There is no law anymore," James said. "You know that. It's anarchy!"

"My Dad," Tristan said, shaking his head. "My Dad wouldn't fight this way."

And now James's face, for a moment, was sad. "Your Dad is dead," he said. "Are you coming? Rachel's in danger."

Tristan stared at him. Leave? Leave the unjust imprisonment behind? Embrace freedom, with all of its risks? Follow after Rachel, and James, and Alex?

He glanced down the corridor: no guard – he was mysteriously absent. He looked at James.

"It's time for me to stop being my own enemy," James said. "It's time to fight for someone else, against someone else: against the real enemy."

And he swung the prison door wide open, and stepped outside.

For a moment Tristan lingered, still in prison: accepting the walls – accepting his unjust fate. James's eyes came to him.

"If you're going to be the martyr," he muttered, "at least do it for the right cause."

And Tristan smirked at him, straightened to his full height, and walked out of the prison.

Alex stood at the bow of the ferry, leaning over the rail.

The ship was moving, through blue water: between the forested hills, past tiny hidden beaches, closer, closer to berthing…

Alex smiled. All the years he had lived in Wellington, he had never thought to sail across the water – he had never known he should want to come.

And yet, this had been waiting, all this time: beauty! Quiet! Peace.

He closed his eyes, he breathed in deeply. The warm summer sun was beating on his face.

Here, he could forget Wellington: here he could live, tucked away, far away from the carnage – far away from the crisis.

He sighed. A hand came to his shoulder – he opened his eyes, and turned.

Rachel was standing in front of him. Alex tilted his head, looking at her. Who was this woman, who had given up all to follow after him? The doctor? No…no, something more.

Family? He held his breath, but she was smiling. She was reaching out her hand.

He looked at her hand – he took it. Family. Was it okay? It was actually feeling okay.

"We're here," Rachel murmured, and she gestured across the bow. "We've arrived."

He turned again, to look ahead: to the houses, on the hillside, and the wharf of Picton.

"What do you think?" Rachel's voice asked. "Wanna stay here for a while?"

"For a little while," Alex murmured, lifting his eyes to the little hills: to a cottage a little away from the rest. From here he could watch the ferries arriving: from here he could guard against his father…

"Just for a little while," Rachel said – and he felt her hand on his shoulder, and reached to grasp it. "And then, time to move on: time for more space."

"More space," Alex whispered. "More distance."

"In time," Rachel murmured – and she drew him, away from the bow, towards a door. They would need to find the right deck to disembark.

John was there, on Rachel's other side. Alex glanced at him. What was he thinking? What was he feeling? He was frowning – and now he caught Alex's gaze.

"I bought the tickets for us," he said. "I have my wallet."

"We don't have much cash," Alex said.

"He'll seize the funds," John said. "Credit cards, bank accounts…very soon they will have no meaning."

"We'll all have to live off the land," Alex said.

"A farming nation, living off the land?" Rachel said, smiling. "Nice."

"He won't want it," Alex said. "Independence will diffuse his control."

"Humanity can survive," Rachel said. "Back to the basics: water, food, shelter…"

"We have water," Alex said, looking up to the sky: to the white fluffy clouds. "Aotearoa...Rainfall..."

"We have the capacity for food," Rachel said, stretching her hand toward the land before them.

"We have houses," Alex said. "We have caravans, and tents. He can't control the weather. He can't control the air."

"Can he not?" John asked. And he grimaced again, and looked away.

Alex gazed at him. John had been forced here: forced across the waters, following after his wife – following after Alex.

"I know he's coming," Alex said, "but...but I still believe..."

"That you can reach him," John said. "That you can redeem him."

Alex held his breath, looking at him: looking at his insight – at his vision.

"Do you not?" he asked, and John's eyes intensified.

"I know what is coming, Alex," he said. "I know that the end is coming."

Alex felt the breathing take him – he looked quickly away, to the idyllic town, standing, peacefully, in the sun. The ferry had drawn alongside the wharf! They had arrived.

"I need hope, John," he said, watching the people standing, oblivious, smiling; waving, on the wharf. "I need to believe that the light is stronger than the darkness."

John's hand came to his shoulder; Alex looked back at him.

"The Light is stronger, Alex," John said, his gaze certain and secure, reaching him. "But the power of all consuming Light is that it reaches into the Darkness and utterly does away with it."

"What do you mean?" Alex whispered.

"Heart surgery," Rachel's voice said, from the side. "He means heart surgery."

Alex glanced to her then back at John, who was smiling.

"If you like," he said to Rachel.

"In heart surgery," Rachel said, "the heart is stopped, and operated on. Then it is shocked again: then its beat is brought back again."

"Heart surgery?" Alex whispered, looking at John.

"The Light will consume the Darkness," John said. "Heart surgery."

"Death to the old man," Alex said. "Birth to a new man."[6]

"Death to the old age," John said. "And new life, for a new age. It's not a permanent end, Alex: only a means to a new beginning."[7]

"But death is still death," Alex whispered, grasping onto John's arm.

"Yes," John said, with sadness, "death is still death."

"And then, new life," Alex said – looking beyond John's eyes, to the wharf: to the sun, the wharf, the beach, the smiling faces... "Childbirth! Childbirth..."

"The delivery will be painful, Alex," John said.

---

[6] Romans 6:1-11 Paraphrased.
[7] Pointing to Revelation.

"Birth-pains!" Alex said. "Birth-pains."[8]

"But, in the morning, the new born child," John said. "Joy! Joy, in the morning: the pain, forgotten. No more pain, or death, or tears…"[9]

Tears welled up in Alex's eyes, and he reached out to touch John's face.

"I will see my father again," he whispered. "I will see him, standing in front of me, no more pain, no more tears, no more darkness – only light! Only light…"

John was silent, before him. He reached now – his fingers touched Alex's face.

"A child," he murmured over him. "You dream as a child."

"That is his power," Rachel's voice said, next to him. "He dares to dream, even in the midst of despair: he dares to hope, even in the presence of overwhelming oppression."

"Don't get me wrong," John said, smiling gently at him. "It's a good thing. Children can see what adults lose the ability to see. To return to childhood: to dare to return…"

"Innocence," Rachel said. "Innocence can overcome evil."

"Innocence can show evil up for what it is," John said. "But to actually overcome evil? That takes more."

"What more?" Alex asked – and John now cast his eyes across the water to the hills beyond.

"Sacrifice," he said. "Overcoming evil takes sacrifice."

And his eyes returned to Alex, he smiled, nodded his head, and stepped away: gesturing for Alex to lead them.

Alex looked ahead. The people were moving, off the ferry. He hesitated, and then he followed them: across the plank, onto the wharf, down and onto the road.

People flooded the shores of Picton. Alex stood a little back, watching them: Rachel and John stood on either side. The water was sparkling, in the sun. Alex wandered forward, onto the beach – he reached down, and cupped sand in his hand: he threw it out, across the water. Then he turned.

People were in front of him. Something was changing: news! News was spreading.

"Parliament's been blown up!" a man cried out.

"It's a mess!" Someone else said. "No leadership! A vacuum!"

"A vacuum?" A third asked.

"It's been some kind of attack!" Someone else cried. "To our foundation! To our Constitution!"

"An attack to our foundation?" Alex asked.

"Wellington is just three hours away," the first man said. "Our Constitution has been blown up! What if the terrorists come here?"

Alex looked over them, and then stepped forward.

---

[8] Matthew 24:7-8; Romans 8:22 Paraphrased.
[9] Hinting at Revelation 21:3-4.

"Are you not ready?" he asked. "If evil should come here?"

They shifted, disgruntled, before him – and then another stepped forward: a muscular man, in his thirties.

"We're not ready," he said. "We're sitters."

"Then what should we do?" Alex asked. "To be ready?"

"We need to find these bastards," the man said. "We need to do them in. We need to block them."

Alex stared at him. "And then what?" he asked. "After doing them in?"

"Take over," he said. "Build our own parliament. Show them who's boss."

He flexed his biceps, and Alex grimaced. It seemed all too familiar...

"What about the good?" he asked. "What kind of leadership are we looking for? What kind of leadership do we need?"

He glanced across the crowd: he seemed to have their attention.

"Are you looking for politicians?" he asked. "Are you looking for democracy? Sure, some kind of political system can be important for order. But what if it's all been taken from us? What do we do now? We have a constitutional monarchy: we have the Queen. But what if we've been cut off from the Queen as well?"

Frowns crossed the crowd. Allies? Could our allies help? How to trust them? To trust that they themselves will not move in: that they themselves will not take over?

"What about another kind of monarchy?" Alex asked. "Beyond our politicians, beyond our systems, beyond our Queen: above them all. What if there's another kind of leadership that will not falter, even if all hell breaks loose – even if everything we have is stripped away: even if the entire world is on the brink of disaster?"

Their frowns intensified.

"Could it be that a greater disaster is coming?" Alex asked. "Is it time for a different kind of leadership?"

They were thinking! He could see they were thinking...

Alex stepped back away from them: he cast his eyes over the water, toward Wellington. His father was coming: he would try to be King – he would try to rule. But there was another Ruler: a much better Ruler.

"What kind of leader will you look for?" he asked them. "Someone who promises you everything? Security, money, prosperity – these can be important, and alluring. But at what cost will he offer them? What would you sell, to gain the world? Truth? Integrity? The lives of others? The souls of yourselves?"

Now Alex turned back to them.

"There is another kind of King," he said. "Another kind of Leader. He is coming: it won't be long. He works in the opposite direction. He promises no money but what you need; no security but that which really counts. He offers no prosperity. He will invite you to sell everything: to even give up your lives. And, in return, he will give you your souls.

"Truth. Integrity. The lives of all.

"Where is the Leader who counts, now that the crisis has come?" Alex asked. "Where is the Leader who demands our all: who, in turn, will win for us what really counts – our all?"

"Who is this leader?" A woman called out. "Will he run for a new kind of Parliament?"

Alex smiled sadly at her.

"Is he not all around you?" he asked. "Has he not always been right before you?"

"Christmas?" another woman asked. "We've just come back from church."

"Shouldn't we fight?" A man asked. "The Army! It's some kind of terrorist group: shouldn't we be finding them, and putting them away?"

Alex grimaced at him. His father! His father would use this...

"Don't fight," he said, "at least not with physical weapons. How about fighting with love? With goodness? With generosity, charity, compassion – with truth.

"What chance has terrorism, in the face of forgiveness?" he asked. "We could overcome terrorism with grace. We could overcome hatred with love. We could overcome crime with justice, but a true kind of justice: not one that is secretly seeking retribution – a kind of justice that is seeking to restore the enemy as well as ourselves..."

"Restore the enemy?" Someone asked. "Like shit. I say we find them! I say we do them in!"

"On Christmas Day?" Someone else asked. "After church?"

"Forget church," the muscular man in his thirties said. "This is War! Someone's attacked us! We need to fight back! We need to form a response!"

"No," Alex said instinctively. A response? They would try to kill his father: fighting fire with fire. "You can't fix this by becoming the same," he said. "You can fix it by becoming better – by transcending the threat, and undoing it."

"Why are we listening to you?" Someone asked. "You're just a boy."

"Please," Alex said. "This is just what the enemy wants...this can only lead to more destruction."

"Follow me!" the burly man called out. "This is an emergency meeting! We'll gather forces, across New Zealand: we'll find the enemies, and deal to them!"

Alex stared at him – at the anger in his face – and then Rachel was alongside him.

"Do something," she said.

"Do what?" he whispered. "They want War!" And now tears filled his eyes: how could it be possible?

"Declare yourself," Rachel said. "Shine the light clearly, don't hide it: let the ones who want to follow, follow."

Alex swallowed: already? Declare himself? That would put himself at risk, and yet...and yet, before him, another movement was rising.

He thrust himself onto a rock. Rau! Suddenly he remembered Rau. He took in a deep breath, and then began.

78

"This isn't the right way!" he said loudly. "Anger, retribution – hatred. How can these things seriously solve anything? No!" he said. "We should follow the better way! We should follow the truth!"

Faces were turning toward him, away from the other man: he continued.

"There is a better leader," he said. "There's a better Way. It's not about self – defence, at the end of the day: why would it be? There's a much more important victory to be won than mere survival. Forget clinging to our own lives: we need to let them go, for something better. There's a greater kind of life coming: a kind of life that is stronger than death."

And now he stretched out his arms before them.

"Retribution?" he asked. "I've already tried that. I lived and breathed it, once – I know all about it. But this isn't the way to freedom: this will not bring us peace. This will not bring us the victory.

"Hold steady," he said. "Hold steady, and wait. Think…who is the real enemy? Think, and engage with the real enemy, but not with weapons, not with fists…with…with…"

And now he searched around himself: a symbol. What to give them?

He reached into his pocket, and drew out the five deformed bullets.

"With sacrifice," he said – and he threw the five bullets in front of them, on the sand. "With Joshua Davidson's sacrifice."

And now he stepped off the rock.

Rachel's arm came around his shoulders – he glanced up to the tears in her eyes.

"Yes," she said. "Well done: you nailed it."

He shrugged, and looked back to the bullets – people were bending over, to pick them up: they were fingering them, confused.

He wandered over to them.

"It was me," Alex whispered, and tears pricked his eyes. "I shot Joshua Davidson. He took my bullets into his chest: willingly, he took them! He died. But then…then he came back. He gave these bullets, the bullets I had sent into his chest, to John. And John gave them back to me."

The eyes shifted to John, who nodded.

"It's true," he said. "I saw Joshua alive. He gave the bullets to me."

"Alive?" someone asked. "How can that be?"

"He's stronger than death," Alex said. "He can carry our death, and bring us through to life."

They fingered the bullets: they considered his words.

Alex watched them, curious: what were they thinking? What were they feeling?

"A different kind of leader," a woman murmured, looking down at the bullet in her hands. "A different kind of King."

Alex smiled at her – and then he looked up, into the disdain of the muscular man.

79

"An assassinated King?" he said. "Forget that. Parliament is taken: I say we rise up – I say we join together, and storm the rubble, and rebuild. The next ferry!" he said. "Who's with me, to catch the next ferry, back to Wellington?"

Alex stared at him: at the shouts that suddenly went up, behind him – at the men that gathered around him.

"Are you crazy?" he asked him. "Go back into ground zero? You'll be killed! The enemy is stronger than you!"

"Not if we all join together," the man said. "Strength in numbers."

"Sure, there is strength in numbers," Alex said, "but you need an Ally…"

"Who's with me?" the man asked.

"Don't!" Alex said. "Don't be foolish!"

"Who's with me?" he asked. "And who's with this youth?"

Awkwardly Alex shifted before him. A horn sounded. The ferry! The ferry was preparing to return.

"How much carnage do you need?" Alex cried out to them. "Before you can see that we can't do this on our own? Some forces are greater than humanity! Some kinds of evil cannot be resisted unless we first submit to the Light!"

The muscular man smirked at him. "You do things your way, and we'll do it our way," he said – and he strode toward the ferry, with a throng of men following.

Alex stared at them, and closed his eyes tightly. Another killing! Another mass killing was coming…

A hand was on his shoulder: John! He knew it was John.

"Continue," John said. "Continue, through the darkness."

"He will kill them all," Alex whispered. "I should go: I should go on the ferry with them."

"No," Rachel said, her hand on his other shoulder. "No."

"I'm trying to save them," Alex said. "Why can't they see? I'm trying to save them."

"Save who you can," Rachel's voice said. "Save all that you can, from the coming darkness."

And he opened his eyes – and a crowd standing were before him.

Surprised, he gazed at them. An older man was close by: grey balding head, gentle face.

"I've been watching the Joshua Movement with interest," he said. "I heard about the killing, at Oriental Bay. Are you from the same Movement?"

Alex glanced back at Rachel and John, and then returned to the man's face.

"We are the same," he said. "I met with Rau: we are in unity. I have come to share with you what I myself received: that Joshua died, and then he came back to life."

"You are only sharing what we have already known for two thousand years," the man said, with a gentle smile. "Only a translation: only a re-interpretation."

"I am," Alex said. "Only interpreting for a new people: only translating for a new land."

"Then, welcome," the man said. "Join us. Happy Christmas."

And he grasped his hand, and led him forward, through the people and off the beach.

A little wooden church was before them. Alex gazed at it: at the cross above.

"This is an interdenominational church," the man said. "We are a small town, and so all of us share the same church building: Catholic, Anglican, Methodist, Presbyterian, Baptist, Pentecostal…"

Alex wandered in: a crucifix was set up on the altar, over white linen, with an empty wooden cross behind.

"I heard about the killing of the Anglican Bishop of Wellington," the man said. "But the Church will continue…"

"Yes," Alex whispered. "The Church will continue."

"Whatever form it takes," the man said. "Whatever culture, or language. Whether visible or hidden, the Church will continue."

Tears filled Alex's eyes. He wandered up to the altar: he sank down to his knees, before the railing and crucifix, and bowed his head.

"The blood of the martyrs," he whispered, "is the fertile ground for the Church."

And he prayed, for Mark, for Rau, for all the others on Oriental Bay: and he also prayed for James Connor, for Parliament, for New Zealand…

"Peace be with you," the man's voice said, and Alex felt his hand on his shoulder, and the man was returning the bullets of Joshua back to him.

"Peace be with you," he whispered back – and now he rose to his feet, slipped the bullets back into his own pocket, turned, and walked back down the aisle.

The bay of Picton was before him. The sun was still shining. The ferry had left. A crowd was still waiting outside the little church.

Alex swallowed. John and Rachel were standing on either side of him. Alex hesitated – and then he reached out, and laid a hand on each of their shoulders.

"Christmas," he said. "Peace be with you."

"Peace be with you," both replied, turning to him – and he felt each hand laid on his own, and he closed his eyes. Breathe! Receive peace. He breathed, and then opened his eyes and moved forward, into the crowd.

Tristan stood with James at the ferry terminal.

The ferry was drawing closer, having returned from Picton. Would Alex, Rachel and John be on it? Tristan was certain not. And yet he had a sense of foreboding...why? Why?

He looked to James, who was frowning, looking at the ferry.

"We should take cover," he said.

"What?" Tristan asked.

"We should move!" James said – and he grasped Tristan's arm, and drew him into an empty office.

Tristan flicked him off, and moved himself toward the door: opening it slightly, to look through the crack.

The ferry had drawn alongside the wharf. The retractable ramp was moving toward the hull: attaching itself. Passengers were starting to walk down the ramp.

"We need to get on board," Tristan said. "We have to catch this one, if we want to get to Rachel – there may not be another."

"He's using it," James said, from behind him. "While it suits his purposes, he's using it."

"Who?" Tristan asked.

"Kensington," James said – and Tristan turned to look at him.

"Kensington?" he asked. "You mean, you believe he's alive again?"

James grimaced at him. "It's hard to keep that kind of bastard down," he said.

"Bullets aren't strong enough?" Tristan asked.

"So it would seem," James said. "We already tried that."

"For five years!" Tristan said. "Five years, in the Army, trying to make peace – trying to facilitate peace, with weapons..."

"This is a different kind of enemy," James said. "A different kind of war."

And now Tristan looked again through the crack to the people disembarking.

There were women, holding the hands of children – seeming oblivious! Oblivious to what had happened: to Parliament having been blown up – to the nation being in crisis. There were men, next to the women – but now there were other men: anger in their faces, determination in their stance as they strode toward the exit: toward the heart of Wellington.

"We'll get the bastards!" one cried. "To Parliament!" And now another was lifting up a New Zealand flag.

Tristan stared at it: the Union Jack, the stars of the Southern Cross. Home! He had fought for this flag! He had fought for his home. Others were lifting their voices – Tristan felt drawn into the crowd. Fight! Rebuild! Raise the flag in the centre of the rubble of Parliament: rebellion! Rebellion, in the face of the terrorists!

He went to open the door, but James's hand was on his shoulder, restraining him.

"No," he said.

Tristan peered out at the crowd. "No?" he said. "But this is our land! This is our home!"

And then, before his eyes, there was an explosion.

The door flew open: Tristan was thrown back into the room, over James, to the ground. And, in front of him, through the door, was carnage.

Tristan dragged himself to his knees, and to his feet. Outside, rubble! Dust! Bodies, in the rubble – hands reaching out, others still, blood…

"Oh my God!" he cried, and he reached instinctively for his gun, but he had no gun – and now, before his eyes, the young men were screaming; the bloody faces, and his shooting, in the Middle East…

"Tristan!" James's voice said from a long distance – and Tristan felt himself being dragged up against a wall: felt himself being shaken. He started to see the face in front of him: the tense frown. James! His comrade!

"We have to move!" the face said, and Tristan shook his head, staring at him.

"Have to help," he whispered. "We have to help them…"

"You can't help them," James said. "You're too shocked."

And now Tristan was being grabbed – and now he was being pushed forward.

He stumbled, one foot at a time. Bodies were around him! Groans! He reached out blindly to the pain – but James pushed him beyond it.

"Onto the ferry!" James said. "Up the ramp! Now, soldier! We have lives to save!"

"People are still alive…?" Tristan whispered – and he shook his head, and straightened himself up, and moved forward.

The broken ramp was still attached to the ferry! The faces were white, the voices lifting in panic.

"Move back!" James called to them. "Back onto the ferry! Detach the ramp!"

Tristan moved across the ramp with James, and a cabin crewman ushered the others back onto the ship, reaching to detach the ramp.

"To the Bridge," James said. "Now."

And Tristan followed him, down a corridor, up flights of stairs, to the Bridge.

The skipper was before him, staring out of the starboard window at the terminal, his eyes wide.

"What the hell just happened?" he whispered. "What caused the explosion?"

"This is War," James said. "Wellington has been taken over: it's no longer safe. You must cruise back to Picton: it's the only hope for the people on board."

"Terrorism…?" The skipper stuttered. "My job…I can't just take the ferry back…"

"This is War," James repeated. "There is no ordinary job anymore. The old rules can't apply anymore. You must act to protect your passengers, skipper: that is the highest priority. Forget your job."

The man stared at him, and then down at his clothes – and at Tristan. Tristan reached down to his own grey pyjamas.

"You're criminals?" the skipper asked, and James grimaced. Irony!

83

"See for yourself," he said. "About two hundred are dead on the wharf. There are no police, there is no army: what will you do next?"

The skipper frowned at him, and Tristan moved forward.

"Please," he whispered. "We didn't cause the blast."

His eyes moved over Tristan's face.

"I believe you," he said – and he reached for his controls, and Tristan felt the ferry move under his own feet.

He sank against the console: he looked out of the Bridge windows. The ferry was pulling away! Away from the carnage, into the centre of the Harbour.

"Civil War?" he whispered, trembling. "Is this the beginning of a divide between the North and the South?"

"When you have delivered these people," James said to the skipper, "don't return."

"Anarchy," the skipper said, frowning. "You are making me into a criminal."

"I am not making you into a criminal," James said. "A law simply doesn't exist for this situation. Would you sacrifice your life for the sake of a lesser law?"

Tristan closed his eyes. What was that: theft? Theft of the ferry, to save the people? And yet, calamity! Calamity, at the ferry terminal!

"Dad..." he whispered, and he remembered the Anglican bishop. What was right? What was wrong? He couldn't tell anymore! He couldn't tell...

He moved away from the skipper and James: he stared out the window. They were passing the neck of the Harbour – they were moving beyond, into open waters: into choppy waters.

Picton was ahead. Was Rachel there? The doctor? Could the doctor help? Could anyone help?

"Anarchy..." he whispered. "There is no stability anymore. There is no authority."

And he sank down against the console, drew his knees up to his chest, and cried.

The ferry was drawing near to Picton.

Tristan lifted himself to his feet. What could he find here: answers? In this tiny idyllic town, so close to the mayhem? He wandered out of the Bridge – he walked down steps, and drew near to the ramp. The people...they were silent: uncertain, their faces a blank page. What were they doing there? What were they going to do? They needed some kind of leadership.

James stepped forward, from behind Tristan.

"When you disembark," he said, "gather together on the beach, and we'll form a plan about how to proceed."

Tristan stared at him. James? James was stepping up to the mark, now? In the midst of hell, he knew what to do?

Army...his army training was kicking in: his army leadership. But Tristan...he could not lead.

84

He lifted his eyes to the hills – there was a little church. Had the others gone there?

The ramp was lowered – James was taking the lead. Tristan wandered down the ramp, to the wharf – he wandered down the wharf, to the street. The others were filing onto the beach…Tristan wandered the other way, up the hill, toward the little church…

Alex was there. Tristan stared at him, at his blonde curls, and his watchful blue gaze – he swayed with relief. Alex was alive! He was actually still alive.

Alex rushed to him now – he was reaching out to grasp Tristan's arms. "What are you wearing?" he asked, with laughter that sounded to Tristan's ears like sobs.

"Kensington put me in prison," Tristan said, grasping Alex's arms in return. "But I escaped, with James."

"Is Kensington on the ferry?" Alex asked, looking past him.

"Not yet," Tristan said. "I know that for certain. We told the skipper not to return."

"But there's another ferry," Alex said. "Two other ferries…"

Tristan closed his eyes. "I'm sorry, Alex," he whispered. "I'm sorry I thought it was your fault."

"It's okay," Alex's voice said. "You had to know: you had to be certain."

"We have to leave, now," Tristan said, looking back at his young face. "We have to go, before he brings another ferry out: before he sends someone here."

"What about all the other people who came?" Alex asked.

"James is dealing with them," Tristan said, "but I just need to protect all of you: just you, even if it kills me."

And he wrapped his arms around himself, and started to cry. His father was gone! Like his sister! Like…like his mother.

He felt Alex's hands on his shoulders. A brother! At least he could still fight for this brother. He was alive! At least, in this moment, he was safe.

"Where are the others?" Tristan whispered.

"Here," a voice said, and he looked to see Rachel.

Her face…beauty! Why, always, such beauty to him? He breathed in her gentle blue gaze, wet with tears.

"You made it," she whispered.

"Only just," he breathed – and now he found himself shaking again, even in the summer heat.

Her hand came onto his arm: steady! She was steady.

"Easy," she said, and her kindness made him erupt with weeping.

Now her arms were moving around him. Tristan quickly looked around: John – was John okay? He was there, green eyes quiet, watching, kind, accepting…

Tristan closed his eyes, and received Rachel's love. Friendship! The beauty, the innocence, the healing…

He buried his face in her shoulder for a moment, he breathed deeply, and then he moved himself away.

85

The church was before him. It was quaint: a small old wooden house, with a little steeple on top – small, simple, open…He wandered inside, down the little aisle, to the altar – he reached out to touch the bronze crucifix. He breathed deeply, and then turned and wandered back out again: standing on the hill, looking across the bay.

James was still on the beach, with the ferry passengers.

"What will happen to them?" Rachel asked.

"They will need to integrate," Tristan said. "Probably move further south, for safety."

"And us?" John's voice asked – and Tristan looked into his sad eyes.

"Run," Tristan said. "We will have to run."

Alex was shifting on his feet, and Tristan glanced at him.

"What?" he asked.

"It doesn't make sense," Alex said. "To keep running, keep running…"

"What else are we to do?" Tristan asked. "We have an enemy who can't be defeated with weapons."

"That doesn't mean he can't be defeated," Alex said, and Tristan smiled quietly. There was something about him: something powerful – something that raised possibilities beyond what others could see.

Tristan suddenly felt hope, looking into those intense blue eyes: hope beyond himself.

"Then show us, Alex," he said, and he gestured before them all. "Show us the right way."

"I can't do it on my own," Alex said. "He would take me down: I'm not stronger than him on my own."

"Then have all of us," Tristan said, gesturing around, to John and Rachel. "Have all of us, to help you to defeat the enemy."

"Thank you," Alex said. "But I really have no idea what to do next."

Tristan grinned at him. "Need some practical help?" he asked.

"Looks like you could do with some practical help too," Rachel said, gesturing to Tristan's prison clothes, and Tristan threw her a foul look.

"Want to make me some?" he asked, and she flicked her hand at him, and his grin widened.

"What about James?" John asked – and now Tristan looked back down to the beach, and frowned.

"What do you make of him?" John asked. "Is he an ally? Is he a threat?"

"Both," Tristan muttered, watching him organise the crowd. "He has great skills, and, in some ways, great strength, but there is a darkness about him as well."

"Don't I know it," Rachel muttered, and Tristan looked at her: at her troubled gaze, down to the beach.

"Is he really your brother?" he asked, and she swallowed.

"Yes," she said. "He is."

"So what do we do?" John asked. "Do we act together? Do we act separately?"

86

"Separately," Rachel said quickly – and Tristan glanced between her and James.
"I'm with you," he said quickly. "You know that, Rachel. I saw what he did."
"As, of course, am I," John said. "I'm behind you, in whatever you feel you need to do."
"And yet…" Alex was wandering forward on the hill.
"What is it?" Tristan asked.
Alex was frowning, looking out toward James. "Something," he muttered. "Something in him. Something good."
And he shrugged his shoulders, and turned back to them.
"So," he said. "What next?"
"We move," Tristan said. "Quickly. Quietly."
"Without showing the crowd?" Rachel asked – and Tristan glanced back down to James.
"I'll tell him," he said. "I owe him that. I'll tell him we're going, but I won't say where."
"He'll follow," Rachel said. "He won't stay here for long."
"The crowd…"
"He'll do what he needs to do," Rachel said, "and then he'll do what he really wants to do."
"And what is that?" Tristan asked, holding her eyes, and she swallowed again, looking at him.
"I don't know," she muttered. "But I do know this: he didn't come here for that crowd."
Tristan frowned. "His own survival."
"Not only that."
Tristan shifted on his feet. "I'll protect you," he said. "I'm responsible: I told him where you went. I'm sorry, and I'll protect you."
Rachel held his eyes with sadness. "Just don't go getting yourself killed for me," she whispered. "I'd die."
"I'll do my best," Tristan said, smirking. "Now, let's get moving."
And he gathered them, and turned, and led them down the hill.

CHAPTER THIRTEEN: Reflections

Rachel stood at the water's edge, in Picton.

The ferry still sat in front of her: motionless, empty. Was there room for a second ferry to dock at the wharf, on the other side? She frowned. They should leave: soon.

She reached a hand into her pocket, to her cell-phone. She frowned. Two and a half years ago, she had teetered on calling the police: two and a half years ago, James had put the gun to her head.

Where was he now? She lifted her eyes across the beach of the sand. The crowd had gone: where? Integrated into the community: into the town. They would spread, outward and down...for what purpose? Escape? Survival? Some further purpose?

What was James planning?

She swallowed – and now John was standing alongside her, following her gaze across the town.

"Gone," he said. "He's disappeared."

"Into the woodwork," she said. "Out of sight..."

"...but not out of mind," John finished.

"I love him," Rachel said plainly, her eyes settling again on the church – and now she glanced at John's face: at his sad smile.

"I know," he said simply back. "Of course."

Rachel frowned at him. "What do you see in him?" she asked. "A criminal? Illness?"

John's sadness intensified. "I see a tarnished man," he said. "A man capable of good and bad."

"What would Joshua have done with him?" Rachel asked. "What would Joshua have said to him?"

"To choose the good," John said quickly. "To be the good."

"God allows us to choose the bad?" Rachel asked. "God enables us to choose the bad?"

"There's a danger to freedom," John said. "There's a responsibility given to us with the gift of choice."

Rachel looked out again across the water: to the sunlight, and the chop – to the gentle waves, lapping on the sand.

"Isn't it better not to be given the choice?" she asked. "Isn't it better to create a world of love, and peace, and never allow the possibility of anything else to enter the picture...?"

And she wandered over to a rock – to the shellfish, growing on the rock.

"Why not protect against predators?" she asked. "Why not always cultivate pearls?"

"He is cultivating pearls," John murmured to her. "Pearls take grit."

"But too much grit destroys," Rachel said.

"That's true," John replied.

"It's a risky business, putting grit into the equation."

"It is," John said.

"What if it turns out badly?" She lifted her eyes to the hills of the Marlborough Sounds: to the green forest, to the blue waters. "What if this is all swept away by our grit?"

She frowned again, and looked down at her cell-phone: scrolling through the contacts. James! His cell-phone number. Her father...

"Alex says Kensington will be able to locate the cell-phones," she said. "Even if they're switched off."

"Joshua was never big on cell-phones," John said.

"James would be able to find me." She lingered on his number.

"Do you want him to find you?" John asked.

"I don't know," she whispered. "Should I? I don't know whether to trust him."

"Neither do I," John said.

She rocked on her feet – she fingered her phone. Then, decided, she threw the phone into the lapping waves, and watched it sink under water to the sand below.

"That's it," she said. "I have to trust, now: I have to trust in God's sovereignty, over my own: in his control, over my own."

John pulled out his own phone – he also threw it into the water.

"Basic humanity," he said. "Basic communication."

"Basic transport, basic food, basic shelter..."

John's hand came to her. "Basic entertainment," he said, and now he was grinning.

She smiled at him – she squeezed his hand.

"Is humanity defined by the clothes?" she asked. "By the fancy phones, the internet, the money?"

"Humanity transcends these things," John said, "just as God transcends humanity."

Rachel smiled, looking out again across the water: taking a deep breath of the sea breeze.

"Freedom," she said. "I feel freedom."

"With freedom comes cost," John said. "The chance to save: the chance to kill."

Rachel swallowed. "The chance to live; the chance to die."

"What will we choose?" John asked. "When we are given the choice?"

And now he stooped to the sand: and now he lifted a lost golden watch.

"Look, Rachel," he said. "To God, the end is as the beginning."

"Yes..." Rachel murmured, reaching to finger the watch. The arms had stopped, but the gold was still somehow shiny.

"In the beginning," John said, "was the Word: and the Word was with God, and the Word was God."[10]

---

[10] John 1:1. Scripture taken from the HOLY BIBLE, NEW INTERNATIONAL VERSION ®. NIV ®. COPYRIGHT © 1973, 1978, 1984, 2011 by Biblica, Inc.® . Used by permission. All rights reserved worldwide.

"Christ," Rachel murmured.

"With God in the beginning," John said. "He came into the world: the world did not understand him. But the world also did not overcome him."[11]

Rachel smiled gently down to the watch.

"He came to his own," John said, "but his own did not recognise him."[12]

"The Creator comes to the created," Rachel said. "Dwells with them: lives with them. Dies with them."

"And then comes back," John said.

"God with humanity," Rachel said. "God here, on Earth, with humanity."

"Where did things go wrong, Rachel?" John asked. "When did God stop dwelling with humanity?"

Rachel frowned, fingering the face of the watch.

"Adam and Eve?" she asked.

"A child's story," John said. "So I believed."

"And now?"

John smiled sadly, looking across the waters. "Now it is the greatest profundity," he said.

"Why?" Rachel asked.

"Because..." John paused, looking around himself – combing the beach, Rachel knew, for another symbol. What to use? She could read his thoughts. He wandered off, and then he returned. "There," he said, and handed her a small slightly rusty spade.

Rachel turned it over in her hands. A spade?

"It can be used for gardening," John said. "To grow veges, and fruit."

"Or to bury the dead..." Rachel murmured.

"Or dig them up again," John said. "Dust. From dust we came, to dust we will return."

"Why?" Rachel asked. "Why death?"

"Because we took too much, Rachel," John said. "We bit off more than we can chew. In Genesis, God warns Adam and Eve not to eat from the Tree of the Knowledge of Good and Evil. Eve eats, and passes it to Adam, even though God told them they would surely die."[13]

"Literal?" Rachel asked. "Metaphorical?"

"Both are as one," John said. "Literal or metaphorical: we can't handle our own knowledge of evil, and it will lead to our death."

Rachel grimaced at him, and looked back down at the spade in her hand.

"Nukes?" she whispered. "From dust to dust?"

"Whether nuclear weapons or some other means," John said, "our future in this age is limited. Our wisdom is not as strong as our knowledge."

---

[11] John 1:2,10 Paraphrased.
[12] John 1: 11 Paraphrased.
[13] See Genesis 3:1-24.

"We have grown too powerful," Rachel murmured.

"We will use the tool for good," John said, taking the spade. "We will plant, we will grow, we will build bigger spades, and we won't see the full consequences: just as Eve didn't see the full consequences, when Satan invited her to eat the fruit. She didn't see the full consequences, Rachel, of experiencing good and evil…"

"Why did she take it into herself?" Rachel asked. "Why did she seek it, if God warned her not to?"

"Why do you think?" John asked – and Rachel looked down to her own hands, and turned them over.

"How did Satan reach her?" John murmured. "In the story? How Eve first, and then Adam?"

Rachel reached for the spade with her hands – she made a digging motion.

"A garden…" she murmured.

"Fruit," John said. "The fruit of life. Why knowledge, Rachel? Why the grasp of morality, independent of God?"

Now Rachel lifted her face to the sky: to the sunlight, to the blue, to the small white clouds. She closed her eyes.

"Freedom," she whispered. "Growth. Wisdom! To grasp God, to see beyond…"

"Will you not see too far?" John asked. "Will you not die with the burden of what you see?"

And now his hand reached her shoulder: and now a vision burst further before her eyes. Explosions! Nuclear explosions, shock waves, dust, thrown up into the air! Violence! Death…

Gasping, she sank to her knees.

"He will do it again," John said, and his hand left her shoulder, and the vision disappeared.

"Who?" she gasped, throwing the spade onto the sand.

"The end will be as the beginning," John said. "A representation! A translation."

Rachel trembled, on her knees. "What do you mean?" she whispered.

"Be ready, Rachel," John said. "Don't make the same mistake Eve made. She was the Mother: whether literally or metaphorically – the Mother of all humanity."

And now John was taking her hand, lifting her to her feet and turning her.

Tristan was waiting for her, with Alex alongside. Tristan looked white.

"What is it?" Rachel breathed – and Tristan handed her his cell-phone.

A news article was on the screen: an image. A red mushroom cloud, in the distance, on the horizon: a nuclear weapon, deployed! On US soil!

"No," Rachel whispered. "Oh, no…"

"They will respond," Tristan whispered. "They must."

"No," Rachel said. "They mustn't."

"It's Kensington," Alex said. "His tactics: his influence."

"He moved our Parliament out of the way," John said.

"We had knowledge," Alex said. "We were mediating. We were blocking his purposes."

91

"Peace keeping," Tristan choked. "We were peace keeping, in the Middle East..."

"And now it begins," John said.

"Assimilation or annihilation," Alex said.

"Over six hundred thousand killed, Rachel," Tristan said, his forehead creasing into an intense frown. "The US Government must respond."

"No," Rachel breathed – and she turned away from them, and sank down to the sand.

John sank down next to her: his shoulder was pressed into hers.

"What is the answer, Rachel?" he murmured to her. "What is the solution?"

She closed her eyes and buried her face in her hands. What was the solution? Mass murder...how to respond? How to respond?

"Take it," she whispered. "Take the hit, and don't fight back."

"And be hit again and again?" Tristan's voice asked from behind her. "Rachel, you can't be serious! You can't expect that: not from anyone!"

And now Rachel turned, and looked up to Alex.

"What do you say?" she asked, and his young face smiled sadly.

"Take the hit," he said. "Don't become the same."

"Six hundred thousand dead!" Tristan cried. "Take the hit? Impossible!"

"The knowledge of good and evil," John muttered. "The experience of evil. How to contain it? How to stop it once it is unleashed?"

"Prevention," Rachel murmured, gazing into Alex's face: remembering Kensington's assault. "The true answer is prevention."

"But what if it's too late?" Tristan asked. "It's done, Rachel! It's happened! The people are dead!"

Rachel rose to her feet, and stared out across the water.

"Justice!" Tristan cried. "You know about that, Rachel? I remember you crying for it to me! When I...when I shot Joshua..."

And now, suddenly, he was silenced.

Rachel turned to him: saw the humility in his face – the silence in his eyes.

"What is true justice?" she asked. "Eye for an eye? Tooth for a tooth? Six hundred thousand civilian lives for another six hundred thousand civilian lives? Is that true justice?"

Tristan shifted on his feet, and now his eyes were looking over the water.

"If it was," he muttered, "I would already be dead."

"Humanity destroying all of humanity isn't justice," Rachel said. "It is self-defeating self-defence."

"We should let go of our lives instead," Alex said. "Be willing to die, not as a means of killing others: but as a means of preventing the killing of others."

"Let go of our lives," John said, "in order to truly gain them."

"Freedom!" Rachel said – and suddenly she smiled. Death? Freedom to die? A freedom to die in order to be truly free to live?

"Just stand back?" Tristan cried. "Stand back, and let the holocaust happen?"

"No," Alex said – and now all eyes were on him. "Don't stand back: step forward. Step forward, and be a voice for what is right – step forward, and shine light, and seek to overcome darkness, but, at the same time, be willing to pay the price."

Rachel gazed at him: the young face, the idealism – the power of his own convictions. Was humanity lost now? Was a nuclear holocaust inevitable? Perhaps. But there was something in Alex's face: something that gave her hope.

"Let's step forward," she said. "Let's uncover Kensington. Let's do what we can in our own land."

"Where?" Alex asked. "Where?"

"Where the people are gathered," Rachel said. "Let's reach as many as we can."

"Nelson," Tristan said. "And then, Christchurch, Dunedin, Invercargill…"

"Let's go straight toward Christchurch," Alex said. "Kaikoura."

"Why?" Rachel asked.

"Time is short," Alex said. "It feels right."

"All right," Rachel said. "Let's head toward Christchurch."

"He'll follow," Alex said. "He'll know."

"But we'll do it anyway," John said, and Rachel watched Alex's eyes fixed on John with a sad smile.

"Yes," Alex said. "We'll do it anyway."

And Rachel walked off the beach, shook the sand off her feet, and moved on to follow Alex.

CHAPTER FOURTEEN: Encounters

Alex stood on the rock of Kaikoura Peninsula.

In front of him in the distance, to the left, was the town of Kaikoura, with the Kaikoura ranges behind. The mountains were showing only a little snow.

Alex drew his eyes back to the sand and sparkling blue waters of the peninsula. He kicked off his sneakers and socks, in the heat, and wandered a little into the ocean.

Beauty…Privacy. There was no one around, in this spot, but seagulls and distant seals: no one to report him. The water was cool, on his feet: refreshing. He had a sudden urge to rush fully into it: he held himself back.

On the rock behind him was Rachel. He glanced at her face: her slight watchful frown. John was nearby, sitting himself down on the rock: dangling his feet over the edge. Tristan was closer on the sand, his cell-phone out; his frown intense.

The trains had been shut down. So soon…so soon Kensington had asserted his control. The army had moved into Picton, even as they had slipped out. Now the marine connection, between North and South Islands, was being heavily watched: heavily guarded.

Alex stared down at his feet, in the clear waters. It was New Year's Eve. Six days…it had taken them six days to walk and hitch their way down to Kaikoura…

His feet were bleeding and aching. He sighed. Bathe? Bathe fully here? They were out of money: there would be no paid accommodation and shower.

He shrugged, pulled off his T-shirt, threw it on the sand and wandered into the sea in his shorts, throwing himself deep into the water.

The sea flooded over his curls. Refreshing! He came to the surface, turned himself over and floated on his back.

The sun was above him: bright and high in the sky. It would burn them, if they didn't find shelter soon! He should protect the others. He closed his eyes, took a deep breath, floating on the ocean, and then heaved himself back to his feet and trekked back onto the sand.

"Wellington's declared a military state," Tristan said as Alex stood dripping in the sand.

"You were right," Alex muttered back to him in return. "It is refreshing going for a swim in clothes. You should do it again."

"Are you telling me I need a bath?" Tristan asked, smiling wryly at him – tugging at his prison shirt.

Alex shrugged. "If it was only me…"

"You do need a bath," Rachel's voice said to Tristan – and now she was holding out Alex's T-shirt to him. "But don't you boys know you should be bathing in fresh water?"

"We take what we can," Alex said, shrugging. And now he saw Tristan's troubled gaze return to his cell-phone.

94

Alex pulled his T-shirt over his wet body, and wandered up to John, sitting on the rocks.

"We should get out of the sun now," he said.

"Yes," John said.

"He will find us," Alex said. "He'll know Tristan is missing, and James: he will find Tristan's cell, and track it."

"Yes," John said simply, "he will."

Now Tristan's eyes were on him. "Without my phone," he said, "we'll have no connection with the outside world."

"No," Alex said.

"We'll have no warning," Tristan said. "No time to run: no preparation to fight."

"We already know he's coming," Alex said.

"You don't understand!" Tristan said, his face taut. "The international scene! Russia, Alex! We have to watch Russia!"

Another nuclear missile…Tristan feared it! Alex grimaced at him.

"We can't prevent Russia responding," he said. "As an ally! As an ally to those innocents America has now taken."

"How can they do this?" Tristan whispered, his body tense in the heat of the sun. "As if they're playing a frickin' war game! And yet…and yet how can they not?"

Rachel's hand was moving to Tristan's shoulder.

"One day at a time," she murmured to him. "There is still sun. There is still blue sky, and beauty, and life, and love."

"Blue sky," Tristan choked, his eyes looking upward. "But for how long, Rachel? For how long?"

"For as long as we have," Rachel said gently – and Tristan swallowed, and reached to turn off his phone, and he slipped it into his pocket.

Now Alex turned to Rachel.

"Have you seen James?" he asked – and Rachel frowned, her gaze shifting across the water to Kaikoura.

"I thought I saw him, once," she said. "Down a side street, away from the crowd."

"He is watching you," Alex said, and Rachel swallowed.

"Maybe," she said.

"You love him," Alex said, and Rachel flushed before him.

"I…I…" she stuttered.

"He's important to you," he said, and Rachel turned her face away.

"From a long time ago," she whispered. "A long time."

Alex searched her pain – then suddenly grasped her hand.

"Come with me," he said, smiling.

"What?" she cried.

"Come!" he said – and he drew her behind him, over the rocks and sands, and up the steps of the cliff face.

"Where are you going?" Tristan's voice cried behind them.

"Out of the heat!" Alex called back to him, still grasping hard onto Rachel's hand: hearing her breathing, behind him.

The track was ahead of them – he cut across the track, across the grass, between trees: Rachel followed him. He knew Tristan and John would be behind: he knew they also would follow, but not all the way – only Rachel would be able to follow him all the way.

"Are you afraid of danger, Rachel?" he asked, moving faster: breaking through the tall grass, drawing them both onto the other side of the peninsula. The southern cliff was before them: the ocean beyond.

She was panting, alongside him: her eyes moving across the deep blue, sparkling in the sun, her face bathing in yellow light.

"Not if there's a higher reason," she said next to him – and he grasped her hand again and grinned.

"There is a higher reason," he said – and now he drew her down the steps of the cliff-face, to the sand and rocks below.

They stood on the sand. There was no one around: no one to save them. Alex looked out to the deep blue.

"The canyon, Rachel," he said. "This is the Kaikoura canyon." And he gestured out to the ocean. "Under the water, out there: a channel, sixty kilometres long, over one kilometre deep – it joins, Rachel, with the deep ocean floor: hundreds of kilometres of access to the Pacific..."

He turned back to her blue eyes: wide, lit with fear and hope.

"Come with me," Alex said – and now he stripped off his T-shirt again, and threw it on the sand.

Rachel's eyes dropped to her own T-shirt and shorts, wearing his belt, with a grin.

"If there's a rip," she said, "it will take me down."

"You won't be taken down," Alex said. "Trust me."

Rachel's gaze returned to him: her eyes sparkling.

"Swim?" she whispered. "Swim, way over my depth? Swim, into the vast awakenings of the full depths of the ocean?"

"Swim," Alex said – and she kicked off her shoes, and he drew her with him into the water.

"Rachel!" Tristan's voice cried out behind them. "What are you doing? The world's in danger! How can you just impulsively risk your life following after him?"

The water was lapping at their knees. Alex turned to look back – to see Tristan standing on the sand, grasping at his own hair, his face distraught. John was standing behind him, reaching out a hand to his shoulder. Alex could see: John understood! His face was calm, though sad.

Rachel turned toward the shore.

"It's for a higher purpose," Alex whispered – and now Rachel turned back: and now she thrust herself fully into the water.

Alex swam. The waves flooded over his head – he lifted himself again to breathe. Rachel was alongside him, a strong swimmer, but she was waiting: waiting on him to set the direction. He looked up to the sun, he took a deep breath. Faith! He wasn't directing! He wasn't guiding.

"Have your way," he whispered, and he saw Joshua, in his mind: his brown eyes – his gentle smile.

"Shine my light," he said. "Carry the cost."

"I will shine your light," he whispered to him, over the waves. "I will carry the cost."

And he dove down under the wave, and started to kick.

Water flooded past him. He gasped, above the water, and dove again. A current was grasping him: he grasped out for Rachel's hand – the current grasped them both.

They were drawn, together, forward – and then, suddenly, the blue deepened.

He turned himself, on his back: he stretched out his arms. Cool! The water was beautifully cool, after their effort! Rachel was on her back, beside him, still grasping his hand: her eyes closed, her face radiant in the sun, pointing to the sky.

Childhood! Brother and sister! Alex laughed freely. She was a sister.

There was a movement beneath them: a gentle tickle on his back, which also made Rachel shiver. The water around them had changed to grey, and now, suddenly, they were being flicked up in the air by the tail of a humpback whale.

Alex gasped, as Rachel cried out in delight: they fell back down to the water, came to the surface – Alex laughed, while Rachel shook her wet hair, and now Alex wrapped his arm around the tail, and his other arm around Rachel, and they were being dragged up and down through the water.

The whale drew them toward the beach.

"Don't get caught!" Rachel's high voice cried out to the whale – but he flicked them off, in the direction of the sand, and swam back into the depths.

Alex reached down with his feet: the sand! He stood, and reached out a hand to Rachel, and lifted her to her feet. She was grinning, and he laughed. What had just happened? And now he turned to the beach.

Kensington was standing on the shore.

Alex stiffened: his grip on Rachel tightened.

"Don't be afraid," she murmured to him. "He no longer has the strongest power over you."

"I haven't done what I needed to do," he whispered – and he lifted his eyes to the mountains beyond.

Not much snow…and the many fault lines…

He lowered his gaze back to Kensington: the tall figure, dressed in a black suit on the hot summer day.

"It's a new year tomorrow," Rachel's voice said alongside him. "A new season."

"The new season will cost," Alex said to her – and now he released her hand, and walked forward ahead of her, out of the water.

Kensington's blue intense gaze was on him as he walked to stand, dripping, half naked, before him. Alongside was another of his father's men, standing with a gun to Tristan's back. Tristan's face was rigid, his teeth clenched. John was standing on the other side, as if unnoticed – his green eyes still calm, finding him: focusing him.

"You are clothed with another now," he said, but his voice wasn't heard as Kensington moved to take up all of Alex's vision.

"Come with me," Kensington said. "Enough with this childish frolicking – we have work to do."

Alex looked up at his father's hard face. He felt no fear! Surprised, he held his father's gaze. He was back! Back from the dead! And yet…and yet Alex was not surprised to see him.

Mention the death? Mention it? He glanced at Tristan, the one who had taken his father's life – at his fear. People were gathering behind Tristan: a crowd was forming. People were talking in high, strained voices, pointing! Pointing at Kensington.

"Parliament has been overrun!" Kensington said, lifting his voice to the crowd: his eyes still on Alex. "Religious extremists have struck at the heart of our home land!"

Alex held his gaze, dripping on the sand. Religious extremists? He would blame Joshua – he would target the movement.

"It is true," Alex said, raising his voice to meet that of his father. "It was a religious extremist who assaulted our land! For what is religion but a following of the treasure of our hearts? Who is our God, but the one we hold highest above all?"

Kensington's gaze flickered slightly. "The extremists have taken control of our fault lines!" he said. "The Hope Fault, in this very region, is their first target!"

And he pointed behind him to the mountain range.

"Do you know?" he cried out. "Have you discovered it yet? The sand and silt lying under these waters, laid down by the great canyon below: it will slip, with a massive earthquake! It will trigger a massive tsunami back, onto the coast!"

"He's mad!" Tristan cried out. "He will kill us all! Run! Run for your lives, away from the coast!"

"No!" John's voice suddenly called out. "Joshua warned us a tsunami is coming! He didn't say to run: he said to be ready! Faith is the swimming! Joshua is the boat for the flood! Don't miss the boat! Learn how to swim!"

"Mad!" Kensington said, his eyes on Alex. "The Joshua Movement is mad! They have taken control of the Hope Fault – they have taken our land under siege!"

And now he gestured to the mountains, and now Alex felt a tremor under his feet.

He stared at his father's face: the control! The strategy. Kensington would be taken by the flood: but he would survive it! He would survive it, when all else would die: he would use the carnage to extend his grip on the nation.

Fear seized Alex: the tremor, under his feet – it was getting stronger! The crowd was starting to react.

Someone suddenly appeared, to Alex's left, in the distraction: he lifted a rifle to Kensington's head. James Lester! It was James.

"We killed you," he said, his face drawn and hard. "I had to see your face for myself: I had to see the truth."

Kensington smiled darkly at Alex, with the gun to his head. "You know the truth," he said. "You can't kill me. You can't overcome me. Every bullet will make me stronger."

"Say the word," James said, glancing at Alex. "This bastard had you at gun point: he has Tristan at gun point. Say the word, and I will shoot him again."

"No," Alex said. "Put down your weapon."

James shifted awkwardly on his feet, fingering his rifle: stepping back.

"What the hell is going on here?" he asked. "A man can't return from death, can he?"

"Joshua Davidson did," John said. "Never to die again."

"Christ," James said, gesturing his rifle to him. "You're telling me this shit is for real?"

And he stared back into Kensington's face. "If you can resurrect then Joshua can resurrect, and then…then…"

And his face went white.

Kensington gestured again to the mountains.

"I overheard his plan," James said. "I checked the Hope Fault. I could find no explosives."

"His power isn't natural," John said. "He has joined with another."

"I don't believe in fairy stories," James said. "I don't believe in ghosts."

"Then believe in delusion," Kensington said. "Believe in your own control over your own fate."

"Enough," Alex said, straightening. "Stop badgering him. You have come for me."

Kensington's eyes darkened. "I have," he said, his voice suddenly soft: hidden from the crowd. "And you will follow me, or I will use you as an example for all the land." And he gestured around, to Tristan, to John, to James, to…to Rachel…

Alex frowned. Rachel! She was standing up alongside him, now: dripping wet, looking at Kensington.

"You won't have him," she said, and Kensington laughed.

"Will I not?" he asked.

"Over my dead body," she said.

"If that's what you want," Kensington said, and he suddenly grasped James's gun.

"Rachel!" Tristan's voice cried, and Alex swiftly moved in front of her.

"No," he said. "You'll expose yourself."

"Of course," Kensington said, "but how easy it was to frighten you." And he handed the rifle back to James.

"I wasn't frightened," Alex said, and Kensington smiled.

"I wasn't talking about you," he said, and he glanced sideways to Tristan before looking back to Alex.

"Your followers are weak."

"They're not my followers."

"Then what are they?"

Alex looked at him and resisted grinding his teeth. "They are my friends," he said.

"Leave them behind," Kensington said. "We have bigger investments."

"Investments?" Alex asked.

"The World," Kensington said, and he gestured around: to the land; to the sea. "It's being handed to us. A new age. But the old must be dismantled first."

And he stretched out his arm toward the mountains – toward the fault lines.

"Stop!" Alex said. "Do this and I die!" Surely he could reach him? Surely connect with him through his own blood line?

"Not if you join with me," Kensington said. "Not if you also drink from my chalice."

And now he pulled out of his pocket a small spade.

"Dust to dust," he said. "Let's rebuild. Let's make it better."

Alex frowned, looking down at the spade in his hands. It was innocent, wasn't it? Innocent?

"He wants to plant using the ash of the dead as fertilizer," Rachel said. "Don't listen to him, Alex. Don't be enticed."

"Come into the Light," John's voice said. "Humanity cannot transcend itself. Humanity is broken."

"Is humanity really broken?" Kensington asked, reaching for the spade – bending to dig it into the sand, and lift the sand up again: flicking off the sand. "You can be immortal, Alex, with the power I have found. You can be like God."

Alex frowned, as his father put the spade in his hand. "We can make it better," he said. "We can make it right."

Alex stared into his eyes. Right? His father wanted what was right? He shook his head, confused – but then, suddenly, Rachel hit him in the side.

He gasped, and fell to his knees. The knife! The knife, his father had thrust into his side! He felt it, again! He saw his father's face, in the Debating Chamber: control! Control!

"See who is standing in front of you!" Rachel's voice cried. "Remember the cold touch of his gun!"

The altar! He was being pressed back, a gun to his temple: a sacrifice on the altar of his father's self-reverence!

Now the same face contorted in rage above him.

"You bitch!" he cried to Rachel, and now he strode toward her, but Alex thrust himself to his feet and ran toward the crowd.

"Look!" he cried. "Evil is here! Evil is all around you! Choose what is right! Be ready for the Light! Don't fear for your lives here: fear for your souls!"

And now the quake began.

It began as a gentle rumble, under his feet. He gasped, and the crowd shifted.

"The tsunami!" Alex cried out. "The tsunami is coming, but Joshua is the boat for the flood! Death is not the end! Don't be assimilated into evil: be made into good!"

The quake was getting stronger. Voices were rising. With tears Alex continued.

"Don't be afraid!" he cried. "The one who is more powerful than this is coming! He will make all things right again! Hold on, through the floods! Hold on, though the earth shakes, though the world heaves, as a woman in childbirth…"

Now he reached out, to grasp their shoulders. Would they die? Would they all die now, together?

Rachel…He looked back for her: where was she? With Kensington?

She was on the ground, knocked off her feet – John was reaching for her. Tristan was running toward James, in the disarray, and Kensington…Kensington had gone.

The shake eased – and then it stopped.

A cheer went up in the people. It was over! The threat, for now, was gone. And yet…and yet, what was that? What had just happened?

"It was Kensington," Alex said quickly. "He has taken over Parliament: he was responsible for the bombs, and the shake."

"But who is he?" a young woman asked. "Who is this Kensington?"

Alex hesitated, and then responded.

"He is my father," he said – and now he moved forward, and the crowd surrounded him, and he told them everything he knew: of Joshua's death, of his return, of Alex's hope for the future – of his father, of Light and Darkness, and of God, above humanity.

They listened; he shared until he could speak no more. They wandered away, back to their homes, wondering about the future: wondering about an eternal future.

Alex sat still, in the sand – and then he remembered Rachel. He quickly rose to his feet, and went to her.

She was lying on her side, her knees pulled up to her chest.

"What did he do?" Alex hurriedly asked, kneeling down behind her. "What did he do?"

John's hand was on her shoulder – Tristan was standing further away, with James, both frowning.

Rachel was staring out ahead of herself – and now, suddenly, she grasped his hand and pulled it to her face.

She was drawing on it: drawing with her finger on his palm.

Alex frowned, tilting his head. What was it?

666.

Swallowing, Alex stared at her invisible image on his palm. The number of Man. He sank down next to her.

"What did he do?" he whispered.

"My mind," she whispered back. "My heart."

"Tarnished," Alex said. "Fallen."

"He is a flame," Rachel said. "An unrelenting flame."

"My father will stop at nothing," Alex whispered, but Rachel was shaking her head.

"I'm not talking about your father, Alex," she said – and he swallowed, looking at her eyes.

"It's repeating," John said. "A representation. A translation."

"The end returns to the beginning," Alex said.

"The end and the beginning are one," John said.

"As though time has stopped for God," Rachel whispered.

"But where did he go?" Alex asked: and he looked around, but his father had disappeared.

Alex rose to his feet. He looked over the peninsula. A hand was on his shoulder – he turned toward Tristan, and then looked out across the sand.

The humpback whale was lying stranded on the beach.

Alex frowned, staring at it. "We should try to move it."

"We can't," Tristan said. "It's dead."

"But how can it be dead?" Alex asked. "So soon?"

And now he noticed other life floating up on the sea: dolphins, sperm whales, dead...

Tristan's face was white, before him: he stretched out his cell-phone before Alex.

On the screen was a headline: a nuclear exchange! Russia and America...

"No," Alex whispered.

"We don't have long now," Tristan whispered – and James, next to him, was silent.

"How much time?" Alex asked.

"I don't know," Tristan said.

"Let's keep walking," Alex said. "Christchurch! Let's just make it to Christchurch, before the end..."

"What's the point?" Tristan asked. "We're all hungry."

And Alex smiled through his tears. "Hope," he said. "The point is to bring the people true hope, before it's too late."

And he grasped Rachel's hand, and drew her to her feet.

She was swaying slightly. He leaned into her face: he pressed his forehead to hers.

"Love," he whispered to her. "Faith, hope and love, but the greatest of these is love.[14] You know it's true, Rachel: you know it."

She smiled gently at him, pressing her nose to him.

"The greatest is love," she repeated after him. "Through hell and high water: it's all meaningless without love."

And her body straightened, and, with new resolve, she walked forward alongside him, holding his hand.

---

[14] 1 Corinthians 13:13 Paraphrased.

CHAPTER FIFTEEN: Food and Drink

Rachel stood in central Kaiapoi.

In front of her was The Letterbox Sculpture: scattered red letter boxes extending up to the top, interspersed with green street name signs: a memorial to the Canterbury earthquake of 2010 – over a thousand homes lost.

She lifted her eyes to the top of the pole, and frowned. Surely Kensington wasn't that much of a bastard? Surely he wouldn't bring more buildings down on the heads of those already scarred?

"We should move on," Alex murmured next to her. He was standing still, looking a little grubby in his same T-shirt and shorts, his right hand in his pocket, holding onto something.

"Wait," Rachel said, looking around the streets: looking for shops. "We need food."

"Just water," John said, behind her, "from the river, down this street. We can do without food a little longer."

"No money," Tristan said – and Rachel turned to look at him. His eyes looked haunted, his hand clutching onto his cell-phone.

"You need food," Rachel whispered, and Tristan tensely shook his head.

"No," he whispered.

His face and arms were burnt – somehow he was more burnt than John or Alex. Rachel grasped his hand, and drew him down the street.

"Come," she said. "Water."

His hand was trembling in hers. What had he read? Some other semblance of doom. She drew him down the street, Williams Street: she crossed the road, and drew him down to the river. The heat! It was too hot.

"Here," she whispered – and she reached down, and pulled off his leather shoes and wet socks, and kicked off her own, and drew him in.

He gasped with the cool on his sore feet: she cupped water in her hands and sprinkled it over his face, reaching again to cup more and lift it to his lips.

He drank, and she led him to cup his own hands: to drink! To drink.

"Hope," she murmured over him, as he sank to his knees in the water. "Every day is a gift! Each day is a new opportunity."

"I'm not ready to die, Rachel," he choked, beneath her – and she laid a hand on his bowed back.

"I don't believe God created us only to destroy us," she said. "There is life beyond death: there is a new beginning."

"I don't have your kind of faith," he whispered. "Only a new faith! Only a baby faith..."

She touched his burnt face with her wet hand.

"Then trust beyond what you can see, Tristan," she said. "Trust in what others have seen."

Tristan looked up at her, from his knees, his face creasing in confusion.

"What others have seen?" he asked.

"Joshua, alive again," she said. "Life, stronger than our death: even death brought about by ourselves."

"The nukes," Tristan whispered. "Backwards and forwards, backwards and forwards: millions are dying..."

"Let it go," Rachel said. "You can't change this, Tristan: you can't stop it."

Tristan closed his eyes tightly. "I saw war, with my own eyes," he whispered. "I saw the explosions, I joined in the firing: I saw the blood. What is war, but hell on earth? What is a human driven holocaust, but the ultimate of human failing?"

"Six, six, six," Rachel whispered to him. "But beyond six is seven. Beyond humanity is God."

"Beyond humanity is God," Tristan whispered – and he rose to his feet, and walked out of the river.

Rachel followed him, onto the land. Alex had sat himself under a tree: he had started to talk with some people. Rachel noticed he had the deformed bullets back in his hands. They had remained safe, even with their swim! He had pulled the crucifix and empty cross out again from under his T-shirt.

John was lingering near him: clearly listening, but also murmuring under his breath – looking up at the trees, to the sky. Rachel wandered past them to a lady passing by. She seemed oblivious to any trouble: shirt and shorts, sunglasses and hat.

"Excuse me," Rachel asked her. "We've been hitching and walking from Picton. We're hungry, but we have no cash and our credit cards aren't working."

"Try the market," she said, and she gestured across the bridge. "It's on the other side of the river, and down a bit: locally grown food!"

"The river..." Rachel murmured – and now she grasped Tristan's hand again, and moved forward.

They walked across the bridge. The water was flowing, clear, beneath them.

"Fish," Tristan suddenly said – and he moved ahead of her, and she watched him stride off the bridge and to the other edge of the river.

He was pulling out something from his pocket: what was that – a pocket knife? His eyes scanned the water, and suddenly he was moving, fast: suddenly he was drawing a salmon, stabbed, out of the water.

"For the market," he said, grinning up at her, still on the bridge.

"No way!" Rachel said.

"Bet you can't do it again," another voice said from behind her, and Rachel stiffened. James! His voice! The gun to her head...

She closed her eyes tightly. Death! She breathed.

"Stay away from her," Tristan's voice said.

"You guided me here," James said. "You came with me to protect her."

"There's freedom here," Tristan said, his voice ever closer. "A tiny oasis of freedom, in a world at war. I won't let you harm her: I won't let you intimidate her."

105

And now Rachel opened her eyes to see Tristan standing next to her on her left, salmon in one hand, knife in the other.

James laughed from her right side. "If I still had my rifle," he said, "you'd be horribly overpowered. But, no: Kensington grabbed it."

"Then you have no defence," Tristan said. "You have no weapon."

"Only my own fists," James said – and now, suddenly, he lunged at him.

Rachel gasped as James knocked Tristan off his feet, pinned his wrist to the ground, and knocked the knife out of his grip. He knelt over his waist, pocketed the knife, and reached to seize the salmon.

"There," he said over him. "Time to get off your bloody high horse."

Now he transferred the salmon from right hand to left, stood over Tristan, reached to grasp his hand, and lifted him to his feet.

"My knife," Tristan said, reaching out his hand.

"I'll get more fish for the market," James said.

"I don't trust you," Tristan said. "We don't have a common enemy here."

"No," James said, "but we have a common interest."

And now he gestured to Rachel.

Tristan was frowning. Rachel looked between them. What was going on? Common interest? She glanced down the bridge, to see Alex and John quickly approaching.

"Go to the market," she said to Tristan. "Go with the others. Take the fish."

"I don't want to leave you alone with him," Tristan said.

"He's my brother," Rachel said.

"So am I," Tristan said.

Rachel smiled gently at him: the hunger, the burns; the instinct to protect his family.

"Go," she whispered to him. "I need to sort this."

"Not without my knife," Tristan said – and his gaze was over her head at James.

Rachel glanced up at James's face. He shifted on his feet slightly: he shrugged.

"Fine," he said, handing the knife over. "But I won the tussle: I want it back afterwards."

"If you think I'm going to willingly give you my weapon again," Tristan said, "you've got rocks in your head."

James smirked. "Anything goes now, Lieutenant Blake," he said. "At least, until the army extends its grip."

"Not anything goes," Tristan muttered, pocketing the knife. "Even if all hell breaks loose, some things remain the same."

And he grasped the fish back from him, gestured to John and Alex, and turned to walk off the bridge.

Rachel caught Alex's face, as he passed: the frowning smile. John's eyes lingered on her: serious, knowing.

"Do what you have to do," he murmured as he passed, and then all three were off the bridge.

She was alone with James.

Fear took her. She stared down to the course of the river – she took a deep breath. He was next to her: he also was staring out.

"You never visited me again in prison," he said, and Rachel shifted slightly.

"I'm sorry," she said. "I did mean to, but…things got complicated."

"Evidently," James said, and he gestured all around. "Paradise, in the midst of hell. But what comes next, Rachel? Our enemy cannot be defeated."

He was reaching now: he was taking her hand.

Rachel shuddered and shook him off. She glanced up in fear at his face: at his grimace.

"You're a bitch," he said.

Tears pricked her eyes – she looked away again to the river below.

"You're not exactly Santa Claus yourself," she said.

"You put me in prison."

"I didn't mean to."

"You had my career on the line! My life on the line!"

Rachel closed her eyes. Crying! Crying now, on the verge of…of what?

"If you want to kill me," she whispered, "just do it. Do it now, before the others come back."

James was still, next to her: quiet. Rachel opened her eyes: staring at the water. She knew he would be capable of killing: there was no need for a weapon.

"Doesn't anything go?" he muttered. "When all hell is breaking loose, when life is reduced to mere survival?"

"Not anything goes, Doctor Lester," Rachel said, and she noticed his face contort alongside her. "Even on the point of death, not everything goes."

And now she reached out and took his hand.

She could feel him trembling. Would he remain? Would he pull away? What had happened with his new family? Abuse! Abuse…Could he return to his old family?

He stood, stiff, staring at their hands. She had left the hairclip in her stethoscope for him deliberately: didn't he know that? Didn't he know she had given him the means to escape imprisonment?

"I don't understand, Rachel," he said. "What do you want from me?"

"I want your redemption," Rachel whispered to him. "I always have, James! I always have."

"There is no redemption," he whispered back. "How can there be? My life is stuffed."

"There can be a new start," Rachel said. "A new man."

"And what happens to the old man?" he asked. "An execution? A death sentence? Purgatory?"

"We don't believe in Purgatory," Rachel said. "Our family's Anglican. We believe in grace."

107

"I'm Catholic," James said. "My new family was Catholic. Purgatory makes sense to me. Suffering! Suffering for my sins."

"Not punishment!" Rachel protested. "Christ has carried it! Christ has carried the punishment: he's carried the curse that we might live."

"Do my crimes not deserve punishment?" James asked. "I'm up for it! I'm up for the whipping..."

"No," Rachel whispered with tears, tightening her grip on his hand. "It's about forgiveness! It's about..."

"...purification," James said, and now he returned her grip: and now he also was holding her hand. "It's about purification."

Tears filled her eyes – she reached out with her other hand to touch his face.

"I love you," she said, and pain took her, and his face contorted and he looked away.

"You shouldn't," he said, still holding her hand. "You should protect yourself."

"But if we only protect ourselves," Rachel said, "how can we help anyone else? What's the point of life, if it is only to save ourselves?"

Now James smiled wryly, looking out to the water. "You're a romantic," he said. "I'm a realist."

"I'm a realist too," Rachel said. "I know the cost of being a romantic. I know the cost of offering love. But I still choose it."

"I know," James said. "I like your way better. But life has toughened my skin."

"I know what can soften skin," Rachel said – and she reached her other fingers to the hand she was holding, and started massaging his callouses.

He gasped. He drew his hand away.

"It hurts," he whispered, and Rachel smiled sadly.

"The medicine can feel as bad as the disease," she said quietly, "to begin with."

"I remember you," he choked. "You were beautiful!" And his eyes were wide, staring at her: almost child-like! And then the moment was gone.

He reached into his pocket: he drew out a nylon thread, and hook.

"Here," he said curtly. "Attach this to a stick, and use anything for bait: worm, snail, insect, fly...Tristan was lucky before."

Rachel stared down at the hook and looked back up at him.

"Do you have another?" she asked.

He shrugged, and broke into a wry grin. "I'm a stubborn bastard," he said. "I'll find a way to survive."

And then he quickly squeezed her hand, and turned away, disappearing back over the bridge.

Rachel stared after him, astonished: where was he going? Away. Always away. But he would be around: she knew, he would still be watching. And yet now...now she wasn't afraid of him.

She remembered his gun to her head. She took a deep breath, and smiled, and looked to the other side of the river. The others were coming! The fish was gone:

108

they had traded it, for a loaf of bread. But they could keep fishing! Keep trading. They could survive.

If they wanted to, they could stay there, in Kaiapoi…and yet…and yet…

Rachel's eyes moved to Alex: his gaze was on her. They needed to move! To keep moving, into Christchurch: to uncover Kensington in front of the crowd.

They would die! Surely they would all die. And yet…

Alex was smiling as they approached her, holding onto the home baked bread. Tears pricked her eyes. Love! She loved him. He bounded up onto the bridge: he opened the paper wrapping. He broke a piece off the end, and gave it to her.

"Here," he said. "Communion."

"The last supper?" Rachel said wryly, as she received the bread. "Where's the wine?"

"Such little faith," Alex muttered, and he reached behind his back and drew out a bottle of red wine.

"Canterbury Pinot Noir," he said, and Rachel laughed.

"Seriously?" she asked. "But we had no money!"

"A lady gave it to me," Alex said thoughtfully. "For free."

And he reached, broke open the foil and twisted off the cork.

"No glasses," Rachel said, and Alex shrugged. "We do what we can."

And he offered it to her.

Tristan appeared behind Alex: his eyes searching over the bridge.

"Where did he go?" he asked. "What happened?"

Rachel smiled sadly at him. "It's okay," she said. "He's okay."

Tristan's eyes settled on her. "You're safe?" he asked.

"Is anyone safe?" Rachel asked, and Tristan's gaze darkened, and he looked away.

"Sorry," Rachel said. "I just meant…"

"Tomorrow is the day," John said, now standing next to Tristan: his green eyes on her. "The day of confrontation."

"The army is already there," Tristan said, staring out at the river. "If we want to announce Kensington in public, we'll only have a few minutes before they remove us."

"A few minutes will be enough," John said. "It will be more than enough."

"I know what to do." It was Alex. His face was gentle, and at peace. A child! He looked like a child. "I know how to reach him."

And now he was reaching for the crucifix sitting on his chest.

Rachel frowned, looking at him: at his trust.

"You believe he can be reached," Rachel said.

"I do," Alex said.

"But what if you're wrong, Alex?" she asked. "What if he's beyond redemption?"

A shadow flitted over Alex's face for a moment. Rachel stood very still: was he vacillating? But then the light settled again in his eyes.

109

"I'm not wrong," he said. "I know what I must do."

And now he reached for the bottle of red wine in Rachel's hands, and he drank from the bottle.

He handed it next to John: John drank quickly from it. John handed it to Tristan. Tristan stared at the bottle in his hands, closed his eyes tightly, with pain, and then opened them again.

"So be it" he whispered, and he drank from the bottle.

Finally the bottle was back in Rachel's hands.

She gazed down at it. Red wine: the colour of blood. She closed her eyes. Joshua! Joshua, shot, in the street, in front of the crowd! Pain took her: she accepted the pain. She opened her eyes: she looked into the blue eyes of Alex. What was in his mind, at this moment?

Shine the Light, Joshua had said to him. *Carry the cost.*

"Forgive me," Rachel whispered in front of him: to Joshua, to Christ; to God. "Forgive me for all my weakness: forgive me for all my doubt."

And she drank from the bottle, and closed her eyes, and offered herself into the greater destiny of the morning.

CHAPTER SIXTEEN: Christchurch

Alex stood in Cathedral Square, Christchurch.

The old Christ Church Cathedral stood tall to his right, its stone tower reaching up to the sky. Alex looked at the iron cross at the top of its spire. The tower had partially collapsed, in the earthquake of 2011: the rest of the tower, rendered unsafe, had been demolished in 2012. The entire cathedral had seemed set for demolition: and yet here it stood, once again, reinstated.

Alex smiled – then he cast his eyes across the square.

The Army was guarding the public place, and the church. Soldiers stood at ease with rifles hanging from their shoulders, and troubled frowns on their faces. A crowd was gathering in the square – why? Something had drawn them.

Tristan stood near Alex, with his back to the soldiers, holding Alex's gaze.

"There are massive casualties overseas now," he said. "The thing's escalated into a full blown World War. It's mayhem, Alex: our troops are over there, but cut off – we have no idea who is still alive and who is dead."

He reached out his cell-phone to show him, but then he took the phone back again, jabbing at its screen.

"Oh, shit," he whispered.

"What is it?" Alex asked.

"No connection," he said.

Alex shrugged. "That's the internet."

"No," Tristan said, jabbing at his phone. "I can get the New Zealand Herald, but I can't get beyond."

"The news sites overseas have been hit," Alex muttered, and Tristan shook his head.

"No," he said, "it's not localized. Amazon's been down for a while, and Facebook…All of Facebook…"

"Here," Alex said, and he grabbed Tristan's phone sped his fingers over the screen. New Zealand links were intact, but international links…they were patchy…

"It's a mess out there," Tristan said, his eyes stern. "We're losing contact."

And now voices went up in the crowd.

"I can't get through!" someone cried. "My daughter's in London, and I haven't been able to reach her: the network's down!"

"Same with my brother!" someone else cried. "I can't get through to Germany!"

"Japan!" someone else called out. "Something's wrong with Japan!"

"And Iraq," a fourth voice said.

"My wife is still in Algeria," an African man said. "I tried to get her out…"

"My children are in Washington DC," a young woman said. "Are they dead? Are they all dead?"

The eyes of the crowd were looking at each other, and Alex looked over them. The World! They were a scattering of the World, drawn together in one courtyard.

What could he say to the World, in this time of utter crisis?

He glanced at John – at his sad knowing smile. He looked at Rachel – at her wet eyes. He opened his mouth and stepped forward, but then, suddenly, Kensington was in front of the crowd.

Images were before them: images projecting into the sky. Mushroom clouds – massive explosions: cities, decimated – bodies instantly charred. Children, caught in their play: caught where they were, standing. The cities could not be recognised – the colour of their skin was taken into death.

"Look!" Kensington's voice cried out. "See what humanity can do!"

Alex stared at the many explosions, speeding up before his eyes: city after city after city destroyed…He swayed on his feet.

"The same enemy is here!" Kensington cried out. "The same enemy took our democratic freedom!"

Now his eyes settled on Alex. "The Deception bombed Parliament," he said, "but there is still hope! A new day, after the old is swept away: a new worship! A new spirit."

And he lifted a symbol high into the air.

Alex peered at it. What was it? Tristan was shifting in discomfort alongside him.

Moulded in gold, attached to the mace of Parliament: 666, and the all-seeing Eye. The symbols of his father's Shrine.

"Shit," Tristan said. "That's the same symbol that bastard tattooed onto my sister's wrist."

"Divinity," John's voice said behind him. "It's a claim to divinity."

"Join me," Kensington said, "and I will protect you! Become like me, and no weapon will touch you! No enemy will take you! But betray me, and you will be consumed by the acid rain!"

And he shook the mace and eye, with 666, to the heavens: and the clouds began to gather, and the heavens began to rumble.

Alex stared at his father, tears filling his eyes.

"Satan," he whispered. "Surely it is Satan."

A hand came to his shoulder – he looked to his side: Rachel! She was weeping: her blue eyes red.

"Let him go," she whispered. "He is lost, Alex! Forever lost!"

"No," Alex whispered back. "I must hope! For the sake of everyone; for the sake of him! I have to try!"

And he stepped forward, toward the beast.

Kensington's arms were raised to the sky: an image was appearing of clouds gathering, over the nations – dark clouds.

"Do you think you are safe?" he cried out. "Away from the conflict: away from the carnage? You are not safe! The clouds will come: darkness will cover the Earth! You will not be spared: you or your children! The cold will take a hold: it will freeze your hearts – it will chill your bodies. It will steal your crops!

"The rain of life will bring death! The sun will turn black: day will be turned into night.

112

"All will die, if you do not turn to me! If you do not put your trust in me!"

He pointed the mace to the image of the clouds, and they dispersed – and behind them was blue sky.

The crowd were staring at him: lifting their voices.

"How can you save us?" they cried. "How can you spare us from the fate of the entire World?"

"Follow me," Kensington said, pointing the mace to the crowd: sweeping around the crowd. "Let me change your minds," he said, pointing to a woman's head. "Let me change your hearts." Now he pointed to her chest. "Let me have the work of your hands: let me have the desire of your souls."

And now he pointed the mace to his feet, in front of the woman.

"Kneel," he said. "Follow me, in spirit, thought and act, and I will save you."

Alex stared, as the woman looked around herself at the others: bewildered. She was young: she was afraid.

"No," Alex said – moving alongside her: laying a hand on her shoulder, and moving her away. "There is only one God; only one Spirit worthy of our souls."

And now he turned and, before the crowd, laid himself on his face before the Cathedral.

"Can you see it now?" he cried out in front of them, lifting his head. "Evil is poised to take you! Death is near! Don't be afraid of nuclear weapons, or nuclear fallout, or a nuclear winter, or even the end of this age: fear for your own hearts! For your own minds! Fear for your own souls!"

He thrust himself back to his feet in front of them.

"Choose the Light!" he cried. "Even if you are surrounded by nuclear cloud on all sides, don't surrender to the Darkness! Choose the Light!"

And he reached down to his T-shirt, and tore it off, and stood before his father half-naked, stretching out his arms before him: exposing his chest.

"There is an Ally greater than the Enemy," he said to him with tears. "There is a weapon stronger than the evil of our own hearts."

And he grasped the crucifix from around his neck, broke the chain, and thrust it out in front of his father's face.

Kensington's face shifted. He stared at the golden crucifix – his forehead creased in confusion.

"Your mother," he whispered. "That was your mother's crucifix."

"She's still alive," Alex whispered back with tears. "Mum is still alive."

"No," Kensington breathed. "You didn't see…you didn't see her…"

"I did," Alex whispered. "I saw her…"

And now, suddenly the memory was before his eyes: his mother! His mother, in their lounge! The gun! The gun to her head. Her eyes on him, afraid! Afraid, dreading…

"I know who it was," Alex whispered, frowning – stretching for the memory. Who was holding the gun? Follow the hand, the arm – look up the arm…

The face was turned to him, frowning: the intense blue eyes. Kensington!

113

"Oh my God," Alex whispered – and he fell to his knees. His father! His father's face, shocked, staring at him: seeing him! "It was you!" Alex cried. "It was you!"

And now his voice lifted into a wail: loud, hard. "Satan!" he cried out. "You killed my mother! You shot her!"

And his words travelled across the whole crowd.

Kensington's face shifted again, into shock! The same shock Alex had seen at seven. He was staring down at Alex, on his knees: staring at the crucifix. Then he set his jaw, reached behind his back, and pulled out James's rifle.

"If you want to change the World, little shit," he said, "you have to make sacrifices."

And he lifted the rifle, pointed it to Alex's chest, and fired.

Alex gasped! Pain! Bullets, to his naked chest! His body was being thrown back.

"No!" Rachel's voice screamed above him. "Bastard! Everyone can see you now! Everyone knows who you are now!"

Alex choked for breath – and now Rachel's face was above him, weeping: she was tearing off her own T-shirt, to press it into his wounds – she was reaching her hand to his head.

"Peace," she sobbed above him. "You made them see! You made them see who he really is! Rest in peace!"

Flashes were happening, before his eyes. His father! The gentle smile, the warmth of his eyes, before...before...

"No," Alex whispered, reaching out to desperately grasp her arm: dragging her closer. "I remember, Rachel! I remember who he really is..."

And he struggled to reach into his own pocket: the bullets! The bullets of Joshua.

"It was my fault," he sobbed, grasping her hand – putting the bullets into her hand. "My fault. I should have stopped him!"

"You were just a child..."

"Stop him, Rachel!" Alex pleaded, clinging to her arm. "You have to reach him! You have to save him!"

Her blue eyes, overflowing, were staring down at him.

"But how?" she whispered – and his vision went hazy.

"Rachel," he choked, and he grasped out for her, but couldn't find her. Darkness was coming: the pain! The pain was fading...

"Alex."

Someone was speaking his name. He tried to shake his head: he couldn't. He couldn't see. He peered into the darkness.

"Where am I?" he asked.

"You don't know?" the voice replied. "Then what will you do?"

Alex hesitated. There was nothing? Nothing but darkness? How to respond?

"Trust," Alex whispered. "I will trust, beyond the darkness: beyond death."

"Your tsunami has come," the voice said. "But I am the boat for the flood."

And now a hand was on his shoulder. Alex opened his eyes – and in front of him, stretched out as far as he could see, were mountains.

"Oh!" he gasped, and he shifted on his feet, and stretched out his arms, and breathed in the mountain air. Snow was under his shoes! Pure white snow covered the peak behind him. A blue-green lake filled the valley a little in the distance, lifting up to the green foothills, and then to the snow tipped peaks ahead.

"Paradise," he whispered. "I am in Paradise."

And he swayed on his feet, and fell to his knees.

The hand was still on his shoulder. He bowed his head.

"You know this place," the man's voice said: he was familiar! He seemed familiar.

"Yes," Alex breathed. "It is Treble Cone."

"It is your favourite place," he said. "In all the Earth."

"Yes," Alex whispered. "It is magnificent! The beauty, the majesty…"

Now the hand was on his head.

"You have entrusted me with your thoughts," he said. "With your feeling."

"Yes," Alex whispered.

"We are here," he said. "In your mind. I am with your spirit: I am enabling you to see."

"Is it just in my mind?" Alex asked.

"Your body has been taken," he said, "for now."

"No eyes," Alex murmured, looking again at the mountains, "and yet I see."

"You see as I see," he said. "You see as I know you would see, in your body. We are here. We are truly here, at Treble Cone: I have brought you here."

"I trust," Alex said. "I love."

And now he looked up to the man who was standing next to him, with his hand on Alex's head.

It was Joshua.

Astonished, and yet also somehow not surprised, Alex gazed up at him.

He smiled: a gentle familiar smile. "Your life is in my hands," he said. "You have known it for a while."

"Yes," Alex whispered. "I have trusted in it."

"I am a representation," he said. "Only a representation of a much greater Truth."

"Yes," Alex said. "I understand."

"I appear to you in that representation: to connect – to be known, as you can know."

"Yes."

Now Joshua looked out to the mountains, standing over him.

"A time is coming," he said, "when the mountains will be laid low, and the valleys lifted up."

"Yes," Alex said.

"Will you allow me to do it, Alex?" he asked. "Lay your precious mountains low? Lift up my valleys?"'

"Yes," Alex whispered. "I will allow you to do it."

"Heart surgery," Joshua said, smiling sadly. "Humanity needs heart surgery, to truly live. And the surgeon must be trusted, for how else can he bring about healing through pain?"

"My father," Alex said, still on his knees before him, suddenly remembering Kensington before him, firing the gun: suddenly stiffening. "Send me back! Send me back, to save him."

The hand was still on his head – the brown eyes were finding him.

"Alex," he said firmly. "You have to let your father go."

"No," Alex whispered, shaking his head. "He can still be reached! He can still be saved."

Joshua tilted his head, watching him. "Do you think I don't have him in hand?"

"But…" Alex stared at him, confused. "Isn't it his choice?"

"It is," Joshua said. "Just as it is also our choice."

"Salvation…"

"He must consent to the heart surgery, Alex: to not do so is conquest, not liberation. There is no other way: he must consent or he must be overcome. True life can only be received through trust."

"Conquest or liberation."

"Am I an Ally or the Enemy?" Joshua asked. "Either way, Alex, the weapon will be dropped."

Alex frowned, and stared down at Joshua's feet.

"I don't understand," he said. "Why choice? Why suffering? Why were we contaminated in the first place?"

"You will understand," Joshua said, "in time. Rachel."

"Rachel?" Alex asked, confused.

"Rachel," Joshua said again.

Rachel stared down at Alex, lying dead at her feet: bullets in his bleeding chest. Agony! Agony! The child – Kensington's child! He had done it! Kensington had shot his own son!

Fury took her. Shoving the bullets of Joshua Alex had given her away, deep into her own shorts pocket, she moved before Kensington.

"Look!" she cried out to the crowd, gesturing to him. "See the one who believes he is fit to lead you! He shot his own wife and child: see the full weakness of Man!"

She glared at him, but now Kensington was staring at Alex. Why? What was he thinking? What was he doing with the rifle?

It was swinging, from his hand, backwards and forwards: directionless – for a moment, purposeless.

"Stand down," James's voice said, next to her. "It's done. It's finished."

116

"No," Rachel said – and fury took her, and consumed her, and her vision turned red. "No!" she cried. "It's not over! It will never be over, until I have what is right! Until I have truth! Until every innocent one killed is brought back to life! Until every murderer is brought to justice!"

And she jabbed her finger at Kensington.

"You will never rule!" she cried out. "You will never rule, as long as there is breath in my lungs! As long as there is a beat to my heart, I will use it to fight you!"

Kensington's face formed into a scowl.

"Fine," he said, lifting the rifle. "Have it your way."

And he fired.

Rachel stared at him: at the gun, pointing toward her – and then, suddenly, there was a movement.

James was in front of her. James!

"No!" Rachel cried out. "No!"

The bullets! They were entering his chest! They were killing him.

His body was thrown against her: she caught him. She lowered him to the ground.

He was gasping: his body shuddering. The blood! More blood!

"My damned gun," he gasped. "I knew it would backfire…"

Rachel reached to the wound over his heart. Clothing? Her T-shirt, on Alex? All she had left was the bra, but what did it matter anymore? What did etiquette matter?

She pulled off her bra: she pressed it into his bullet hole. Stop the bleeding! She was naked: she didn't care.

"I'm so sorry," James gasped, under her: his body jerking slightly. "I'm so sorry for putting the gun to your head."

Pain gripped her: she reached to grasp his hand to her chest. His blood was on her! His blood…

"What do you think?" he gasped, staring up at her. "What do you think of my solution?"

And Rachel stared down at him, in agony.

"Oh dear God," she whispered. "Purgatory?"

"Eye for an eye?" James whispered. "Suffer the effect of the crime on yourself?"

"No," Rachel whispered, sobbing as his jerking intensified. "No! Freedom! Freedom."

"Now I can be free," he gasped. "Now I've reversed it."

"No," Rachel pleaded. "I want you to live! I want you to live."

His body stiffened: his gaze filled with fear, staring at her. His fingers lifted to her cheek – and then he fell back, dead.

Rachel stared at him. She stared at Alex's body, a few feet away. She felt numb. Then, suddenly, rage filled her.

"No!" she screamed out. "You bastard!"

And she thrust herself to her feet, rushed to Kensington, grasped James's rifle out of his hands to her own side, and thrust it up to Kensington's head.

117

"Rachel!" Tristan's voice cried out behind her. "Don't!"

"We knew this would be the cost," John's voice said quietly from behind her. "We knew this day would carry death."

Kensington's body was shaking in front of her: his eyes, for a moment, filled with fear. Rachel stared at him: pressed the gun harder into his temple.

"Kneel," she said. "Beg for your life."

"Rachel," John's warning voice said behind her. "Don't become the same."

"Kneel!" Rachel yelled – and Kensington knelt, before her. His eyes looked erratic – he was staring about himself, at the crowd.

"You killed your wife," Rachel announced over him. "You killed your son. You killed my brother. You blew up Parliament. Why should I let you live?"

"Rachel," Tristan's voice said, shaking. "This isn't us. This isn't civilisation."

"Why should I let you live?" Rachel yelled, prodding him harder.

The blue eyes were staring up at her. She hated him! She loathed him! He was a murderer: nothing else! Nothing else.

But then...

Rachel.

The familiar voice. She shifted uncomfortably. The bullets! Joshua's bullets, in her pocket: beneath her naked and blood stained chest.

She held the rifle with her right hand – she reached with her left hand into her right pocket, and pulled out the bullets.

Now Joshua's face was in front of her, dying.

"It's done!" he whispered, smiling widely. *"It's sorted!"*

The bullets! The bullets Kensington had sent, into Joshua's chest! Into the grave.

Tristan's face was in front of her now, white. Guilty! But forgiven. It wasn't the same, was it? Not the same? A psychopath? Evil incarnate? Surely Kensington should be removed? Surely he should be stopped?

She stared down at Kensington, on his knees before her. What was he doing there? She stared at her own hand, holding the gun to his head. James! She had become the same as James. She looked at Kensington's face.

He was afraid, but there was more. In that moment, for a moment, there was something else.

"Kill me," he whispered. "Before he comes back."

"Oh my God," Rachel whispered over him. "You still have insight."

And she staggered back away from him, and dropped the rifle to the ground.

She felt to her knees: she lifted her face to the sky, and screamed. John had moved between her and Kensington: Tristan also had moved between, pulling off his grey prison shirt – handing it to her.

She covered herself: she surrendered herself into agony. The Army: where was the Army? They were there, standing, powerless: rifles hanging at their sides.

"Save us!" Rachel cried out, up to the sky. "We have no idea what to do! No idea how to save ourselves!"

And she dragged herself to her feet, and staggered toward Alex.

The crucifix, the golden crucifix, was lying, dropped, on the ground.

She stooped, to pick it up – she sank down at Alex's side.

A boy...he was, at heart, just a young boy. Beautiful! Innocent. Agony grasped her again – she reached over to draw his blonde curls away from his blood stained forehead.

"I'm so sorry," she whispered over him. "I'm so sorry, I'm so sorry, I'm so sorry..."

Weeping took her, and she bent over him and kissed his forehead, and she grasped him to her chest and rocked, wailing, over him.

Kensington was watching her. Numbly, she let him watch. What did she care? What did she care if he could see her?

She cried – and he stood still, blocked by John and Tristan. Then he turned, looked over the crowd, and simply walked away.

CHAPTER SEVENTEEN: The Sanctuary

John stood very still, in the courtyard.

Clouds were gathering again, overhead. Cries were going up in the crowd: the fear was tangible – John could taste it. Panic! Panic was seizing the people. Where had Kensington gone? What was he going to do next?

They were running, but to where? To whom? Random directions, all directions, clinging to some semblance of hope: driven by desperation.

And the Army…the Army were motionless.

John looked over the courtyard of chaos – he passed his eyes over the Cathedral, standing quiet and empty, reaching up to the sky: its tower, its spire, its iron cross, penetrating into the dark clouds.

"Enter," John whispered, looking up into the darkness – looking at the cross, surrounded by darkness. "Enter into our pain; enter into our corruption."

And now he turned back.

Rachel was on her knees, poring over the body of Alex: her arms wrapped around herself, clothed in Tristan's prison shirt, her own body rocking backwards and forwards on the pavement. James's body lay nearby. Tristan was pacing, his face drawn: his eyes fixed, his hand reaching in his pocket for a weapon. He drew out a pocket knife. He stared at it, his face contorted, and then he threw it away.

John walked over to him – reaching to grasp his shoulder: taking up his distraught gaze.

"The Cathedral," he said clearly. "We need to take Alex and James into the Cathedral."

"You think they'll be safe there?" Tristan asked, his eyes haunted. "He has penetrated another Cathedral! He has destroyed…"

And now Tristan's body stiffened – and now horror took his gaze.

John reached for his other shoulder – tightened his grip on both.

"Listen to me," he said, searching out Tristan's eyes. "There is only one sanctuary now: there is only one place of rest."

"Death?" Tristan breathed, and now he sobbed, and John grimaced with Tristan's pain. "Is death the only place of rest?"

"No," John said, still holding him tightly. "Death is not the final destiny, Tristan: life! Life is still coming. Help me! I need your help! Rachel needs your help. We need to move our friends into the Cathedral."

Now a glimmer entered into Tristan's eye.

"Friend?" he muttered. "You think that bastard James was my friend?"

He broke into a wry smile, with tears, and drew himself up.

"Okay," he said. "I'll do it. I'll move the bodies."

And he walked over to James's body, and knelt down next to him.

John lingered on his face for a moment: lingered in his grief.

"You fooled me, you bastard," Tristan said over James, his face contorting again; his words almost a moan. "I didn't see that one coming at all. Could have

120

warned me you were going to play the hero, instead of killing her: I would have let you have my knife."

And now his face suddenly changed, and he was crying – and quickly he reached with his hands to cover his face: to hide his tears.

John drew his eyes away – privacy! Give him privacy. And he turned to Rachel.

Agony. John felt her pain, as a knife penetrating to his gut. Her body was rigid, on her knees, rocking…rocking.

He moved to her: he knelt down on the other side of Alex's penetrated body.

The boy…he looked down at his dead white face; at his blonde curls. He had done it! He had confronted Satan himself, in his own father. He had exposed him, before the World, and yet…and yet…

John searched the closed eyes. Was this the end? The boy shot by the tyrannical man: revealing the enemy, only to succumb in the end to his greater power – only to surrender into death?

John frowned, and reached out to touch the curls. Life? Life after death…?

"There is no God," Rachel whispered beside him, rocking in agony. "There can't be."

"Come," John said, reaching to take her hand.

"Where?" Rachel whispered, her tear swollen eyes upon him

"To the sanctuary," John said. "To the place of rest."

And he lifted her to her feet alongside him, and drew her toward the Cathedral.

Rachel was tugging on his hand, from behind.

"His body!" she said. "I won't leave his body!"

John looked sadly back at her. "Tristan will bring him," he said. "We will lay them both down at the altar."

And he drew her after him, across the courtyard, through the panicking people, away from the crowd – into the Cathedral.

The church was silent.

John wandered up the aisle, drawing Rachel behind – between many wooden chairs, between white stone arches, glancing up at the stained glass windows on either side, and then forward: to the inner sanctuary – passing choir seats and candles on both sides, closer, closer to the altar.

Tristan was sitting against the communion rail, with his back to the altar – staring outward, toward the inner nave of the church, his hand on the dead chest of James.

He started a little as John approached.

"Where's Alex?" he whispered.

"Still out there," John said, gesturing behind.

"I'll get him," Tristan said – and he dragged himself to his feet, and moved down the aisle.

John stood at the communion rail, looking at the white linen covered altar – at the bronze cross on top.

121

This cross was empty.

"The resurrection," John whispered, looking at it. "There is still hope."

And he turned back to Rachel, and stretched out his hand.

She shifted on her feet, before him – she stared down at his hand.

"What?" she whispered.

"Give them to me," John said.

"Give what?" Rachel whispered.

"Alex's treasure," John said, and tears pricked his eyes.

Rachel frowned at him, confused – and then her swollen eyes widened. She reached into her shorts' pocket – she drew out the deformed bullets, and the golden crucifix, and laid them in John's hand.

Weeping threatened John: he closed his eyes tightly – he closed his fist around the bullets and crucifix.

"Where's the other one?" he whispered.

"What other one?" Rachel's voice asked.

"Mark's!" John said, and now the tears took him and the pain, and he let them, and opened his eyes and quietened his own voice. "Mark's cross. The empty cross."

"Alex is still wearing it," Tristan's voice said from behind him – and John turned, to watch Tristan lay Alex's body down next to James, before the communion rail.

Tristan's face and chest were stained with Alex's blood, as he knelt next to Alex's body. John reached to grasp his shoulder, and then knelt on the other side.

He hadn't noticed it before: on the naked, penetrated chest – the plain golden cross. Mark's cross.

He reached out to lay a hand over the cross – over Alex's chest. He closed his eyes. Joshua! He could still remember Joshua, shot by Tristan, lying dead between the Beehive and St Peter's Cathedral.

"I don't want to leave him," Rachel moaned behind him. "I won't leave him."

John had stayed! Had stayed with Joshua's body.

"I understand," he murmured to Rachel, "but we have to leave him."

"Bury him!" Rachel's voice insisted. "Bury them both."

"There's no time," Tristan said. "If we bury them our own bodies will be thrown alongside."

"He'll return," John said, opening his eyes – looking up to the bronze cross, and the stained glass windows behind. "Kensington is going to return, twice as strong – wounded, but not defeated."

"We can't leave them here!" Rachel said. "We can't leave them to rot!"

And now her voice choked – and John looked back to her.

She was swaying on her feet, covered in Tristan's prison shirt – face swollen with weeping, long hair a mess around her contorting face.

John reached out his hand to her again.

"Come," he said.

"What?" she whispered.

122

"Come to me," he said – and she tentatively reached out her hand.

He took her hand – he held it. She was trembling, she was vulnerable; she was, in this moment, weak.

He reached out to her hair – he stroked the knots away from her swollen face. He stepped closer to her – he brushed his lips across her wet swollen cheeks.

"Come to me," he whispered, and she gasped, and her breathing lifted.

"Tristan," John said, turning his head a little behind.

"We don't have much time," Tristan's voice said. "Are you sure you want to spend it doing this?"

"I'm sure," John said. "Love, Tristan. Love is the only thing worthy of death."

"Then I'll guard the doors," Tristan said. "Even if it kills me."

And John watched him walk down the aisle, with naked chest, through the doors, and they swung shut behind him.

He was alone with Rachel.

Her eyes were wide – her blue more intense through the tears.

"Do you trust me?" John asked her.

"Yes," she whispered. "I trust you."

"Do you trust my God?" John asked – and Rachel's eyes moved past him, over his shoulder, to the altar behind his back.

"If Love is indeed stronger than Death," she whispered, "then I can trust in God."

"Love is indeed stronger than Death," John said – and he reached and pulled off his shirt.

Rachel's eyes came to him – moved over his chest. Her breathing was deepening – her eyes deepening.

"We're in a church," she whispered.

"We're in the presence of God," John said, reaching to Tristan's prison shirt – tugging gently at it. "I'm not ashamed of our bodies, Rachel. I'm not ashamed of our love."

And now he pulled off Tristan's shirt.

She was exposed, before him: as she had been exposed, before Kensington – as she had been exposed before the dead body of Alex.

"Come to me," John whispered. "Join with me. Death cannot defeat Love – the temporary Darkness cannot separate us from eternal Light."

"Come to me," Rachel whispered, "and I will give you my all. One body. One heart. One soul."

"One spirit," John whispered – and he stepped into her body, and fully undressed them both, and made love with her.

Ecstasy. She clung to him, in the pain. Ecstasy, again! He lifted her, he knew her, he reached her agony – he channelled it into her delight. So much pain! Relieve it! Relieve it!

123

She was pleading – he gave, into her pleading. He gave, and gave, and held himself back, but now she was turning! Now she was drawing him. Now, he was pleading! Now, she was releasing him.

Bliss…a few moments of bliss.

He drew her into his arms: he held her. They were naked, together. They were one. They were fulfilled.

But then, suddenly, the doors of the church burst open.

Kensington was striding down the aisle.

Rachel gasped: naked! Naked! They had just made love! But John felt no shame.

He stepped in front of her: he faced Kensington, naked. He glanced down – the bullets of Joshua, deformed, were on the ground, with the crucifix.

"It's all repeating," John whispered to Rachel. "The end is becoming as the beginning, to undo the curse."

And he lifted his eyes to Kensington.

He was dragging Tristan alongside him, one arm around his naked and bloody chest – he dumped him at John's feet.

"There," Kensington said. "That's what I think of your body guard."

John looked down at him. Tristan's eyes were almost swollen shut, his cheeks cut and bruised, his chest beaten. He was gasping for breath, reaching out – reaching out, to grope for John's ankles.

John crouched down – he reached out to grasp his hand.

"Peace," he murmured over him. "Peace, Tristan. You fought your hardest. The rest is out of our hands now."

"The weapon is coming," Tristan whispered to him. "The most dangerous of weapons. The World will never be the same again…"

"Why didn't you kill him?" John asked Kensington, looking at Tristan's pain: at his heaving for breath.

"Because I wanted him to see my conquest," Kensington said – and now he gestured to Rachel.

"No," John said instinctively, blocking her body with his own. "You will not have her."

"That isn't your choice," Kensington said to him, "you know that. The choice belongs to her."

And now, suddenly, the Cathedral disappeared.

CHAPTER EIGHTEEN: Marriage

Rachel stood on grass.

Surprised, she looked around herself. The ocean was stretched out before her, vast, deep blue. She was standing on a peninsula, at the top of a cliff-face – she stretched out her arms, she lifted her face to the warmth of the sun. She was naked! She was naked, and didn't care. Freedom! Freedom. The grass was soft on her toes.

She turned, and a man was standing before her. He was tall – he was smiling. He was wearing a black suit, in the sun, but he wasn't sweating.

There was something about his eyes – his blue eyes.

"It's beautiful, isn't it?" he asked, and she turned again, drinking in the vast paddocks of grass, and then the ocean. "You can have all of this if you join with me: if you become mine."

"All of this?" she said playfully. "Is it not already mine? Has it not already been given?"

"No," he said, his face shifting slightly. "It's not. It has not."

He extended his hand, and there was a little spade on top.

"Dig, Rachel," he said. "Dig in the dust, and see how far you can go. See how much already belongs to you."

She took the spade – she playfully went to her knees, and started to dig.

There was grass, and then soil. She searched further – little earthworms. She studied them, and lay them aside, protecting them – and still she dug, and dug, until there was a small hole in the Earth.

"How far can you go, Rachel?" the man asked. "I'll bet you can reach the other side, if you keep trying."

She glanced up at him: what was he doing? His arms were lifted to the air – his face drawn in some strange expression. She felt afraid – she went back to work: she dug harder. There must be something! Must be something important to find – something important he wanted her to find.

She hit something: what was it? She dug around it. A skull! It was a human skull. Shocked, she thrust herself to her feet. Naked! She was naked! She wrapped her arms around herself.

His eyes were on her: dark eyes – penetrating eyes. His arms were pointing up to the sky. Clouds! Clouds were forming! The clouds were changing! She looked up, into the swirling clouds – she turned, to look across to the ocean's horizon. Darkness! Dark clouds, on the horizon!

"Death," the man said to her. "You have been given the Curse of Death. Dust! From dust you came, to dust you shall return!"

The warmth of the sun had gone: now there was a chill! She shivered – she stared into his eyes.

"All of the World is being reduced to dust," the man said. "All of the dust is coming to you, Rachel! The Death of the whole World, to block out the sun! To chill your naked innocence – to choke the life in your lungs."

The clouds were gathering, on the horizon! The darkness was deepening.

"Dig, Rachel," the man said. "Dig, to see if you can find the source of life. Dig, to see if you can find the knowledge to save yourself."

And he stood back, in his suit, and gestured to the ground.

Rachel frowned at him.

"You save me," she said, "if you have the knowledge – if you have the source of life. You save us all."

The man smiled. "Keep digging," he said. "Find it for yourself."

She returned to the soil, frowning – she dug and dug, around the body, until her hands were bleeding: and then she hit another object.

Surprised, she poked at it with the spade. Glass. She dug around the object – she pulled it out.

It was a jar. There was something inside: something strange – a small light brown lump, its surface soft, edible...

"It almost looks like medicine," she muttered.

"Very good," he said. "Medicine for your soul. Medicine to take into your body."

She fingered the jar – reached to feel the lid.

"What is it?" she asked.

"Knowledge," he said. "A new kind of knowledge for a new kind of humanity."

"A new humanity?" she asked.

"You can be the Mother," he said, smiling, "and I'll be the Father. You can start a new generation, as my Bride."

She stared at him. "Your bride?" she asked.

"Eat," he said, gesturing to the jar. "Here is the knowledge you were looking for. Here is the empowerment you need."

Rachel rose to her feet, holding the jar. Mud was on her fingers: her body was exposed.

"This isn't right," she said. "The goodness was already there before: the sun was shining, and I was free."

"What is true freedom," the man asked, "but to be given the choice? What is true knowledge but to have what others have?"

"What is true freedom?" Rachel asked, turning to look out again to the horizon. "Isn't it to trust beyond what we can see?"

"See it for yourself," the man said. "You have the means: you are carrying it. Reach for the stars – claim the knowledge for yourself."

"What if I'm not equipped to carry the knowledge?" Rachel asked, fingering the jar: looking out to the clouds. What were they: nuclear? Nuclear clouds? Her memory was starting to return. Was that nuclear dust? "What if the knowledge should consume me?" she asked. "What if it should consume us all?"

"It will not consume you," the man said. "Don't you want to be like Joshua? Don't you want to be as God? Knowing good and evil?"

"Wisdom," Rachel whispered, staring into the jar. "The knowledge of good and evil brings wisdom."

"Is wisdom not what you wish for?" the man asked. "Is it not what a woman is made for? Don't you want to pass your wisdom on to your husband? Don't you want to save the World? Isn't your greater wisdom needed?"

And now she looked up, and John was there.

His face was pale, and drawn. He looked in pain. Why? Why in pain? His body was naked – and, at his feet, was another, his face buried in his arms.

"Look!" she said to him, gesturing to the jar. "The World's in trouble, but we can fix it."

"No," John choked, shaking his head. "Don't do it: don't take it in. Don't take him in."

"But it can save us!" Rachel said, and she opened the jar, and reached inside.

The medicine! Light brown, light, on her hand.

"It will kill us," John whispered. "Please, Rachel – don't do it."

"It won't kill you," the man said. "If you don't take it, you will all die."

And now he was moving toward her – and now he was taking off his jacket, and his shirt.

"If you don't take me in," he said, "you will all die."

Rachel stared at him – at his face. He was hard! He was hard. He was taking off his trousers.

"Please," John whispered to her. "You're not seeing straight: you're not seeing what's in front of you."

"If I take him in," she whispered, "I become the Mother of the new humanity."

"He will infect you," John whispered. "He will infect me, through you, and all our children: and all your children. We will all die."

"We're all going to die anyway," Rachel whispered with tears – and now she looked down at Tristan.

He was choking: choking for breath, in his arms.

"Wouldn't I do it?" she whispered. "To save you? To let you live?"

And now Tristan lifted his face from his arms – and now his eyes, almost swollen shut, found her. He was reaching – reaching with his hand: finding her left hand, placing something in it.

The bullets…the deformed bullets, and the crucifix. Joshua! Joshua's death, to save Tristan! Christ's death…

"I'd rather die," Tristan whispered to her, "than see you corrupted! Than see you fall to him!"

Rachel stared at him – at the tears forming, in agony, in his already red eyes – and she suddenly straightened. Pain! Pain was there for a reason: to help humanity to see! And death…death was also there for a reason.

She grasped the deformed bullets in her left hand, with the crucifix; she moved the jar to her right hand, and held it with the light brown medicine. And now she turned back to the man.

127

He was clear before her, standing tall and naked, his eyes set on her.

It was Kensington.

Shocked, she stared at him. He wanted her! His eyes were moving over her body: over her soul.

"Give in," he said, "or I will take you anyway."

His darkness was showing, through his skin: who was this? Kensington? Satan? She shuddered. Rape? He would rape her?

"You don't own me," she choked. "Even if you should take me, you will never own me."

"If I take you," he said, "no-one else will ever have you again."

She swallowed, holding his cold eyes – suddenly seeing what she had not seen before.

"That's not true for me," she said, "and it's not true for you either."

His face flickered and then hardened again.

"Take the medicine," he said. "Take it of your own free choice."

"No," Rachel said. "Tell me the truth."

"What truth?" Kensington asked. "What is truth?"

"The knowledge of good and evil," Rachel said. "The knowledge that took you down."

Kensington's eyes widened.

"Taste it for yourself!" he said. "Taste it, before you claim to know anything about me!"

"I have tasted it!" Rachel said to him "I am tasting it! You are thrusting it down my throat, but I will not have it! I will vomit it back up! I will give you back your life instead!"

And now she thrust the crucifix out in front of his face.

The man stood before her, naked, suddenly bewildered, staring at the crucifix.

"Do you see it now?" Rachel asked, searching him. "Can you remember the truth? You have a wife. You are already married."

"Married?" he whispered. "I'm already married?"

Robert…Rachel was starting to see him, exposed, before her: the man! She suddenly knew his name: could see the man.

"Tell me the truth," Rachel said.

"My wife…" he whispered, staring at the gold. "The thief…The thief has her…"

Rachel held her breath. A thief?

"What thief?" she whispered. "Who is the thief?"

Robert's face was contorting, still fixed on the crucifix.

"I can't stop him," he whispered. "He's got the gun to her head."

"What's he doing?" Rachel whispered.

"Rape," he whispered back. "He's raping her."

Now Rachel faltered before him, but then stood straight. The jar! The knowledge of good and evil! She wrestled it now, under her right arm: she wrestled the light brown medicine back into it.

"Did you see her?" she whispered. "Did you kill her? Did Alex see you?"

"No," he whispered, still staring at the crucifix in front of him. "That's not what Alex meant. I love her…"

"Then, what…?" Rachel stared at him, fixed in the moment: as if all of time was standing still, in this one moment of exposure – in this one potent exposure of truth. "What did Alex see?"

Robert's face was blushing: his blue eyes were human.

"I couldn't save her," he whispered. "I couldn't stop him."

"Then why…?"

"God killed her," he said. "God makes everything happen. God is the enemy."

He was hardening again – she quickly reached out to grasp his arm.

"Alex saw you kill," she said. "Who did you kill?"

Robert hesitated, and then spoke. "The thief," he said. "I grabbed his gun, after he shot her: I shot him. And…and everything changed after that…"

Rachel fell back a step. This? This was the truth?

"Death," she whispered. "And the knowledge of evil. It passes on and on…"

"Yes," Robert said, staring at her. "The curse passes on; Satan's power over us passes on and on…"

"But what if we have the solution?" she asked with tears. "What if the solution also has been passed on, from generation to generation?"

"A solution to evil?" he asked. "A cure for the curse? What could it possibly be: more death?"

"A kind of death," Rachel said. "A different kind." And she opened the jar, thrust the bullets inside with the light brown medicine, and closed the lid.

Kensington's eyes were on her.

"Don't," he whispered. "If you do this, I die. You don't know his malice: you don't know the pain he can inflict."

"The malice of Satan?" Rachel asked. "The pain of despair?"

"You don't know," he whispered, "how much it costs to try to stop it. The agony of trying to stop the curse – do you think I didn't try? Much easier to give in! To let him have his way! To forget how things were…"

"To die," Rachel whispered, with tears.

"To return?" Robert said. "To try to stand in the light, now? Now, after all these years?"

"Choose the pain!" Rachel said. "Choose the cost. Do away with the knowledge of evil: do away with it!"

Joshua! Joshua taking the bullets into his chest! Into death! Into the grave.

Now she handed him the jar, and Robert stared down at it.

"The bullets," he muttered. "The bullets I sent into Joshua Davidson, through Alex and Tristan."

"Undo the evil," Rachel said. "Choose the pain."

"Face it all?" Kensington whispered, clutching onto the jar. "Face the knowledge?"

"Purgatory," Rachel said. "You are Catholic, remember? You believe in Purgatory."

Robert stared at her. He looked down at himself, naked – he looked at her. He stared out toward the horizon: the gathering clouds of death.

"Purgatory," he whispered.

"It's about purification," Rachel said – and Robert's eyes widened, in sudden fear.

"He's coming," he whispered. "I can feel him coming!"

"Who?" Rachel asked.

"He's coming!" John's voice cried out, from behind her.

And then, suddenly, there was a flash of light.

Rachel gasped. Light surrounded her: Light passed straight through her.

"The weapon!" Tristan's voice cried out, from the ground. "Oh, God, Rachel: it's nuclear! It's nuclear…"

Nuclear? Fear seized her – she listened out for an overwhelming explosion: she waited to die, from incineration or the blast, knocking her down. She searched the horizon for the mushroom cloud. But none of it came.

Instead, she was penetrated by the Light: instead, agony took her.

She sank to her knees: gasping, she lifted her face up to the sky.

"Rachel!" Tristan's voice cried, lifting into a wail. "Rachel!"

Where was John? He was there, beside her, on his knees: his face lifted, his naked body gasping, penetrated by the Light.

"Hold on," he whispered. "Hold on."

"Hold on?" she whispered – and now she was being lifted to her feet: and now Joshua was standing in front of her.

"Hold on," he said, and he reached out, and touched her shoulder, and the Light intensified.

Her body stiffened. What was happening? Joshua was smiling – he moved his other hand to her head, and now she remembered standing with him, outside of North-East Hospital, where he had healed so many patients.

The DNA! He had scribbled it down, on the paper: on both sides of the paper. The code! The original code, before it had been changed: he had turned the page, they had introduced aging into the code. Mortality! Death.

But now, in her mind, he was turning the page back over: back to the original! No aging! No death…

Nuclear!

"Hold on," Joshua said in front of her, and she clung to the hand on her head. The Light! It was penetrating into her cells! It was penetrating into her very DNA.

"Radiation?" she gasped. "Is it radiotherapy?"

"No, doctor," Joshua replied, smiling. "Another kind of energy entirely."

"The knowledge," Rachel gasped. "What about the knowledge…"

And now both of his hands were on her head – and now he was drawing her eyes to his own.

"Your soul," Joshua said, and his Light penetrated her, and she gasped.

Her father! She saw him, standing in front of her: tie loose, leaning against the hospital bed in the ward, smiling at her. Now he was lying, dead, on the floor at St Peter's. Dead! He was dead.

She wept, and Joshua murmured over her.

"Trust," he said. "Trust in me, beyond the pain of losing your father."

"I will trust," she said – and the vision moved on. James! His gun to her head. He was going to kill her! She was going to die. She held her breath.

"Keep trusting," Joshua murmured. "Keep trusting in me, even beyond the threat of your own death."

"I will trust," she breathed, "even in death."

And now he moved her on further. James, killed! Killed by Kensington!

"No," she pleaded. "No." And she reached out to grasp onto Joshua. "Why?" she pleaded. "Why?"

She was trembling, and his grip on her intensified.

"Must you know why?" he asked. "Must you know?"

Tears filled her eyes – she struggled to hold his gaze through the tears.

"I can't see," she whispered.

"But I can still see," his voice said, and she closed her eyes and clung blindly to him.

"I will keep trusting," she whispered. "I will trust in your vision, beyond what I can see."

And she held to him, and her eyes were closed, but he was still moving her mind further.

Now Alex was kneeling before Kensington: his chest naked – his arms stretched out.

"Oh my God," Rachel whispered. "Oh my God, don't let me see."

"The knowledge," Joshua said. "The knowledge of evil."

"It's too much," Rachel whispered. "It's too much for me to carry."

And now Kensington was shooting Alex – and now his young body was being thrown back.

"Oh, God!" she cried. "No!"

And she was grasping the weapon: and she was pressing it into Kensington's temple.

"Beg for your life," she was saying. *"Why should I let you live?"*

She stared at herself, naked, pressing the weapon into Robert's temple – she thrust herself away from Joshua, staring into his eyes. The Light! It was burning her! It was burning!

"Why should I let you live?" Joshua asked. "Why should I let any of you live?"

The weapon! The Light was the weapon!

131

"Are we allies, Rachel?" Joshua asked her. "Are we allies fighting the same enemy: the evil of your own souls? Or am I your enemy?"

"We are allies," Rachel whispered – and she stepped forward, closer to his Light, and knelt down before him.

"Change me," she whispered. "Whatever the cost! Whatever the cost."

"We will change you," Joshua said. "Whatever the cost."

And he laid his hands back on her head.

Rachel was back, on the street, between the Beehive and St Peter's Cathedral, in Wellington. Joshua was there, staggering, in the intersection! He was wearing the ancient crown: he was sweating blood. Darkness! Rachel could see, watching again, as from outside: the darkness of the World, drawn to him! Her darkness, drawn to him. Crushing him.

Tristan was standing in front of him, lifting the rifle, his face drawn – and now he was firing: and now Joshua's body was thrown back.

He was lying, on the ground, bleeding: dying.

Rachel went to her knees beside him. His hand found her: his eyes, in pain, found her.

"It's finished," he said. "It's over."

"It's over?" Rachel asked, reaching to stroke his bloody face.

"It's done," he said. "My body and my blood, Rachel. It's over."

And then he gave up his life and died.

Rachel looked into Joshua's eyes now. The Light! The Light, in and through him: dancing around him – drawing in everyone he touched.

He was touching her. With tears Rachel received his touch.

"Master," she whispered. "You are the Master of everything good."

He smiled, and Rachel gazed at him. Love! She loved him. The Light drew her: drew her to her knees before him – drew her into worship.

She was clothed by the Light. She was safe in the Light.

She was one with him, in the Light.

She was whole.

She rose to her feet – he was taking her hand, and turning her around. Where were the others? John was there, on his knees; his eyes closed, his face radiant. Bliss! He looked in bliss. The Light was around him, hiding his nakedness: the Light was penetrating through him.

Tristan was near John, on his knees. Rachel wandered over to him – reached out to touch his face. The bruising had gone! His eyes were wide open, staring around himself: reaching out to try to touch the Light.

Rachel almost laughed, looking at him: he looked like a child, trying to capture a dandelion. Let him try! The Light eluded him, but captured him: captured his imagination – unleashed his freedom.

His eyes found hers: tears! Tears and joy.

132

"It's gone," he whispered.

"What's gone?" Rachel asked him.

"The guilt," he breathed. "The burden…"

"Such a heavy burden," Rachel murmured over him, and Tristan smiled at her, and he suddenly reminded her of Joshua.

She took his hand – she squeezed his hand. But now Tristan was rising to his feet – now he was turning her.

"Rachel," he said, and she looked forward.

Kensington! He was there, on his knees: his face was contorted – his mouth drawn in a silent scream of agony.

Rachel stiffened. Anguish! She moved forward – she reached out to touch his shoulder.

"No," Joshua's voice said, behind her.

"But he's in pain," Rachel said.

"You can't save him," he said – and now he reached out, and laid a hand on Kensington's shoulder.

His body stiffened, under Joshua's touch: his voice became audible, his scream filling the air. The Light! The Light was burning him!

Joshua went to his knees before him: laid both hands on his shoulders.

"Don't die," Rachel whispered to Joshua. "Not again. Not all over again."

"Either the Darkness will be consumed by the Light," Joshua said, his gaze returning to her. "Or the Light must undo the Darkness. One offering, Rachel: one offering for all who would receive my help."

And he pressed his head forward, against Kensington's forehead, and breathed in, and his face contorted, and Kensington groaned, gripping onto his arms.

Blood! Rachel clenched her fists: drops of blood were appearing again on Joshua's face. The Darkness! Kensington's Darkness! It was being drawn to him: drawn to Joshua – drawn to the Crown, collapsing him between Parliament and the Cathedral.

To God, the end was as the beginning.

"No," Rachel breathed. "No."

Kensington was gripping the jar, in his right hand – he had shaken it! Shaken the bullets, inside the jar, with the knowledge of good and evil. He had dispersed the knowledge, amongst the bullets: he had made his choice.

Joshua was grasping him now: saving him now. Rachel watched, gripped, as Joshua breathed in Kensington's darkness. Robert was sinking against him, now! His head was sinking down against Joshua's chest.

"Oh, God," he whispered, and he released the jar, and it fell from his hands, smashing to the ground.

The knowledge of evil, the light brown medicine, dispersed away. The deformed bullets were scattered on the ground.

Robert sank down to the ground, curling up: curling up as a foetus.

133

"A new life," John's voice said from behind her. "For him, the entirety needs to start again."

And Rachel left Kensington curled up at the feet of Joshua, like a small dog to his master, and turned away.

The Light! The grass of the field was lit, penetrated; alive. The Light was filling the sky – hugging the ocean, playing with it. Life! Rachel could see a humpback whale lift up into the sky and fall back down onto the water.

The clouds! The dark clouds on the horizon had dissipated. Instead, the Light sped across the waters, over the sea.

Rachel gazed after the Light.

"The rest of the World?" she whispered.

"It's a new day," John said, "for the entire World."

And Rachel smiled, and blinked – and suddenly she was back in the Cathedral.

Light filled the church, flooding through the stained glass windows – flooding through the stone walls and out again, to the courtyard and beyond.

John was there, his face radiant, his green eyes lit: naked, and yet wholly clothed, standing before her.

Tristan was still sitting on the ground, his face healed and bright, looking about himself in wonder.

Kensington was curled up, naked, not yet clothed: his eyes closed, the Light moving through him.

Rachel reached for Tristan's abandoned shirt lying on the floor – she reached to drape it over Kensington's waist. Then she rose to her feet.

The bodies: James and Alex! They were lying, at the altar! She gazed at them.

Then, suddenly, the earth began to shake.

CHAPTER NINETEEN: Death and Life

Alex lay in darkness.

Gasping for breath, he tried to grope about himself, but he couldn't move. The darkness pressed in through his sight: the darkness pressed into his mind.

"Where am I?" he asked.

"In Death," a voice answered. He tried to turn his head, to look: he could see nothing.

Cold penetrated him: a vast deep cold. Fear seized him.

"Am I alone?" he asked. "Are there others?"

"Would you wish for there to be others?" the voice asked.

"No," Alex said. Others, in Death? "No."

"And yet, you are not alone."

Now someone appeared, before him: Joshua, lit from within.

Alex gazed at him: relief! He felt relief, looking at his face. But Joshua? In Death, with him?

"I am the boat," Joshua said, "for the tsunami." Now Joshua's hand was moving, reaching toward him.

"Breathe, Alex!" Joshua commanded. "Breathe!"

And Alex sucked in a deep breath, and gasped, and opened his eyes.

Light! Blinding Light! He turned his face away – he closed his eyes. His body! He could feel his body! Breath, filling his lungs: the hard surface against his back.

Shaking! His body was shaking!

"Alex?" a voice cried out. "Alex?"

He opened his eyes: Light! He shut them and opened them again. The voice – who was it?

Rachel's face appeared over him: her blue eyes wide – her brown hair around her shoulders. Lit! Her face was lit! Her eyes…they were bright, with beauty and tears.

The World was shaking around them. Alex gazed up into her face, and reached out to touch her cheek.

"Salvation," he whispered. "Death is being overcome."

"The Light," Rachel replied, crying over him. "The Light is overcoming the Darkness."

Tears were spilling down her cheeks: Alex reached out to stroke them away.

"No more tears," he whispered. "No more death, or crying, or pain…"

She broke into a radiant smile, and Alex was struck, looking at her. Light! Light!

She reached down to pull him up, to his feet, and he reached down to finger his own naked chest. Bullet holes! He had been shot! But now the bullets were gone: now the wounds were healing, the tissue filling in, even as he watched.

The Light was surrounding him – the Light was penetrating into him. His heart! His lungs. His brain…

135

He breathed in again – he felt the Light in his mind. Clarity! Peace. The mind of another! The Universe of another...

Intrigued, he reached out to seek His thoughts, and then he turned.

John was standing in front of him. John! His green eyes were intense with joy.

"Victory," he cried. "The weapon has been dropped – the enemy has been defeated!"

"The enemy," Alex murmured, reaching to grasp a hold of his arms, "of the darkness of our own souls: the Death resident in our own nature."

"We are remade," John said, with a wide smile. "We are reborn."

"Like a woman," Alex murmured, "giving birth..."

John was grasping his hand now – he was turning him. There was another body lying on the shaking floor: who was it? Alex peered down: James! It was James Lester! He frowned. Bullets! There were bullets in his chest: there was blood, staining his shirt.

"Dead?" he asked. How? "I don't remember..."

He struggled to recall: what had happened? James had been shot? And now John was grasping his hand again: turning him again.

Lying on the floor, naked, was his father.

Alex gazed down at his face. He was alive! But curled up, his eyes tightly closed: the Light moving around him.

"Oh," Alex breathed. "What's happening? What's happening?"

"Do you remember?" John asked.

"Remember what?" Alex asked.

"How you died?" John asked.

Alex gazed down at his father. His face! His face was human! No dark intensity, no...no...

"Oh," Alex gasped, and he fell back a step. The eyes! The blue intensity, the hatred, the gun pointing toward him.

"If you want to change the World, little shit," he said, *"you have to make sacrifices."*

The gun was firing! The bullets were landing in his chest.

Pain! And yet...and yet the pain was fading...

John's hand was on his arm.

"Do you know what happened to him?" John asked, gesturing back to his father.

"No," Alex said, confused, looking at his closed eyes. "What happened?"

"Death," John said. "And then a rebirth."

"A rebooting," Alex murmured, gazing down at him. Kensington! But not only Kensington: Robert! His father's name was Robert.

"Dad," he whispered, kneeling down next to him – reaching out a hand to his head. "Are you in there? Are you still in there to be saved?"

His father didn't stir. Alex knelt quietly next to him: the shaking around him was settling. He looked up to the altar, with the bronze cross. The stained glass windows: they had shattered, with the shake! He could see blue sky, beyond: blue

136

sky, lit with the Light…He remembered another time, another Cathedral, with windows he had shattered with a gun…

"Alex," someone said, and he looked up. Tristan! It was Tristan. He was grinning – he was reaching out a hand.

Alex reached for the hand – he let Tristan pull him up to his feet. Tristan was strong! His young face was radiant in a different way from John's: his eyes twinkling.

"Freedom," Tristan said. "How does it feel, little brother, to finally be free?"

Alex smiled back at him, still grasping onto his hand.

"It's a relief!" he whispered – and Tristan's eyes shifted for a moment into memory.

"Yes," he whispered back. "It is a relief."

Then he returned: then the innocent mischief was back in his eyes.

"So, did you see anyone I know when you were dead?" he asked, and Alex stared at him and laughed.

"Well, no!" he said. "I…I don't know if it works that way…"

"Sure it does," Tristan said, his grin widening. "What's Paradise, without your loved ones?"

Alex's eyes moved automatically back to his father.

"But what if our loved ones are lost?" he asked. "What if they are beyond salvation?"

"I don't believe that," Tristan said. "Not of my loved ones."

Alex glanced back to him: to the treasure in his eyes. Mark! Mark Blake! And…and Selena…

"I agree," Alex whispered to him. "But it's not my choice. I didn't see them. I don't know, Tristan."

Tristan's face coloured a little, but then his smile returned.

"I know," he said. "You're alive again, and so Joshua's going to bring them back to life too."

Alex reached out to touch his face. Faith! Tristan had faith.

"Then find them," Alex said. "If you are so certain, go." And he gestured out of the Cathedral doors.

Tristan's eyes filled with tears, looking at him.

"Go back?" he whispered. "Go back into Ground Zero?"

"Use your faith, Tristan," Alex said. "Use what you already know to be true. Go back to Wellington: find them alive."

And Tristan's face contorted with tears. "Hitch?" he asked. "After everything that's happened, hitch again? Back up the coast, across the water, back into the explosion…?"

"The end returns to the beginning," John said, alongside him. "But this time do it in the Light."

"In the Light," Tristan muttered, smirking slightly. "Wish I still had Rau."

"You have Joshua," John said.

137

"Yes," Tristan whispered. "Now I actually do have Joshua."

And he turned away from them, and walked down the aisle and out through the doors.

The tremors had settled.

Alex looked up, to Rachel. She was standing quietly next to James, looking down at him. Was he dead? Would he stay dead? Alex wandered up to her, and stood alongside.

"What of the Dead, Alex?" she asked. "What of those locked in darkness forever?"

"I don't know," Alex whispered, remembering the Darkness: remembering the cold. "We are not the Masters of Death and Life."

"I know we're not the Masters," Rachel said, reaching for a stethoscope around her neck that was no more. "I know eternal life is beyond our domain."

"I would wish…" And now he hesitated, and then continued. "I would wish for all to be saved."

Rachel's hand reached out to take his.

"I know," she whispered. "So would I."

"Even my father?" Alex asked, and her eyes met his: tears filled her blue, and she nodded.

"Yes, Alex," she whispered. "Even your father."

And relief filled him.

She was looking down at James again: her face was contorting with grief.

"Bury him?" she asked. "Bury him with the other Dead?"

"Not in your life," James's voice said – and Rachel was staring down at him: her grief turning to laughter.

"What?" she cried. "What are you saying to me?"

Alex looked, a lump rising in his throat. Alive? He was alive?

James's eyes were open, brown, surprised. He was still lying at their feet, shifting a bit awkwardly on the ground – a wry grin slowly forming on his face.

The bullet holes! The bullet holes in his chest had gone.

He shoved himself quickly to his feet – he stood before them, reaching to tug down on his shirt. The Light! The Light was forming around him – moving through him.

His face changed: he swayed slightly, on his feet, with the Light. Then he stood still.

Rachel was staring at him. Alex watched, captivated, as she stared. And then she spoke.

"Well?" she asked. "Who are you now?"

He looked a little confused. He looked around himself, at the Cathedral: at the shattered windows. Then he turned back to Rachel.

"Who am I?" he asked. "I am your brother."

Tears filled Rachel's eyes and spilt down her cheeks.

138

"You're alive," she whispered. "You're alive."

"I guess so," James said, reaching to finger his own chest – and now he looked toward Kensington, on the floor.

"Is that him?" he asked, and Alex nodded.

"That's him," he said.

"Not dead?" James asked. "But also not alive?"

"I guess not," Alex said. "But I'm still hoping he will live."

"Purgatory," James muttered – and he looked back to Rachel.

His face darkened for a moment: a memory! An experience gone. And then it passed.

"Life," he said. "It's different from what I expected."

"Yes," Rachel said.

"Love is different."

"Yes."

"I…" And now James hesitated and then continued, reaching out to touch her arm. "I feel free."

And now, suddenly, Rachel's arms moved around him.

James hesitated for a moment, as if astonished: uncertain what to do. And then, slowly, his arms moved around Rachel.

"Is this what it feels like?" he asked. "To be held?"

"This is what it feels like," Rachel's voice whispered.

James's eyes were lit, looking over her shoulder: looking at Alex.

"I like it," he whispered, breaking into a smile: a smile that seemed strangely unfamiliar to Alex – a whole new universe, suddenly opened up. "I like it a lot."

Alex gazed at him – at the dawning love in his eyes: at the growing freedom.

"That's good," he whispered to him. "That's very good."

And now he turned away from them, back to his own father.

Robert was lying on the ground: still curled up – his eyes still closed.

Alex knelt again next to him, and reached out his hand to his head.

"Dad," he whispered. "Wake up."

Robert's body was naked, but now he was clothed: now the Light was covering him. Alex looked over his clothed naked body, and returned to his face. He was breathing! His chest was rising and falling.

"Not dead," Alex murmured, "only sleeping."

And he reached his fingers to his father's hair.

What was in his mind? What was in his heart? What was happening to him?

"Daddy," Alex repeated. "It's time to wake up."

The white face was quiet. Alex noticed Rachel, on the other side – he looked up to the tears in her eyes, as she watched him.

"Is it a coma?" she whispered. "Some kind of coma?"

Alex frowned at her, and then looked back down to his father. A coma? No – it couldn't be. Not like this, neither dead nor alive, forever. No.

139

He groped around for something to help – he found the empty cross on his own chest. He reached, and undid the cross, and lifted it out in front of his father's face.

"Look, Dad," he whispered. "There's life after death. I believe it! I have it! And I believe you can have it too, if you just reach out! If you just reach out to take it!"

Rachel was sinking to her knees, on the other side of his father: reaching, lifting up the crucifix, with the deformed bullets.

"His death," she whispered. "He has accepted his own death, with Joshua's death, and after the crucifixion comes the resurrection, with Joshua…"

"Now, Daddy," Alex said, holding the empty golden cross in front of his father's face: letting it swing before him. "Now's the time."

"The child shall lead them…" John's voice murmured, behind him – and Alex peered into Robert's face.

His father's eyes opened. Holding his breath, Alex watched him. Robert was staring at the cross, the blue gaze trying to focus.

"Empty?" he choked. "No longer a crucifix?"

"No longer a crucifix," Alex whispered.

His father's face contorted. "Your mother," he whispered, and sobs began to rack his body. "I remember your mother."

"She's alive," Alex said. "I know my mother is alive."

"Alive?" Robert whispered.

"Alive," Alex said. "The time for the crucifixion is over."

Robert stared at the empty cross in front of his face. "Death," he said. "Death is finished. Redemption is won. Now comes the resurrection."

And he reached out and grasped the empty cross to himself.

Alex gazed at him in wonder. He rose to his feet – he reached out his hand to his father.

"Come," he said – and Robert looked up to him.

"Where?" he asked.

"To freedom," Alex said. "To life in abundance."

"I will come," Robert said – and he rose to his feet, and stood over Alex.

Alex gazed up at him. This man! This man had terrified him! This man had almost crushed him. He remembered: chalices of blood! The guns, and the beating. But the memories, they were starting to fade! They were starting to dissolve away, in the Light…

The altar…the altar where his father had shoved him back: where he had pushed the gun to his temple…

His father's eyes were on the altar ahead, now: his forehead creasing into a troubled frown.

"Did I…?"

"You did," Alex said quickly. "But it's over now."

"I…" Robert turned quickly toward him – reaching out toward Alex's chest, his eyes widening. "I…"

"Peace," Alex said, taking his hand: drawing it to his own healed chest. "It's done. It's finished."

Robert was gazing at him, Alex released him – and then Robert lifted his eyes to Rachel.

She looked astonished, her eyes moving over his face.

"You," Robert muttered, gesturing to her. "I led you to destruction too: like a lamb to the slaughter."

Rachel took a deep breath. "You did," she whispered, "like a ravenous lion. But God had something much greater in mind."

"Something greater," Robert murmured, "for the lion and the lamb."

And then his eyes returned to Alex.

Alex smiled at him. Robert's eyes were misting, looking at him. Alex looked at Rachel: her eyes also were misting.

He stretched out his hands to both. Then he walked up to the altar, knelt down on the floor before the communion rail, turned himself, and lay down on his back – looking up to the stone dome above him, flooded with the Light.

"It's beautiful," he whispered.

John was standing nearby, watching him from above: smiling down at him. James was standing on the other side, quiet: silent.

Alex looked away from them back up to the Light, through the dome.

Now Rachel was appearing, next to him on his left side – lying on her back, looking up to the dome with him: reaching to take his left hand.

"I've never done this before," she said, and Alex glanced at her, gazing up: her pretty face brightening with what she was seeing. "You're right, it is beautiful."

"I knew it would be," Alex murmured to her. "I knew God would be worth the pain of the wait."

"You did know," Rachel said.

Alex smiled back up at the Light – and then there was a movement to his right.

His father was lowering himself down next to him: laying his tall body down on the ground.

Alex trembled – and now his father was reaching out to take his right hand.

"Show me," his deep voice murmured, and Alex kept gazing up to the dome.

"Light," he whispered. "Light, everywhere: around, and through, and in all things. God's Light! God's purifying Light."

"I see it," Kensington said, and Alex turned to see the tears pouring from his eyes, as he looked up. "I can see!"

Weeping took Alex. He squeezed his father's hand: his father squeezed back.

"What do you see?" Alex asked.

"Light!" Robert said. "Light, and life. Love, and longing…"

"A longing fulfilled," Alex said. "A life complete."

"A life complete," Robert said – and his face broke into a radiant smile.

Alex propped himself up on his elbows – he looked at his father's face. Memories! Suddenly they were flooding back! Smiles of love! Eyes of warmth, and comfort. Protection! Gentleness from the big hands.

"I can see you," Alex said – and Robert's eyes came to him, and his father smiled, with bright happy blue eyes, and the past and present became one.

"And I can see you," he replied.

"Do you see Mum?" Alex asked him. "Can you remember Mum?"

Robert frowned, and looked back up to the dome. Pain took his face – Alex reached out to lay a hand on his shoulder.

"I can," Robert whispered. "Can you?"

Alex looked at him, and then turned himself back over – looking back up into the Light: searching. His mother…

"I didn't kill her, Alex," his father whispered.

Alex searched the Light, to see through the darkness. The thief! The thief, over her, with the gun to her head…

"It was Satan," Alex whispered.

"The thief stole all our lives away," Robert said. "The Darkness took a hold. But now the Light has overcome the Darkness! But now comes a new day."

"Now comes a new day," Alex whispered. "Now comes a new life."

And he lifted himself from the ground, to his feet – and reached out to lift his father and Rachel alongside himself.

Now John was before him, bowing his head.

"It's finished," he said. "It's done. The lion has lain down with the lamb."

"Yes," Alex said, "but there's still more to be done."

"More?" John asked – and Alex looked to Rachel.

She held his gaze, perplexed – and then her eyes widened.

"Oh," she said.

"It was always going to happen this way," Alex said. "It had to."

"Yes," Rachel said, "you're right: it had to."

And she walked down the aisle and out of the Cathedral.

Alex was left alone, with his father, John and James.

He turned. He looked back to the bronze cross. He looked at the altar. And then he turned around, gazing down the aisle toward the doors.

"Work," he murmured. "There's going to be work to do."

"What kind of work?" James asked.

"The forming of a brand new life," Alex said. "The outworking of a complete change."

"Then form the new life," his father said. "Take the lead."

And he gestured toward the doors.

Alex glanced up at his face: the peace, the knowledge. He glanced at James's face – his silence, the inner quiet.

"Let's do it," Alex said. "Let's form the changes."

142

And he walked down the aisle, with James and Robert close behind.

Tristan walked down the road.

On his right, the ocean gently lapped white foam across rocks, and across sand. The blue of the sky joined with the deep blue of the ocean: the Light enhanced the colour and intensified it.

Tristan paused, on the side of the road – he gazed out toward the horizon. Beauty! Such beauty, like looking through rose tinted lenses, but it was real! Vibrant! Alive. Unblemished.

He wandered off the road – across the sand, into the water. It was cool, on his bare feet: refreshing, and cool. He playfully launched himself further in: dove, under the surface. Cool! Refreshing. He resurfaced, and lay on his back on top, looking up, up, toward the yellow sun…the white Light played with the yellow! Enhanced it, and transcended it.

He took a deep breath.

"Joshua…"

His face was there, before him, now: his friend – the one who had willingly taken his bullets into death: into the grave.

Do it, Tristan, Joshua's voice said. *Play.*

And Tristan laughed, and flicked water up in the direction of his friend, and he rose to his feet, in the ocean, and moved his arms all around, making gentle waves.

It is for freedom that I have set you free.

Tears pricked at Tristan's eyes. Freedom! But the cost! The cost! He still remembered the day, but it was starting to lose its edge: the day he had shot his best friend.

"I love you," he whispered. "I love you."

And I love you.

"With all my heart, soul, strength and mind," Tristan whispered.

A love stronger than death.

"A love stronger than death," Tristan said – and he drew his arms out of the water, and wandered back to the shore.

The street was before him again. It was a long highway, back up the east coast, the way they had come, through Kaikoura, toward Picton, and then…and then on, to Wellington…

Tristan frowned. What might he find there, in the capital? What might he find, in his home? Would it resemble in any way what had been? Would he even recognise it?

A walk, through hundreds of kilometres…his feet didn't seem to get sore anymore, as if the Light was healing him: sustaining him. He didn't feel hungry, or thirsty, though, when he reached down to a little brook to try it, he enjoyed drinking.

His body was lit with the Light. He still expected to see a shirt and shorts, looking down...thought he could still vaguely see them. Maybe it was just a habitual memory...

The road was deserted. A little surprised, he looked both ways and then started wandering in the middle of the highway. No cars. Curious. Just walking – he could manage that! Just one foot in front of the other, on and on: nothing but him and the Light...

He wandered forward: time passed – he didn't know how long. The sunlight was fading: the Light remained. He left the highway again: sat himself on a rock, looking out to the bright pink of the sunset – watching as the yellow light faded, and the moonlight appeared, sparkling on the water. Strange...strange how he could experience the best of both worlds, simultaneously: contrast, darkness and light, but always the Light, governing both night and day.

He liked gazing at the full moon. There was something about it: light, in the darkness – hope, in the fading memory of despair...

"It's beautiful," a voice said.

"Yes," he murmured.

Now he felt someone settling next to him on the rock, taking his right hand.

Surprised, he looked up to find Rachel alongside him.

Her face, illuminated from within, also somehow caught the reflection of the moon.

"Yes," he repeated. "It is beautiful."

She smiled. Tristan noticed her brown hair was tidy: half tied back. He reached out to touch it, and instinctively messed it up a bit.

"There," he said, grinning. "I recognise you now."

She shrugged, and reached back to her hair tie, pulling it out.

"Doesn't really matter," she said. "I'm not sweating with the walk."

"You've noticed that too."

"I don't seem to overheat," she said.

"But the water still feels good," Tristan said.

"Yeah?" Rachel asked.

"Would be nice in the moonlight," Tristan said, gesturing to the dark water in the Light.

Rachel cast her eyes over the water, smiling. The Light was covering her, and moving through: Tristan could hardly see her body or clothes. She was free! Free to swim: free to not swim.

She was reaching now – reaching for something. She pulled them out, and laid them in his hand.

The bullets! It was the deformed bullets from Tristan's gun: the bullets he had used to kill Joshua.

Tristan stiffened, looking down at them.

"How does the idea of war feel now?" Rachel asked. "Soldier?"

"War?" Tristan breathed, staring down at the bullets, confused. "Soldier?"

145

"That's what I thought," Rachel said – and she took the bullets from his hand, and threw them into the ocean.

They landed, with five little splashes – they sank into the depths.

Tristan gazed after them – then he looked back to Rachel.

"What about you?" he asked. "What's changing for you?"

She tilted her head – she gazed out toward the ocean.

"There's…" And now tears filled her eyes: she hesitated, and then continued. "There's no need to judge anymore."

"To judge?" Tristan asked.

She looked vulnerable suddenly. He instinctively reached again for her hand. She was moving toward him: face pressing into his shoulder.

Astonished, he wrapped his arms around her. Crying? Vulnerability? This was all part of it? Something was being unlocked in her: something deep – something hidden. And there was trust…a new kind of trust…a new kind of intimacy.

"What is it?" he murmured over her, gazing over her head to the ocean – reaching to stroke her hair.

"You don't know?" Rachel whispered, beneath him. "You don't know what's coming?"

"Love," Tristan replied. "Love is coming."

"Yes," Rachel said, "but what kind of love, Tristan? Love with whom?"

He frowned, trying to search the Light, moving through the gentle breeze on the waters: the moonlight reflecting off the little tufts…but the Light playfully evaded him.

It was Rachel's journey.

"Only you can find out," Tristan murmured. "Only you can know."

"We have a lot in common," Rachel murmured against his chest. "Do you see it?"

"I see some things," Tristan said. "I've seen them for a while."

"Family," Rachel said. "Our fathers. Your sister; my brother."

"These we already know," Tristan said, "but there's someone else."

And Rachel's head nodded on his chest. "Yes, Tristan," she whispered. "There's someone else."

And now Tristan rose to his feet, on the rock, and lifted her up alongside him: peering out into the darkness of the night – the night lit with the Light.

"Could it be?" he whispered, holding her hand. "Might it be that my mother…?"

And now tears freely filled his eyes.

"It's easier for you," Rachel said. "You…you…"

Tristan searched out the darkness. He could see her again! Her body, lying under the blood stained sheet! Dead! She was dead.

He turned his face away. His father! His father had killed her, but it had been an accident…just a terrible car accident, driving too fast…

"I lost both in the accident," he murmured to her. "I lost both. To claw them both back again…to somehow reach for them both…"

146

"Whereas I…"

Her voice faded. Tristan turned to look at her: the Light! The Light, around and through her, and yet the darkness of night still, outside…

She was staring now into the darkness.

"What do you see?" he asked.

"I can't see," she whispered. "That's the problem."

"And yet the Light is through the darkness, penetrating where you can't see."

"Yes," Rachel said. "But…but I know what's coming…"

Tristan gazed at her. "You're afraid," he explored, searching her. "For some reason afraid to see your mother again, after everything that's happened."

"Afraid?" Rachel asked, turning her eyes again to him. "How can anyone be afraid of the darkness now, with so much Light?"

"And yet," Tristan explored, "you don't know what to do with it."

"What to do with the Light?" Rachel asked, and she looked back away toward the full moon. "How to navigate the darkness?"

Tristan tightened his grip on her hand. "Your stethoscope can't help you now," he said.

"No," she replied, shrugging slightly. "It's quite useless to me here."

"Your moral judgments fail."

"They are redundant," Rachel said, "in Joshua's Light."

Tristan smiled at her honesty. Love! He loved her deeply.

"And yet it's a mystery to you," he said.

"What's a mystery?" she asked.

"Love," Tristan explored intuitively. "What love means, after all that has passed. What connection actually means."

Now Rachel's face contorted, looking into the darkness at the moon.

"A simple tragedy is much easier," she whispered. "Terrible, Tristan, but easier."

"My tragedy was easier?" he asked. "I don't think so…"

"Of course you don't," Rachel said, squeezing his hand. "Of course, you can't. You would wish with all of your heart for your mother to live again: it was heart-breaking that she might have been taken from you. And yet…and yet…"

"And yet what?" Tristan asked.

"Some things are more complicated," Rachel said.

"What?" Tristan asked. "What could be such a mystery? What could be so difficult?"

Rachel frowned, looking toward the horizon.

"The threat has been diffused," she said. "The Light has come. The darkness has not overcome the Light, and it never will, yet…yet…"

"Yet what?" Tristan asked.

"I still have no idea what to do."

Tristan looked at her: at her hair, messy about her shoulders – at her face, lit, peering into the darkness, trying to understand it

147

He held her hand: he smiled at her.

"Welcome to my world," he said.

"What?" she replied, peering at him, quizzical.

"Well, you don't know what to do!" he said, grinning. "I've been living in that state for years."

Rachel broke into a grin, gazing at him.

"Must be a first for you," he said. "Actually not being able to figure it all out. Actually coming to a place of the unknown: not being on top."

"A first, not being on top?" she cried, shoving him affectionately. "You were there, when James had the gun to my head! You saw my response when you shot Joshua."

"I'm sorry," Tristan said quickly, but Rachel was shaking her head.

"No, no," she said. "That's not what I mean…"

And then, suddenly, a new kind of light entered her eyes.

"Oh," she said.

"What?" he asked.

"The carnage," she said. "Walking through the carnage. That's our road."

"Walking through the rubble," Tristan whispered – and now, suddenly, Parliament was exploding before his eyes.

He gasped. The attack? He had seen it? Seen it with his own eyes? How did that make sense? He was sure he had only seen it on the news…

"Oh, dear God," he whispered. "Rachel! Rachel, I was there…"

"Where?" Rachel asked, reaching to grasp his shoulders. "Where were you?"

"At Parliament," Tristan whispered. "Alex! I was looking for Alex. I left Dad in St Peter's, on Christmas Eve. I went into Parliament: I saw the shooters, dressed in black, with silencers. I had no weapon! I knew I couldn't take them alone. I had to find Alex, but I couldn't find him…"

"He was with me!" Rachel interrupted. "Alex was always with me."

"Where?" Tristan asked.

"Away," Rachel said. "I had to get him away. John and I got him away: the work was taking too much of a toll on him."

"He wasn't there?" Tristan asked.

"No," Rachel said. "Not there."

"Bodies," Tristan whispered. "There were bodies, everywhere. More and more bodies. I couldn't stop them – couldn't stop the assassins. And then…"

He closed his eyes. Connor! Rachel's father! He opened his eyes again, to look into the darkness.

"I don't know if you want me to say," he whispered.

"Tell me," she said.

"Your father," he said. "I saw him! I saw him running, out of Parliament: I saw Kensington run after him. I had no weapon! He was crying out, Rachel! Crying out, as he ran, to my father – running into St Peter's, to be with my father…"

Rachel's hands were trembling on his arms.

148

"Did you go in?" she asked.

"I'm so sorry," he breathed. "I couldn't bring myself to go in. I knew they would both be dead when I arrived."

Now Rachel was grasping him to herself: her arms were moving around him. Tristan closed his eyes.

"Must we go back?" he asked. "Into Ground Zero?"

"We must," Rachel said. "Both of us must."

"Then what is your Ground Zero, Rachel?" Tristan asked. "What rubble must you walk through?"

Rachel drew back and smiled sadly at him.

"The same as you," she said, "for my father."

"And for your mother?" Tristan asked.

Rachel frowned, and looked away toward the horizon.

"Bodies dead," she said. "Parliament exploding. Carnage, Tristan! Rubble everywhere."

"Rubble?" Tristan asked.

"Blood," Rachel said. "Corruption, poison: death! Death, everywhere! Everyone's death. Death, instead of life. Smothering, explosive, owning: owning all things – an all-consuming appetite…"

"A beast…" Tristan murmured.

Rachel sat herself back down on the rock – she buried her face in her knees, and wrapped her arms around her legs.

"She brought death," Rachel said. "And yet the greatest death was already resident within her."

"A tsunami…" Tristan murmured. He sat himself alongside her – he reached to lay an arm around her shoulders.

"She changed," Rachel whispered. "Connected, present, a mother – and then gone, and then shooting, and then death."

"You remember her?" Tristan asked – and Rachel lifted her head, reaching to cling to his hand, staring again out into the horizon. The moon! She was looking at the moon lifting on the horizon.

"I remember her," she whispered.

"Your father…"

"Loved her," Rachel finished. "He knew his own weaknesses. He knew his own flaws."

"Your brother…"

"Disappeared," Rachel said.

"And you," Tristan murmured. "What happened to you?"

Rachel's face contorted as she stared forward. "What happened to me?" she whispered. "I disappeared too. Into books. Into work. Into…"

And now her eyes filled with tears. "…into trying to save everyone else."

Her gaze intensified, staring at the moon. And then she closed her eyes.

"Shine the Light," she said. "Whatever the cost."

149

And now Tristan moved both arms around her.

She was stiff: her body was stiff. But then she started to relax in his embrace.

"I admire you," he said.

"Don't," she choked. "I'm a worthless…"

"…piece of shit," Tristan said, surprised. Swearing? Swearing, in the Light? "Yes, I know you feel that way," he said, "but I happen to know that's untrue, and so do you."

"My worth doesn't matter," Rachel said. "It's not the point of life."

"What is the point?" Tristan asked.

"Love," Rachel said. "Light. To shine the Light. To work out the Love. That is what is worthy. That is what is good. I have no need for self-worth."

Tristan drew back to gaze at her. Stoic! She was stoic.

"You are owned by another," he said.

"Thoroughly owned," Rachel said.

"And so am I," Tristan said.

"I'm glad for it," Rachel replied.

"And so," Tristan said, "what now? The morning is coming: the sun will rise, to join the Light."

"We will walk," Rachel said. "Together, we will walk down this road, until we reach the end: until we reach our destination."

"And what is our destination?" Tristan asked. "Where are we headed on our road?"

Rachel's eyes suddenly became lit with mischief.

"To the end," she said. "To Resolution."

"To Resolution?" Tristan asked. "What kind of resolution?"

Rachel smiled at him.

"It's a new year," she said.

"Yes," Tristan said.

"2033," Rachel said.

"Yes," Tristan said.

"Two thousand years after Christ," she said.

"Yes," Tristan replied.

"So then," Rachel said. "It's time."

"Time?" Tristan asked.

"Time," Rachel said, "for the end to return to the beginning."

And now, suddenly, their view disappeared.

CHAPTER TWENTY-ONE: Trust

Wellington.

Tristan swallowed. How had they arrived? The Light! The Light had transported them somehow.

The right time...

They were standing on the sand at Oriental Bay. Tristan looked across the waters, skipping with the Light, to the church on the hill, on the other side – the cross lifting up to the sky.

Rau! Rau Petera was dead!

Tristan turned toward the street: the retaining wall! The tsunami retaining wall had gone.

Rachel was standing next to him, casting her eyes over the sand – looking across the water to the left, toward...toward...

Tristan reached for her hand.

"Let's go," he said. "It's time."

And he led her, by the hand, down the street.

The streets were deserted. Tristan frowned: why should they be? Why deserted? Why not people happily going their ways? He led Rachel along the waterfront, through the streets: he led her down Lambton Quay.

The shops were deserted.

Tristan felt uneasy. A ghost town? Their capital had become a ghost town, in their absence?

Rachel's hand tightened on his.

"Courage," she whispered. "Courage."

"The weapon?" Tristan asked. "The weapon did this?"

"Maybe it wasn't Joshua's weapon," Rachel said. "Maybe it was a different kind of weapon."

His eyes were wandering forward, toward...toward...

He pulled back, but now Rachel was moving forward: now she was taking the lead.

"We're almost there, Tristan," she said – and in that moment she felt like a young child to him: a young girl. "Just a few more steps, and we're home."

"Home..." he choked, and now his father's face was before him, in their lounge: and now Mark was looking out of their windows toward Wellington Harbour.

"It's often choppy in Wellington," Mark said. *"It's often windy."*

"Horizontal rain!" Tristan said.

"Yes, but..." And now Mark's eyes came back to Tristan. *"It's still home."*

"Home..." Tristan whispered – and now Rachel drew him into the opening.

The Beehive – he lifted his eyes, expecting to see the rising ten stories of the grey hive: the windows, the stone. Instead he saw rubble, a metre deep in parts, scattered across the Parliament gardens, and behind, the rubble of Parliament House.

151

Explosions! Explosions! Tristan gasped. Kensington was running across the road, after Connor: setting off explosions, behind his back! Connor's face was white, staring at the explosions – his body, shaking with sobbing…

"A sanctuary!" he cried out. "Oh, please God: a sanctuary!"

And he was thrusting himself up the steps to St Peter's.

Tristan looked up those same steps now. The glass doors were still broken. But the Light…the Light was moving through the shattered doors, beckoning him.

He drew in a breath.

"I saw them in there before," he whispered. "I saw them dead. I saw my father tortured."

Rachel's hand was on his shoulder: the doctor.

"There is no darkness that can separate us from the Light," she said. "There is no darkness that will overcome the Light."

"Is that the Truth?" Tristan whispered. "Or just what we would wish to believe?"

And now Rau's brown face was before him – his gentle smile: his embrace, for Tristan there on his knees, after having shot Joshua.

"Houhanga a rongo," Rau said. "Be at peace, Tristan. 'By his wounds, we are healed.'"

"By Joshua's wounds…" Tristan whispered.

"I saw him dead," Rachel said. "John saw him alive."

"He has come," Tristan said. "He has made his residence within me."

And now he saw Joshua standing, at the top of the stairs, beside the shattered glass – gesturing for Tristan to enter.

"Do you trust me?" Joshua asked, his face gentle: his smile subtle.

"I do," Tristan said.

"More than death?" Joshua asked.

"More than death," Tristan said.

"More than the pain and death of your father?"

Now Tristan held his breath, watching him, and then he thrust himself up the steps to stand alongside him.

"I can carry his pain and death now," he said. "I can do it." And he turned back.

Rachel was behind him, still at the bottom of the steps.

"Come," Tristan said – and Rachel ground her teeth, looking at the shattered doors.

"It's hard," she whispered. "I didn't see him."

"You will," Tristan said. "You will see him."

"I never saw him," Rachel said, her eyes filling with tears. "I wasn't there when he died."

"Come," Tristan said, reaching out his hand to her – and Rachel walked up the stairs to stand next to him, taking his hand.

Tristan turned. The church was dark – there was no interior light. The Light was hesitating: the Light was waiting.

152

"Come," he whispered – and now he walked over the shattered glass inside, and released Rachel's hand.

The Light flooded into the church. Tristan gasped, and lifted his face: the stained glass windows – they were rich with colour, almost overwhelming with intensity: red, blue, green – alive! They were alive!

"Tristan," his father's voice said.

Tristan stared up at one particular window: Christ's second coming – the dead rising to life! The resurrection.

"Tristan," his father's voice repeated.

"Tristan," Rachel's voice gasped – and now Tristan lowered his eyes: and now he looked, down the aisle, to the altar, and the cross behind. Jesus wasn't on the cross anymore! The cross was empty…

And alongside the empty cross, was…was…

Tristan swayed on his feet. His father's face was naked, looking at him: his blue eyes wide. Tristan launched himself down the aisle – he thrust himself forward. Look at him! Look at him, tall, astonished – the Light, dancing around his face: the Light, carrying him…

Weeping took Tristan. He reached out – he grasped a hold of his father's arms: he grasped a hold of his face.

"Alive?" Mark whispered, reaching to touch his face. "You're alive? I'm alive?"

Tristan grasped him into his arms, against his chest.

"Alive," he whispered. "We're alive." And he reached now for his father's wrists. The torture! The marks of torture. The bullets into his wrists! He reached to stroke them, but peered down with Mark to them, and found them gone.

"Alive…" Mark whispered – and now he grasped Tristan's arm, his blue eyes fervent.

"Kensington," he said.

"You wouldn't believe it," Tristan said. "I'd have to show you."

"Alex."

"Safe," Tristan said. "Alive. He went through hell, but he's alive."

"Then…" Now Mark's eyes misted, finding him. "What about…what about…?"

Tristan held his eyes, holding his breath again.

"I don't know yet, Dad," he whispered. "I haven't seen them."

Mark grasped his hand – he turned him back down the aisle.

"They're alive," he whispered, his hand trembling. "They have to be."

And now Tristan noticed a body lying on the ground, next to the altar.

"Oh!" Mark cried out – and he knelt quickly next to the body, reaching out for a pulse. "James! James!" And tears filled his eyes.

Tristan's vision blurred. He looked up, down the aisle, to Rachel: to her pale face.

"Come," he choked – and she came.

CHAPTER TWENTY-TWO: Justice

Rachel stared down the aisle of St Peter's.

Light was filling the church: Light penetrating through the stained glass windows. Tristan was standing with his father, alive again…but…but a body was lying still at their feet.

Mark was poring over the body: praying! He was praying, with tears. Rachel trembled. She walked, one foot ahead of another – she looked at the quiet intensity in Tristan's green eyes. She lowered her eyes to the body at her feet.

It was her father.

Rachel caught her breath. Pain took her: she hadn't grieved! Hadn't had a chance to grieve! And now, here he was, at her feet: dead! Shot! A bullet-hole through his chest.

"Who?" she whispered, swaying on her feet.

"You know who," Tristan said, reaching out a hand to her shoulder. "You already wanted him dead."

Kensington. Rachel closed her eyes. Kensington was alive, and her father was dead?

"Justice," she pleaded. "Justice."

She opened her eyes – and now Joshua was standing in front of her, standing on the other side of her father's body.

His brown eyes were on her.

"Do you remember?" he asked, and Rachel reached her hands up to her face with tears. Grief! Another kind of grief.

"I remember," she whispered. "I'll always remember."

Joshua, shot! Shot, in front of her, while her father stood by: while her father was ordering the execution.

"Life is found in me," Joshua said, gesturing around them to the Light. "I carry the Death, in my own substance: I carry it, that others may live. But what if some might reject the offer? What if some might prefer to shoot?"

"They don't know," Rachel said. "They don't know what they're doing."

"You're right," Joshua said, his gaze intent on her. "They don't know."

"He regretted it," Rachel whispered, tears welling up in her eyes. "When he could see what he had done, he regretted it."

"But he couldn't undo it," Joshua said. "Could he, Rachel?"

Rachel was silenced before him.

"Do you still think it is unjust?" Joshua asked. "For me to allow Kensington to live and your father to die?"

Agony took her. She turned away from him: she leaned heavily against the altar. Her father had shot him: there was no denying this! There was no denial.

"No," she whispered. "It's not unjust."

The Death Sentence? An eye for an eye? If there was ever one who had the right to declare the Death Sentence, it was Joshua himself.

She sank down against the altar – she buried her head in her arms.

"Why not take me?" she asked. "Take my life as payment instead."

"You don't know what you're offering," Joshua said. "You haven't tasted Hell."

"A life for a life," Rachel said into her knees. "That's fair."

"Do you think your life is enough to pay for mine?" Joshua asked – and Rachel looked up at him, trembling.

"Never," she whispered. "Then the debt can't be repaid."

"I have a right to his life?" Joshua asked.

"Yes," Rachel said. "All life comes from God: God has a right to reclaim all of it."

And she looked down at her father's body.

Mark was still praying fervently over him: Joshua was standing, watching him.

"Which would you choose, Rachel?" he asked, lifting his eyes back to her. "My death, or the death of your father?"

"Neither," Rachel said, a lump growing in her throat. "I love you both."

"But if you must choose, Rachel," Joshua asked. "Who would you choose to live?"

Intensity gripped her. "You," she whispered. "I would choose you. I would save you: the innocent one – the right one, with all authority over our choices."

"Good," Joshua said. "You have chosen well: but this is not your choice to make."

And now he knelt down next to her father.

Mark lifted his eyes from his prayer – he stared at Joshua.

"You're here," he whispered. "You've been here all along."

"In his mind?" Joshua asked him, gesturing to James. "In his heart?"

"Not always," Mark whispered, "but in the end. In the end he knew himself: in the end he knew what he had done."

"'A sanctuary,'" Joshua said. "He cried out to God for a sanctuary, in the midst of his failure."

"You are the sanctuary," Mark said. "You are the shelter, in the midst of our failures."

And Joshua laid a hand on Connor's head.

Rachel stared at him, kneeling over her father. He was going to bring him back? But that meant...

"No," she pleaded, kneeling next to him – reaching out to lay a hand on Joshua's shoulder. Blood! His blood. "Please..."

"It's not your choice to make, Rachel Connor," Joshua said. "The choice is between your father and God."

And now his face contorted – and now beads of blood were appearing on his forehead.

Rachel tightly closed her eyes. Death! Death. Joshua was drawing her father's death onto himself! Taking it into his very nature! Consuming it with himself.

"I'm so sorry," she whispered. "I'm so sorry, I'm so sorry, I'm so sorry..."

155

Joshua's body stiffened, beneath her hand, but now it was easing – and Rachel opened her eyes.

Her father was awake. She stared down at him: at his wide eyes, fixed on Joshua.

"You," he whispered. "It's you."

"It is me," Joshua said.

"You brought me back," Connor whispered.

"I did," Joshua said.

"You brought me back because…because you are the King."

And now his body stiffened – and now he launched himself to his feet.

Rachel could read the thoughts in his eyes. The King? As Prime Minister he had assassinated the true King?

"Parliament was dismantled," Joshua said to him. "Everything you feared has come to pass. At one level, you were right."

"Yes," Connor said, "but…but I didn't realize…"

"No," Joshua said. "There are many other levels."

"…that…that to be truly free, you have to let the freedom go."

"Yes," Joshua said – and now he was smiling: now he was reaching out a hand.

"Come," he said. "Let me show you what true freedom looks like."

And he drew Connor to his feet, and walked down the aisle.

Rachel hurried after her father and Joshua – she stood on the outside steps of St Peter's, and looked out toward the carnage: the rubble of the Beehive and Parliament.

"Democratic freedom," Joshua said, "only works under true authority."

"Yes," Connor said, gazing across the courtyard in disarray.

"But where does the true authority come from, James?" Joshua asked. "You are all merely brothers and sisters. Humanity leading itself is only the blind leading the blind. Why wouldn't you all fall into a pit?"

And now he reached out his hand: and now the rubble began to shake.

Rachel stood, fixed, staring. A dream! Surely it was a dream. Surely she would awaken soon. But she knew it was somehow real.

The stone was regathering in the right place. The glass was reforming.

Joshua was rebuilding the Beehive.

Her father was weeping. Another chance! Another chance. The Light was surrounding Joshua, lifting the rubble: restoring the structure.

"Freedom works when it knows its own limitations," Joshua said. "When it humbly acknowledges its own boundaries."

"When it knows when to stop," Rachel whispered – and now her father, wide-eyed, was straightening.

"A Constitutional Monarchy," Connor whispered. "A King…a king endorsing freedom."

"But a freedom with boundaries," Joshua said, smiling at him. "For what kind of King would want his people to lead themselves into the Pit?"

156

And now he was turning to Rachel.

A spade! A little spade was on her hand. She stared at it – she looked up into Joshua's face.

"The knowledge of good and evil," he said. "The knowledge, outside of our Domain."

"Take it," Rachel said, hurriedly laying the spade in his hands. "We can't carry it alone."

"Knowledge without boundaries brings death," he said. "I will take your knowledge: I will undo it."

"Undo it," Rachel whispered. "Make us a new humanity."

"We will remake you," Joshua said. "We will start again."

And he turned, and Parliament was standing.

Tristan was alongside her now: his eyes wide – his face bright.

"The explosion," he said. "It's been undone."

"It's been transcended," Mark said, standing behind him. "It's been overcome."

"A new day," Joshua said. "A new kind of freedom."

"A new day," Rachel whispered – and now Joshua turned away: and now her father was standing in front of her.

His eyes were filled with tears. Rachel stared at him – she started to weep before him.

"Can you believe it?" he whispered, reaching out to touch her face. "How can it be possible?"

"It is possible," Rachel whispered. "And salvation is also a miracle."

"A new life," her father said. "A new kind of life."

"A new kind of life," Rachel said – and she wrapped her arms around him, and held him tight.

His body was trembling in her arms. She held him for a long time: he held her, in return. She looked over his shoulder, at the new Beehive: at the new Parliament, embraced in the Light.

"Freewill," she murmured. "Freewill continues."

"How could it not?" Mark asked. "Freewill is freedom."

"But a freedom that gives up evil, of its own choice."

"Yes," Mark said.

"A freedom that aligns itself with the Light."

"Yes," Mark said.

"Choice," Rachel said. "There is choice."

And she pulled back from her father, walked down the steps of the cathedral, crossed the road, and wandered into the Parliament grounds.

CHAPTER TWENTY-THREE: Confrontation

Rachel stood in the Parliament Grounds.

The Light was moving over and through the pohutukawa trees: new roses and camellias were growing before Rachel's eyes, tucked inside the black iron fence. She reached down: she touched a rose. The deep crimson was lit, from within: she stooped to smell the flower – to drink in its rich fragrance. Then she turned.

Her mother was standing in front of her.

Rachel froze. She stared at her.

Pam was still dressed in that same floral dress in her father's photo on his desk – Rachel still remembered: her own matching shirt her mother had bought her. She felt a bit sick.

Now her mother wandered alongside her: now she was reaching, and plucking the same rose.

"Lovely," she said. "Just like ours at home."

Now Rachel's head was spinning. She desperately looked around herself.

"Rachel," a voice said – and it was Tristan, standing a little apart.

"I can't do this," Rachel whispered to him.

"You can do it," Tristan said. "Courage, remember? Courage."

And Rachel drew in a deep breath, and faced her mother's eyes.

"Your father's proud of you," she said. "Qualifying as a specialist! He couldn't be more proud."

"He died," Rachel said. "Didn't you see? Don't talk about him. Don't talk about anything."

"I think we need some more of these flowers at home."

"I don't think so."

"And when we're done, we'll get some of those, too," And she flicked her hand out towards some camellias. "Pink and purple," she said. "Red and orange. Which colour do you think is best?"

"I don't care what colour…"

"Maybe when your father starts back at his job, we can build a bigger garden – maybe add some lemon trees, and apple trees…"

"Shut up!" Rachel cried out. "Can't you see he died? Can't you see he's back? Can't you see everything he's been through?! What do I care about bullshit flowers?"

She stared at her – at her widening eyes – and then stepped back, flushing. What had she done? Attacked her own mother? In the Light? In Joshua's Light?

She looked around herself, and started to beat her own chest. Guilt! Guilt! There was no answer! There was no solution! Just entrapment! Just entrapment with a woman who could not see; who would not see. Failure! Failure! There was no way forward!

"You're turning into a nasty piece of work," her mother said. "You used to be such a perfect child."

"The perfect child," Rachel whispered, starting to turn around: starting to feel vertigo. "Why am I here? Why have I come?"

"Ground Zero," Tristan's voice said. "You have come to face Ground Zero."

"Ground Zero," Rachel whispered.

"I'm cutting you out of my inheritance," her mother said. "You've turned into a spoilt brat."

"Fine," Rachel whispered. "I'll make it on my own! I'll make it alone."

And she threw herself out of the spinning wheel.

Now she found herself on her knees at Joshua's feet.

"I'm a piece of shit," she whispered to him. "But I know you accept shit back again."

"You should honour your parents," Joshua said. "You should seek what is good for them."

"I am incapable of honouring her," Rachel said, "while she is trampling me underfoot. I am destined to fail."

"Yet I am destined to succeed in you."

"I don't know what to do. I know what should be: I know what is."

"Go back," Joshua said.

"Back where?" Rachel asked.

"The lion will lie down with the lamb, and a child shall lead them."

"The child..."

"Go back," Joshua said – and he touched her head, and Parliament faded away.

Her mother was screaming.

Rachel cowered against the wall in her room. What was wrong now? Her father's voice was rising – now he was slamming the door! Rachel jumped. Her brother: where was her brother? Somewhere in there? Gone? Was he gone?

With trembling legs, she left her room.

Joshua...Joshua was her friend, wasn't he? A wooden crucifix had fallen from its hook in the hall. She reached for it – she lifted it up. She wandered into her mother's room.

Her mother was lying on her bed, hair messy, face wet: eyes distraught.

Rachel looked at her: pain seared her mind.

"What does she need, little Rachel?" Joshua's voice asked. "What does your mother need?"

Rachel tilted her head, looking at her.

"Mummy," she whispered – and she moved forward and drew the blankets up under her chin. "I'll take care of you."

Her mother was starting to cry! Rachel laid the crucified Jesus carefully under the sheets with her mother, and then rushed out. Her doll! Where was her favourite doll? She grabbed her off her bed, rushed back in to her mother's room – laid her doll under the sheets next to Jesus.

159

"There, Mummy," she said. "Everything's going to be okay now, see? Everything's going to be all right."

Her mother's face was brightening! Her eyes were widening.

Hands were drawing Rachel away: arms were moving around her. Her voice lifted into a scream. Pain! Pain! Her mother's pain.

She beat against the chest that was holding her: Tristan! It was Tristan. She fought with the pain. He was handing her to another! To another.

Other arms were moving around her: whose arms? Her father's arms.

"Daddy!" she screamed, beating his chest. "Daddy, Daddy, Daddy…"

The arms were holding her, and her father's face looked white: contorting! Actually contorting with her pain!

She wrestled against him – she sank down to her knees in exhaustion. A child! She was just a broken child.

"What do you see in her?" Joshua asked.

"A woman more broken than I am," Rachel whispered. "A child more crushed."

And she sank down onto her face at his feet, and wept.

Joshua's hand was on her head. "You kept her alive," he said.

"The burden was too great," Rachel whispered into the ground.

"But not now," Joshua said. "Not now, with me."

And she lifted her face, to see him stretching out his hand to her.

"A love stronger than death," he said, his brown eyes dancing. "A Light greater than your darkness."

"A purpose," Rachel whispered, gazing into his eyes. "A path."

"To shine the Light, whatever the cost," Joshua said.

"To shine the Light, whatever the cost," Rachel repeated – and she reached for his hand, and was pulled up.

She was standing on her own feet: she was swaying slightly. Parliament was in front of her, intact. Her father was a few feet away. Tristan was next to her. And…and her mother was still there.

Rachel swallowed. Her mother's eyes were on her: green! Green eyes, frowning…older hands, reaching…

She was wearing a crucifix around her neck.

Rachel gazed at her – she gazed at the crucifix.

"Do you yield?" Joshua's voice asked her. "All of your adolescent rage: all of your youthful agony?"

And now his hand was in hers: and now he had handed her the deformed bullets.

Rachel stared at them: tears filled her eyes. She stared at him: at his gentle knowing smile.

"I yield," she quickly whispered, and she tucked the bullets safely away again into a pocket.

His smile widened.

"Of course you do," he said. "You see? I was destined to win in you. Always I was destined to win."

"Destined," Rachel whispered – and she reached out to touch Joshua's face, as a child, and Joshua's fingers found her cheeks, and he began to wipe away her tears.

CHAPTER TWENTY-FOUR: The Mace

Alex stood in Cathedral Square.

The Light was filling the square – it was moving over and through the Cathedral and out, beyond, into the distance. Alex gazed at it, and turned.

His father was standing in the middle of the square: tall, clothed in white. People were standing, looking at him – he was looking back. He looked down to the white Light passing through his own chest – he reached with his fingers to poke at his own heart, and looked up again at the people watching him.

"Isn't that Kensington?" someone asked.

"Robert," he replied. "My name is Robert."

"What happened to the clouds?" another asked. "What happened to the threats?"

"Gone," Alex said, moving forward toward his father. "That person has gone."

"Gone," his father murmured, looking at him – and Alex stood alongside him. His father reached to grasp his hand: Alex could feel him trembling slightly.

"I'm not used to this kind of exposure," Robert whispered to him. "I'm not used to standing in the Light."

"I know, Robert Kensington," Alex said, "but you will get used to it."

"There was so much darkness…"

"No more," Alex said, grasping his hand more tightly. "The darkness is no more."

He glanced up to see tears in his father's eyes – Kensington released his hand and moved closer to the Light: closer to the crowd.

"I was lost," he said. "I'm sorry."

"You were full of power!" a man said. "What was that power?"

"Satan," Robert said. "The evil of my own heart. Both. Either. I was wrong."

Alex watched at him: watched his exposure. What would the crowd do, in the Light? A man was stooping – reaching, and now raising the mace of Parliament: the symbol attached to the top – 666, and the all-seeing eye.

"Is this yours?" he asked, lifting it high into the air.

Kensington looked up at the symbol – looked up high in the blue sky. Alex stared at it: the Shrine! His father's shrine. Now Kensington was swallowing – now he was walking up to the man.

"Give it to me," he said.

"What will you do with it?" the man asked him. "Use the same power? Conjure up the clouds, and the fear – try to rule over us again?"

"I will not," Kensington said.

"Why should we trust…?"

"The Light has come," Alex said. "The Darkness has surrendered."

"The mace has power," the man said. "It still has power, even with the Light."

"You're right," Kensington said. "That's why I must deal with it."

The man frowned. He searched Kensington's face – he turned to the others in the crowd.

"Give it to him?" he asked. The others shifted on their feet – some were reaching out fingers, to try to touch the Light: to explore it.

The man turned back – and now handed the mace to Kensington.

"Show us," he said. "Show us what to do with Satan; what to do with the evil of the heart."

"I will show you," Kensington said, grasping the mace – and he strode with his long legs across the courtyard toward the Cathedral.

"Here's what I say to the reign of corruption!" he cried out, lifting the mace high to the sky. "Here's what I say to the threat of a human holocaust! The acid rain has been neutralized! The true conquest has come!"

And he turned, dragged the doors of the Cathedral open, and threw the mace inside, closing the doors behind.

There was the sound of a small explosion. Alex stared at the Cathedral; Robert, in front of him, was also staring. The Cathedral shook slightly, and then was still.

Quiet laughter spread across the crowd. Alex moved again alongside his father: Robert looked a little bewildered.

"Go in," Alex said, gesturing to the Cathedral doors.

"In there?" Robert said. "I'm not worthy. I don't belong."

"It's not about being worthy," Alex said. "And of course you belong. Go in. That was the mace of Parliament you just threw in there: the mace that was corrupted, but still represents freedom."

"You're right," Robert whispered. "That mace is important."

And he opened the doors of the Cathedral again, and walked inside.

Alex passed his eyes over the crowd. What were they thinking? Men, women – there were children as well, boys and girls: bathed in the Light, but still uncertain – still questioning.

Leaderless? Were they leaderless?

Kensington's footsteps were sounding – and now the tall man appeared again, in the doorway of the Cathedral, carrying the mace in his right hand: the wooden staff with the golden crown on top – and above the globe, at the top of the crown, was the golden cross.

"Freedom!" Kensington cried out. "Freedom has been restored! Under sovereignty, under authority, freedom has been restored!"

And he strode into the middle of the courtyard and set up the mace, in front of the people.

They looked at the staff. They looked at Kensington. They looked surprised.

And now Robert turned to Alex, with tears.

"We have to go back," he said.

"Back?" Alex asked.

"To Wellington," Robert said. "We have to take this back to Parliament."

Alex looked at him. "But Parliament has been destroyed," he said. Explosions! Explosions to the Beehive and Parliament House.

163

Now Robert smiled. "I decimated it," he said. "I destroyed Parliament. But it has been restored."

"Restored?" Alex asked.

"It's time to return," Kensington said, light in his eyes – and then, suddenly, Cathedral Square disappeared.

Alex stood before Parliament.

Astonished, he gazed up at the buildings: restored! They had been restored! The Beehive was rising up to his left, ten stories, almost pristine, as if new – and Parliament House was alongside, stone strong, seemingly polished.

Joshua was standing in the courtyard.

Alex caught his breath. Joshua! Here...here he had been shot! Here his father, here Alex, here Mark Blake, here Tristan, had all carried out Joshua's execution. What was he doing now? Standing, his face quiet, filled with Light, as if waiting...

Kensington was standing nearby. Alex looked at his face: he was staring at Joshua – there was fear in his eyes! But now the fear was easing – now the Light was intensifying.

His father was carrying the mace in his right hand.

Joshua smiled, and now he reached out his hand.

"Come," he said.

Kensington moved his eyes over the Beehive and Parliament, and settled again on Joshua.

"I will come," he said – and he moved to stand before Joshua.

The brown eyes were on him, filled with Light. Alex watched as his father swayed under his gaze.

"Follow me," Joshua said – and Alex remembered the words his own father had said in Cathedral Square before the crowd, now on Joshua's lips. "Let me change your mind," Joshua said, pointing to Kensington's head. "Let me change your heart." He was pointing to Kensington's chest. "Let me have the work of your hands; let me have the desire of your soul."

And now he took the mace and pointed to the ground at his feet with it.

"Kneel," he said. "Follow me, in spirit, in thought and act, and I will save you."

Kensington looked at him – into the brown eyes, bright with Light. And he knelt before him.

Joshua laid his hand on Kensington's head: he murmured a few words Alex could not hear. Then he grasped Kensington's shoulders and lifted him back to his feet.

"It's done," Joshua said. "Parliament is restored. You will be the first Speaker of the House."

"What?" Kensington whispered.

"Democracy," Joshua said, smiling, handing the mace back to him. "You will safeguard freedom for the nation."

And Kensington fell back two steps, staring at the golden mace in his own hand.

Alex stared at him. The Speaker of the House? His own father? After all the corruption; after all the darkness?

"Beautiful," Alex whispered – and his father was turning to him, bewildered, with tears, and tears filled Alex's own eyes: but it wasn't over.

Joshua was moving closer to the Beehive.

Alex could see a group gathered near the entrance: who was it? Rachel! He could see Rachel, and an older woman next to her, and Tristan! And...and two men...

Alex peered to see – he wandered after Joshua. Who were they? Mark Blake! Mark was alive again, and...and James Connor...

Connor, the Prime Minister, was alive.

Alex looked at his face: white, astonished, staring at Joshua.

"Come," Joshua said – and he reached out his hand to Connor, and drew him back with him, toward Alex, and toward Kensington.

Connor was staring at Kensington: Alex felt a lump in his own throat. His father had shot Connor! He had shot him, and Mark Blake! Mark was following quietly behind: his face with a deep lit peace. He knew...Alex was sure he knew what was coming.

Joshua led Connor and Mark across the courtyard to Kensington.

Connor seemed caught, uncertain what to do: uncomfortable, staring at the tall man carrying the mace. But Mark...Mark was much more comfortable.

He stepped forward now: he reached out a hand to Kensington.

Alex watched his father stare at the bishop. Peace? The one he had tortured and killed was offering him peace?

He hesitated, and Alex wandered forward to him.

"He understands," Alex murmured to his father. "Mark understands what corruption means."

"The bishop," his father murmured – and he reached out his hand, and grasped Mark's hand.

But Connor...Connor was more difficult.

Kensington shifted on his feet before him: holding the mace in his right hand.

"You manipulated me," Connor said, holding his eyes. "You wanted to take over. You blew up Parliament. You shot me."

"I did," Kensington said, before him. "But everything I ever did has been undone, and I'm glad for it! I'm glad for it."

"This is my new Speaker of the House," Joshua said, gesturing to Kensington. "And this is my newly reinstated Prime Minister." And he gestured to Connor.

Connor's eyes were wide, looking at him. "Reinstated for the second time," he whispered. "A third chance at leadership, and I can hardly comprehend it..."

Kensington's eyes were on him. "I'm sorry," he said, and for a moment he seemed to Alex to be choking. "For a time I became as Satan incarnate..."

"That time has passed," Joshua said – and now his eyes were on Connor.

Connor looked between them: between Joshua and Kensington. He looked over Parliament House and the Beehive. Then he looked back to the mace.

"Well," he muttered, with a wry smile on his face, "if I fail this time you've seriously got to change the Parliamentary system. Who knows what lunatics you might get on the Throne?"

And Kensington handed the mace to Connor, and Connor held it for a moment, staring at it.

The Crown, with the cross above the globe, at the top.

"Hmmm," Connor said. "Hadn't really noticed that before."

And he handed the mace back to Kensington, turned, and walked back into Parliament.

CHAPTER TWENTY-SIX: The Legacy of the Thief

Alex looked at his father, holding the mace – standing alongside Joshua.

"Who would have thought," Alex said.

"Well," his father said, shrugging his shoulders. "Is it really that surprising?"

Alex remembered now – his father, on his knees at the communion rail, in a Catholic church.

"What went wrong?" Alex asked.

"You know what went wrong," Kensington said – and now, before Alex's eyes, the gun was to his mother's head.

"No," he whispered. "No." The thief! The thief was there! The thief was...was...and then, the eyes! The eyes, staring back at him, hard, pulling the trigger...

Alex fell: back! Back! But Joshua's hands were grasping him, lowering him gently to the ground; Joshua's face was over him, his brown eyes finding him. Light! Light...

"Easy," Joshua whispered. "It will be all right."

"Death," Alex whispered, reaching out to cling to him. "Death."

"There is also life," Joshua said.

"Death," Alex sobbed – and he closed his eyes, and shook his head. Darkness! Darkness. His father! His father had the thief! His father had his gun. He was...he was becoming the same...

"Oh my God," Alex whispered. "Oh my God."

Rachel's voice was near him now.

"Alex," she murmured. "What are you seeing?"

"The thief," he whispered. "The thief."

"What has the thief done?" Rachel asked.

"Rape," Alex said, writhing, his eyes closed. "Murder."

"Who is the thief?"

Alex opened his eyes – he looked into Joshua's face. Innocence! Light. Life. He lifted himself to his feet, and turned, to look at Parliament: destroyed, and then restored. He reached out to take the mace in his father's hand: the crown, and the cross.

"Satan," Alex whispered. "And our own corruption. Both, bound together in an escalating partnership of death. Satan incarnate: Satan, inherited, passed on through the fallen heart of humanity. The desire and outworking of evil."

"The thief comes to destroy," Joshua said, "but I have come to bring life: life in abundance."[15]

Alex stood before Parliament, the mace in his hand – and now Joshua was turning him.

His mother was emerging from under the trees.

---

[15] John 10:10 Paraphrased.

Alex stared at her. Bright face! Lit eyes. She looked surprised, looking around herself! Clothed in Light, a crucifix lying on her chest.

Alex dropped the mace; his father caught it.

His mother's eyes moved to Joshua, to his father, to the others, and then came to him.

Green. Her eyes were green.

Alex gazed at her, tears choking him, and she walked up to him.

"You," she murmured, reaching out to touch his face. "You're my Alex."

His voice was lifting, before her: lifting against his will, into a wail. Pain! Her pain! He remembered her pain: he carried it, in his very essence! And yet here she was, without pain? And yet here she was, alive? Not dead? Not conquered? Not destroyed by malice, by violation, by…by the thief?

"Alex," she said, in recognition – and now she broke into a radiant smile, and Alex threw both hands over his mouth. Was it possible to die, all over again? But this time, to die of happiness?

He laughed at the thought! A child! He was only a child with her, here, now: only a child, who had been broken, who now, in this place, was beginning to be restored…

She saw his laughter: she laughed with him. Tears were in her eyes – he reached up to finger her tears. Then he stepped back, and turned.

His father. He was staring at her: his face had fallen – stunned. He looked stunned.

She walked up to him: she stood, short, under his height. She reached out to touch his face.

The tall powerful man now broke into weeping: the intense blue eyes were drowning in tears.

Alex cried, watching him – Joshua took the mace, while Robert's hands rushed to his face. The Curse! The Curse was being lifted! The evil was being undone.

Joanna wrapped her arms around him – Alex thought his father might collapse: wondered if he might die. But, no: in this place, in this Light, overwhelming happiness could be sustained! In this place, joy could be breathed in as air, almost tangible – almost able to be touched.

His father's arms moved around his mother: the intense powerful eyes were closed, with his chin on her shoulder. Alex trembled on his feet – he turned away from his parents: he fell back a step.

Rachel's hand came to his. He looked up to her face: to her wonder, and tears.

"Beyond words," she whispered, and he nodded.

"Beyond words," he repeated – and he squeezed her hand.

His father drew back from his mother – and now stood alongside her, holding her hand.

169

"I am the way, the truth, and the life,"[16] Joshua said. "Those who are in me: even though they die, yet shall they live."[17]

And now he was turning away.

Alex looked, and Rachel's hand tightened again on his.

"Oh," she whispered.

"What?" Alex asked.

"Tristan," she said – and Alex looked across the courtyard toward Tristan and Mark Blake. Joshua was approaching them! Tristan's face looked white.

"Oh," Rachel said again. "You have to see this."

And she drew him, by the hand, and moved him forward.

---

[16] John 14:6 Paraphrased.
[17] John 11:25 Paraphrased.

Tristan stared at Joshua, approaching them again, across the courtyard of Parliament. He was coming to them? To them, next?

"Dad," Tristan whispered. "I don't like this. I'm scared."

"Don't be," Mark said, alongside him – reaching to grasp his hand. "Just trust. Trust in him."

Tristan glanced at his quiet blue eyes and looked back at Joshua.

"I killed him," Tristan whispered. "How can…how can I grasp…?"

"I killed him too," Mark said, his older, wiser voice a comfort. "He's over that."

"That's Alex's mother," Tristan said, looking at the woman holding Kensington's hand. "I'm sure of it."

"Yes," Mark said.

"What if…" Tristan choked, and made himself continue. "What if…?"

Mark squeezed his hand tighter. "Life and Death are God's domain," he said. "They are God's choice."

"Dare I hope?" Tristan asked. "Dare I?"

"I dare," Mark said – and now Joshua was standing in front of them.

Tristan shifted uncomfortably on his feet before the brown eyes.

"Listen," he began, stuttering a bit. "That's really great, what you did there, with Alex's Mum, and the whole Parliament thing is awesome, and…and I know I put you through hell and everything, and…and I just want you to know, that if you decide not to…"

"What he's asking is," Mark interrupted, "will you be bringing his mother and sister back to life too?"

Tristan held his breath, heart pounding; watching Joshua's face. Fear? It was still possible to feel fear, in the Light?

"You don't have to," he whispered, stuttering again. "I…I mean, you'll do the right thing…whatever that means, you'll do the right thing…" And now tears were filling his eyes, and his body was shaking.

Joshua grasped his hand.

"Peace," Joshua whispered. "Don't be afraid."

"I'm terrified," Tristan blurted. "You have power over life and death. I love you! I love you! I'll accept it: whatever you choose! But I'm still terrified."

"I know," Joshua said, and Tristan felt his other hand on his shoulder. "Trust me."

"Even if they should remain dead?" Tristan whispered.

"Yes," Joshua said, holding his eyes. "Trust me, with their lives and with their deaths."

Tristan swallowed, looking at him – and then he sank down to his knees before him, and closed his eyes.

"You are the Master of Life and Death," he said. "I will trust you: whatever happens! Whatever happens."

171

"Good," Joshua's voice said above him – and now he was reaching down, and grasping Tristan back to his feet.

"Tristan," a voice said – and he turned around, and there was Selena.

Her white face was radiant, framed by her long black curls. Her blue eyes were lit with an innocent kind of mischief.

"Selena!" he cried – and he rushed to her, and grasped her into his own arms.

"Have you seen Mum?" he asked her, turning quickly, looking around across the pavement. "Is Mum safe too?"

"Easy," Selena said. "Where am I?"

"Back at Parliament," Tristan said hurriedly. "A lot's changed since you left."

"Alex…" Selena asked.

"Yes, yes," Tristan said impatiently. "He's fine! Mum! Where's Mum?"

And he released her, and turned around, and around, searching! Searching, and not finding.

His eyes settled on his father: on Mark's sadness.

"Dad," he whispered. "She's gone?"

Tears were filling Mark's eyes. "I'm sorry, Tristan," he whispered.

"An accident," Tristan said, with deep pain "A road traffic accident."

"I was speeding," Mark whispered. "I shouldn't have sped."

And Tristan reached out to touch his face.

"I'm sorry, Dad," he whispered. "I speed too…"

Mark smiled sadly – but then his gaze shifted, over Tristan's shoulder: then his eyes widened.

"Oh," he whispered. "Thank God."

And Tristan turned.

His mother was standing in front of him.

Tristan gasped. Her body! Her body was before him, in his mind: under the blood stained sheet. Dead! She was dead, and his father was sitting alongside her, face in his hands.

But now…now she was standing in front of him: young and alive.

"Tristan!" she said, her green eyes wide. "Are you all right? Is Selena all right?"

And she turned, to find Selena – to draw her toward herself, and finger her curls.

"Look at you!" she said. "Such a beautiful young lady!"

Selena's blue eyes were wide, staring at her: stunned.

Their mother's eyes came back to Tristan: frowning, concerned.

"What happened?" she asked.

"You died," Tristan whispered, and his mother's eyes moved to his father.

"Mark?" she asked. "I remember we were driving…"

"Teresa," Mark choked. "I killed you…"

"Don't be silly," Teresa said, reaching to touch his arm. "You mean there was an accident?"

Tears blurred Tristan's eyes. His mother was gracious! When he…when he had…

172

"I'm sorry," he whispered. "I'm sorry…"

His father was hugging her – and Selena was pressing in, between them, hugging her. Tristan smiled sadly at his family: standing a little apart, suddenly taken by shame…and then he felt Joshua's hand on his shoulder.

"I'm a wretch," Tristan whispered. "I blamed him. I drove him into darkness."

"No," Joshua said. "You only enhanced the guilt he was already carrying."

"I love him," Tristan whispered. "I love them all."

"Of course," Joshua said.

"It was my fault," Tristan said. "I don't deserve to be a part of this. I ruined it. I ruined it all."

Joshua's hand tightened on his shoulder.

"War," Joshua said. "You were at war. The enemy was pressing in, on all sides: you were firing, in self-defence – you were firing out of desperate survival."

"I don't deserve…"

And now Joshua turned to him: and now the bullets were there, deformed, in Joshua's hand, pressed in to Tristan's hand – held between them in a grasp.

Joshua's brown eyes were on him.

"I forgive you," he said, and Tristan broke into weeping before him.

"I don't deserve…" he whispered, and Joshua smiled sadly.

"It's not about that," he said. "It's about what you need. It's about what I want to give to you."

And now Tristan looked at the bullets in his hand: the bullets he had sent into Joshua's chest – the bullets Joshua had willingly taken. He looked back into the brown eyes.

"I'm so sorry," he whispered.

"I know," Joshua said. "Of course, I know."

And Tristan looked at his family, embracing, and looked back to Joshua.

"You're still human?" he asked. "Unleashing the Light of God, but still human…?"

"Yes," Joshua, said, his eyes smiling. "I am still human."

"Then…" Tristan shifted awkwardly on his feet, glanced at his family and back at Joshua. Should he? He hesitated, vacillated, and then threw his arms around Joshua – drawing him to his own chest.

Joshua's arms moved around him, and Tristan closed his eyes. An embrace! A male embrace. Who was this one to him? His friend. His brother. His saviour. His…his embodiment of God.

"Peace," Joshua murmured to him. "Peace, Tristan."

And Joshua was pulling back, grasping Tristan's hand – and now he led him into the heart of his family.

Arms were around him: bodies were pressing close in, on all sides. His father. His mother. His sister.

Love. Love had been resurrected.

Tristan drew back, from his family. He looked over his father's happy tears; his mother's live beauty, and his sister's light. He looked further over the courtyard, to Kensington, stilled, holding the mace and his wife; to Alex, wandering forward, drawing Selena into his arms.

He looked to the Beehive, restored, looking almost new: to Parliament House, standing strong.

He cried. And then he saw Rachel.

She wandered up to his side: she took his hand. Her face was wet – her eyes astonished.

"Well?" she whispered to him. "Is it done? Is it finished?"

Stunned, he looked at her – and looked back over the courtyard of Parliament. This place had exploded, before his eyes! And yet now…now…

"I…" he whispered back. "I don't know what to say."

"Resolution," Rachel said. "The end of our journey."

"The end?" Tristan asked. "Or just the beginning?"

Rachel smiled, and her face was pretty.

"Are they not the same?" she said. "Is not the end of one season the beginning of another? For you, the end returns to the beginning: and for me, a new season begins."

She was looking up, across the courtyard: Tristan could see John there, his quiet gentle smile for her. But Rachel was turning him toward another.

Across the courtyard, toward the street, in front of St Peter's, stood a Maori man.

Tristan stared at him – and then drew in a breath. Rau! It was Rau Petera! He rushed toward him – over the courtyard, through the gate, onto the street. His brown face was smiling: his brown eyes, with slight wrinkles, were twinkling.

"Rau!" Tristan cried, and he threw his arms around him, and Rau laughed, and embraced him in return.

"Kia ora, 'mate'!" Rau said. "Been doing much fishing lately?"

Tristan trembled. "Oh, Rau," he whispered. "You have no idea! No idea everything that's happened."

"Then I guess you'd better tell me," Rau said, drawing back – searching out his eyes. "Been getting up to much mischief since I've been gone?"

"No idea!" Tristan cried. "You have no idea!"

"Then tell me," Rau repeated.

"Well," Tristan began. "I took Rachel, Alex and John with me toward Parliament, and we heard the gunfire when you were shot, and…"

"Wait," Rau interrupted, grasping his arm.

"What is it?" Tristan asked, as Rau cast his eyes over the courtyard, looking at all the people: being surrounded by the Light.

"Okay," he said. "I think I have it now."

"Already?" Tristan complained.

"But you'll still want to tell me," Rau said, grinning, "so, let's do it in style."

174

"In style?" Tristan asked – and now Rau was pulling a fishing rod from behind his back.

"No way," Tristan said. "We can still do that? In the Light? Thought there'd be no death, or eating animals, or…"

"Well, we'll release them, of course," Rau said.

"It would still harm them."

"Not for long," Rau said. "And, anyway, we'll use plungers."

"'Plungers'" Tristan asked, grinning at him.

"It's something I got from Joshua," Rau said. "Tiny plungers. You suck them in and then you release them. No pain! No damage. Attraction! It's all about attraction."

"You know what this means, don't you?" Tristan asked.

"What?" Rau asked.

"We're going to be surrounded by the blighters," Tristan said. "There'll be no respect! We'll be knee deep in the ocean, and the fish will all around us, as if we're best friends."

"Exactly," Rau said, smiling – and Tristan glanced back to Joshua: to his brown eyes – to his Light.

"Best friends," Tristan murmured.

"You've got to go to the best places though," Rau continued. "Where the fish are! The fisherman should always go to the fish."

"Lazy," Tristan muttered, grinning. "The blighters are just lazy."

"Come," Rau said.

"What?" Tristan asked, and Rau was laying a hand on his shoulder, and Parliament disappeared.

175

CHAPTER TWENTY-EIGHT: Love

Rachel stood in the courtyard of Parliament.

Tristan had rushed across the road – toward Rau. They seemed to have disappeared. His family were standing quietly together, catching up. Alex and Kensington were standing on the other side, with Alex's mother – and Alex had drawn Selena in to see his father.

Rachel watched her face, looking up at the man: watched his face, white, looking down at her. She was reaching out a tentative hand – he was reaching out his own hand, to join hers. How could it be? How could it be possible? This man, who had dominated her: who had killed her. Now, there was reconciliation? Now there was a reversal?

Rachel was taken by the humility in Kensington's face: she was taken by the smile in Selena's eyes.

Miraculous. It was miraculous.

Rachel gazed at them, and then shook her head and searched the courtyard.

Her mother stood quietly next to the garden. Rachel wandered up to her, reached and plucked a blood red rose.

"Here, Mum," she said. "I think this one's nice."

"This one?" her mother asked. "You like this one the best?"

"I do," Rachel said.

"Okay," her mother said. "I'll see if I can grow this one at home."

Tears pricked Rachel's eyes. "Which ones do you like?" she asked, and her mother's eyes moved over the garden.

"Me?" she asked. "I...I don't know..."

"Maybe yellow?" Rachel asked. "Do you like orange?"

Pam looked down at the garden, frowning in confusion.

"I can't remember," she whispered. And now Joshua wandered past her, and touched Pam's arm, and her mother's face seemed to lighten: she looked younger.

"White," she said. "I like white."

"Really?" Rachel asked, intrigued. "Why white?"

"Because they look clean," her mother said. "Pure."

Rachel gazed at her. "And harder to find," she murmured to her. She searched the garden: a white rose! There was a white rose, hidden, behind the colours. She reached for it – she plucked it, and gave it to her mother.

"There," she said. "For you."

"Thank you," her mother said, and now her eyes were searching the garden again.

"Red," she murmured – and her fingers found a red carnation. She plucked it, and held it close to her chest.

Joshua's hand was on her arm – he was leading her away, toward the entrance to Parliament: toward her father.

Rachel gazed after her, and then John was before her.

176

"Well?" he said.

"Well?" Rachel asked – and now John was grabbing her hand: and now he was whisking her away.

He took her to a high place. Rachel looked around herself: Mount Victoria! They were standing on Mount Victoria, alone – grass tipping down the hill away from their feet, the blue waters of Wellington Harbour sparkling in the sun, the Beehive tucked away, hidden behind the high rise buildings of the city, and, across the waters, Lower Hutt...

There was a ferry...a ferry, moving out into the water, in the Light...

John reached for her hand.

"Love," he said. "Time for love."

"Time for love," she whispered, and he drew her body to himself.

They made love. Rachel trembled in his arms, and now he was murmuring into her ear.

"A new generation," he said. "A new season."

"A new generation," she whispered, and she reached down to finger her abdomen.

"No more curse," John murmured. "No more pain, or tears, or death."

"Just life," Rachel whispered. "Just life, in abundance."

"Just life," John said – and he made love to her again.

They lay, amongst the grass, on the top of the hill. The Light surrounded them – the Light surrounded all things.

"I remember," John murmured to her. "Joshua, here in the garden. I remember the cost."

There were tears in his eyes. Rachel reached up to touch his face.

"How long?" she asked. "How long will we remember?"

"Not long," John murmured to her. "The tears are fading. The pain is disappearing. The death resident within us is dissolving in the Light."

"Beauty," Rachel murmured, stretching out her arms – breathing in deeply. "I feel beauty."

"I see beauty," John said, and he smiled at her.

"I see strength," Rachel said, moving her eyes over his solid chin. "I see power." And she breathed in excitement.

She reached out to touch the Light joining them: she searched the heart and the mind surrounding and penetrating them.

"Goodness," she murmured. "Everything around and through us is good."

"Yes," John said, reaching to take her hand. "We are in his image again. We are pure again."

"The end is returning to the beginning," Rachel explored. "We are in a garden: a garden of Life."

"A garden of love," John murmured.

177

"No fruit of evil," Rachel said. "No spade, dig, dig, digging – digging, on and on, at risk of reaching the other side."

"Contentment," John said. "We are content."

"We are content," Rachel whispered – and she reached for him, and kissed him, and drew him to herself.

Light filled her. Light, and love. She drew away from him – she cast her eyes over the water.

The light sparkled; the blue waters touched the sky.

"Thank you," she whispered to the Light. "Thank you."

And she reached to the ground, and gathered stones in one spot. A memory! A memory of Joshua. Then she grasped John's hand, pulled him to her side, and skipped with him down the hill.

CHAPTER TWENTY-NINE: Fishing

Tristan stood on the sand at Ninety Mile Beach.

Rau was standing near him in the water, gentle waves lapping at his knees. He was holding a rod, with a line thrown out into the sea.

"Seriously?" Tristan complained to him. "You want me to use a plunger?"

"Attraction," Rau said, smiling at him. "It's all about attraction."

Tristan fingered his own rod, and the line attached. At the end was a little soft ball with the inside scooped out. It sucked! He touched his finger to it – it attached, and drew him in.

"So much for hunting," he muttered, and he glanced back up at Rau's warm face.

"Do you still feeling like hunting?" Rau asked, looking back at him, and Tristan shrugged.

"I don't know," he said, frowning, looking down at the plunger. "Do I?"

"Killing?" Rau asked. "Do you feel like killing?"

"No," Tristan said quickly – and he looked out across the water. Killing? He remembered, didn't he? Killing? And yet somehow the memory was fading.

"Why would I want to kill?" he asked his friend.

"Nuclear," Rau murmured to him. "Nuclear warfare. You have been changed from within."

"Changed?" Tristan asked.

"Come," Rau said, and he beckoned him into the water.

Tristan looked across the sparkling surface. The Light – the white Light was there, dancing with the water, beckoning him even more strongly than Rau: drawing him in to the depths.

He took a deep breath: he lifted his face to the brightness of the light blue sky. Light! The Light wanted to fill him! The Light wanted to penetrate him.

He threw his rod onto the sand. He waded into the water.

"Hey!" Rau's voice called out affectionately to him. "We're supposed to be fishing!"

"I am," Tristan whispered back to him. "I am fishing." And he dove into the water.

The water was clear, all around him! Fish! He could see the fish, dancing around him: snapper, trevally, salmon, weaving around his arms and legs, unafraid. He laughed underwater, and then rose to his feet, dripping, waist deep, under the sun.

"What's all that about, boy?" Rau's voice called out to him. "Needed a swim?"

"Yeah," Tristan said, grinning back at him. "If you're going to do it, do it right."

"You've changed, Tristan Blake," Rau said. "You're not the man you used to be."

Tristan looked at him. "Who did I used to be?" he asked.

"Afraid," Rau said, his brown eyes insightful. "I still remember your fear."

Tristan looked back toward the sand. The tide! The tide had been coming in.

179

"The tsunami," he murmured, and he looked into his friend's eyes. "The tsunami took me, but there was a boat."

"Ae," Rau said. "There was a boat."

"There was a man, on the shore," Tristan said. "There was God, in the flood."

"Ae."

"Death, and then life," Tristan said. "Darkness, and then Light."

"Te Atua," Rau said. "Te Tamaiti. Te Wairua."

"After death comes life," Tristan said. "After night comes day."

"The Light," Rau said, gesturing all around them. "The Light of te Atua."

Tristan gazed at him. "The Light of te Atua," he murmured. "The Light of God."

And he turned his face into the Light.

Memories…Memories whispered to him now. Shooting! He stiffened. He had shot others, but the shootings were fading. Death! His mother had died, but this memory also was fading. He was carried, from within: he was being changed, from within.

Joshua's face was before him now: his brown gaze, his gentle smile – his hand on his arm.

"Full tide," he had warned. *"It's coming."*

"To hell with your care," Tristan had replied.

Now he closed his eyes: now he shook his head. "What an idiot," he whispered to himself, grinning – and now Joshua was before him again, receiving his bullets.

Tristan looked at his friend, taking his shots: he went to his knees, in the water. Death had been taken into the grave! Murder had been transcended by new life.

"Houhanga a rongo," Tristan whispered, remembering Rau's words, his embrace, while kneeling next to Joshua's dead body. "Peace! You won for me my peace."

The water was all around him now: warm and easy, around his body. He lowered himself beneath the surface: he fully immersed himself.

"The Spirit of Atua is like the ocean," Rau's voice had said, after Joshua's death. *"Pure, life-giving, washing us clean."*

Tristan remembered: his gun! He had still held his gun, in his jacket pocket. He had hesitated to follow. He had lost his gun to Alex, and then to James! He had shot Kensington with Alex's gun, and thrown his own into the Hutt River…

"I believe you," he had said to Alex. *"I believe that Joshua is alive again."*

Under the water, he remembered his baptism.

"No gun," Rau had said. *"No gun holding you back."*

And he had lowered him under the water: a wave had covered his face, murky, and Rau had pulled him up out of the water.

But now he lingered – now he stayed under the surface.

"Tristan," Rau's voice sounded above him, through the water, but he remained.

Death. Rau's death! The shootings. The shootings at Parliament, and the explosions. Kensington, rushing after his father! Certain to kill his father, even as he had killed his sister…

180

Blame, and imprisonment…and yet…and yet an escape…Carnage, at the ferry! And yet, a way to run…

Run! Run! And yet, Alex's way: confront! Confront…

The Holocaust! And yet, Rachel's comfort. And yet John's quiet faith.

"I'm not ready to die, Rachel!" he had said to her, at Kaiapoi, on the eve of certain death.

"There is life beyond death," Rachel had said. *"There is a new beginning."*

Beyond humanity is God…

Alex had confronted his father and been killed. Rachel had confronted Kensington and been saved by the death of James. John and Rachel had joined in the Cathedral! Kensington had come, and targeted them: and targeted Rachel.

Yet…yet something had intervened.

What had it been? Oh, yes: the Light! The offer of the Light.

Rachel had reached Kensington! How? In the midst of his depravity, she had reached him, and…and he had chosen.

Light, instead of Darkness. Pain, instead of corruption. Death, instead of murder, and…and then new life…

The Light had come: a flash! A flash, into their bodies! Into their hearts! And now it was here to stay: raising the dead to life! Illuminating the darkness. Transforming humanity.

Nuclear.

Tristan lingered now, under the water. Rau's voice was calling out to him.

Life, or death?

He looked at the water, all around him: he looked at the fish. He looked up at the sun-light, penetrating the water: he looked at the white Light, penetrating all.

Faith? Faith stronger than death? Faith that would bring eternal life?

He breathed in the water.

He lived.

Rau's hands were reaching for him.

"Tristan!" he cried, dragging him up out of the water. "What are you doing? Don't be an idiot."

Tristan stared at him, swaying on his feet, dripping under the sun. He reached to grasp his friend's arms – he laughed.

"It's all right!" he said. "I can do it. I can breathe through the water. I can live through the tsunami."

"We're still only human!" Rau protested. "Still with lungs! Still with hearts!"

"He lets me breathe water," Tristan said, gesturing to the Light. "He sustains me through the death."

"Lungs are for air…"

"This isn't your typical water," Tristan said. "This isn't your usual swim."

"Not your usual swim?" Rau asked.

"It's a spiritual swim," Tristan said. "A spiritual conquest. Only this time, Rau; only now, because of him." And he gestured toward the shore: to Joshua, standing there: to his lit brown eyes.

Rau followed his gaze. "Fishing," he muttered. "He's still fishing, isn't he?"

"Ae," Tristan said to his Maori friend, his eyes on Joshua's gentle smile. "He'll always be fishing."

"I'll bet he won't use plungers on us," Rau said – and now Joshua was wading into the water toward them, his eyes set on Tristan.

Tristan held his breath, while Rau moved aside. The familiar gaze was searching him! What would he find?

"Look," Joshua said, gesturing across the sparkling water; lifting his hand to the sky. "What do you see?"

Tristan turned to look across the deep blue lit expanse.

"The Ocean," he breathed. "A whole new world."

"Your body was made for swimming," Joshua said. "Your heart was made for soaring."

And now, suddenly, he was grasping Tristan's shoulder.

"This is how you swim, Tristan," Joshua said – and he tugged him into the water.

Tristan sucked in a breath: he dove under the surface, following Joshua – deeper and deeper into the Ocean, holding his breath. But now Joshua was grasping him – now he was pulling him to the surface, turning him onto his back.

He sucked in another deep breath of air. He gazed up to the sky. Light! Light! He lay on the surface, floating.

Joshua was floating with him, by his side. They were far away from the shore: in the heart of the Ocean.

"The fishing is great out here," Joshua said to him. "In the depths – in the clear waters."

And he was shoving him back down under the surface.

Tristan dove again, deep, with Joshua's shove. Sunlight filtered through the water: the Light hovered near the surface. Tristan swam down into the darker waters – he could feel the fish, encircling his arms and legs, gently pressing into his body: he drew them up into the Light. They were all shapes and sizes, swimming all around him: many different colours; many different schools.

He broke the surface – he sucked in another breath. Joshua was floating next to him, in the Light, smiling.

"How many do you want?" Tristan asked.

"All of them," he said, gazing up at the sun. "I want all of them."

"I love these blighters," Tristan said, feeling some nibbling softly at his leg. "They're beautiful."

"I knew you would," Joshua said, closing his eyes, smiling.

"I love this fishing thing," Tristan said. "They're great little swimmers."

"Yeah," Joshua murmured.

Tristan gazed up at the sun: he reached out his fingers to the Light. Ask him? Ask him the burning question of the life before?

"Joshua?" he murmured.

"Yes?" he replied.

"Why all the pain?"

Joshua's eyes opened. His forehead creased into a frown, as he also reached up his fingers to touch the Light. For a moment Tristan thought he could see a faint memory of beads of blood on his face.

"Forget it," Tristan whispered. "It was my fault. It was all my responsibility. I shouldn't even be asking you, after everything you've done…"

"It wasn't all your responsibility," Joshua said, "but I do forgive you."

Tristan looked at his gaze into the Light. Was that it? Was that all that was needed? No – there was more.

"Salvation," Tristan said. "I needed salvation. My soul was stuffed." And Joshua nodded, turning to him: looking at him.

"And always," he said. "Always I will save you."

Was salvation it? No, there was more: more that he needed.

"Redemption," Tristan said. "I needed to be fixed." And Joshua smiled at him.

"That's why," he said.

"What's why?" Tristan asked, gazing at his brown eyes.

"That's why the pain exists," Joshua said – and he turned back into the Light.

Tristan searched him. Redemption? Redemption required pain? He didn't understand, but looking at Joshua basking in the Light, he didn't care that he didn't understand.

"Renew our lives," Tristan whispered, "to bring you glory."

Joshua smiled into the Light, with closed eyes. "We will," he said. "We will renew your lives, forever."

And he reached out to grasp Tristan's hand into his own.

Peace…Tristan felt peace, floating there with Joshua, on the surface of the water: bathing in the Light.

The fish were swimming around them both! Now they were starting to nibble at Joshua.

The memories of war were fading: the shooting! The death. Tristan reached up his own fingers – the Light! It was dancing around him! The Light was beckoning to him.

He eyeballed it: the Light wanted to own him! He could see it in the way it shone! He knew this kind of Light wouldn't go by halves: it was searching for his all. It would take his all.

Was he ready? Was he ready to offer his all?

"Fine," Tristan whispered to the Light. "Have it your way. You do your thing: you win."

And the Light passed through him, and the Light surrounded him: it filled him! It lit him. It held him on the surface. It tickled him.

Tristan laughed.

REFERENCES

Chapter One

Kenneth Barker, ed. *The NIV Study Bible New International Version*. Michigan: Zondervan, 1985.

Chapter Six

Kenneth Barker, ed. *The NIV Study Bible New International Version*. Michigan: Zondervan, 1985.

Chapter Nine

Kenneth Barker, ed. *The NIV Study Bible New International Version*. Michigan: Zondervan, 1985.

Chapter Eleven

Kenneth Barker, ed. *The NIV Study Bible New International Version*. Michigan: Zondervan, 1985.

Chapter Thirteen

Kenneth Barker, ed. *The NIV Study Bible New International Version*. Michigan: Zondervan, 1985.

Chapter Fourteen

Kenneth Barker, ed. *The NIV Study Bible New International Version*. Michigan: Zondervan, 1985.

Chapter Twenty-Six

Kenneth Barker, ed. *The NIV Study Bible New International Version*. Michigan: Zondervan, 1985.